the
CHANCE

Copyright © 2024 by Rae Stone

All rights reserved.

No part of this publication may be reproduced, distributed, or transmitted in any form or by any means including photocopying, recording, or other electronic or mechanical methods without the written permission of the author except in the case of brief quotations embodied in critical reviews and certain other noncommercial uses permitted by copyright law. For permission requests, please contact the author at the address below:

raestone@raestone.com

ISBN: (ebook) 979-8-9888601-6-7

ISBN: (paperback) 979-8-9888601-7-4

Any references to historical events, real people, or real places are used fictitiously. Names, characters, and places are products of the author's imagination.

Cover design: Lori Jackson Designs LLC

Cover photo: Cadwallader Photography LLC

Editing: Heather Caryn

Grymm Publications LLC

To those that said you can't.

Thank you.

Playlist

Theme Song:

Magnetic—Wage War

Playlist:

Check it out on Spotify

Character List.

Not all of these characters will make an appearance in this book, but will be around.

As Above band members

Rex Thompson— vocals, guitar, songwriting

Finland Montgomery— guitar, backup vocals, songwriting

Tobias "Toby" Jeffers— bass, rhythm guitar

Mac Thompson— drums, nickname designator

Leo Keenan— band manager, cat herder

Sentry Security

Ian— Head of Security, Rex's detail

Lugh— Second in command, Toby's detail

Peach— Fin's detail

Jordan Kauffman— Mac's detail

Jonathon— The floater

and more ...

A Note from the Author

AFTER TWO YEARS, finally bringing this book, these characters, to life … it feels unreal and I'm so glad you're here to share in the journey with me.

In this book, you will find some heavier topics meant for readers eighteen years or older. Lots of mistakes. This is all driven by the characters and their paths, and is *not* a reference for real life. There is a list of content warnings after the acknowledgements.

This is an MM romance. It's open door. It's spicy. It's gonna make you want to throw your kindle.

Enjoy the rollercoaster.

Prologue

Mac

Seventeen years old

"I'll give you fifty bucks."

Shaking my head, my wild frizzy curls fall into my eyes. "Bro, no. These are easily worth two *hundred*."

The jock who wants to take up drumming in his spare time shrugs. "You didn't start there, and I have fifty."

"Bullshit," I murmur when Darius pulls out his wallet. "One fifty and we'll call it even."

His eyes roll, but he takes out three of the bills and practically throws them at me before collecting my snare drum in his arms and turning his back to me.

It hurts to watch it go. My stomach cramps.

Ma's gonna be so pissed when she finds out I sold the gift.

But the cash in my hand now means that Rex and I can go to the concert tonight.

It's our favorite band, and they're playing for the first time on this side of the country, possibly for the last tour of their career.

We have to go.

It doesn't take long to snag the tickets from another asshole who tries to haggle more cash out of me, even though these guys all know that Rex and I … we don't come from much. Ma does her best, but feeding two mouths armed with attitude and too many hormones isn't exactly easy. Money and new things just aren't part of our reality.

Just like the thrift store shit hanging from my too-thin shoulders, featuring the very band we're gonna see tonight. It's got holes in the armpits and is so faded that the black has become a weird version of washed-out grey, but it's still my favorite shirt.

"Rex!" I call as I bound across the field where my twin brother waits for me after school. His backpack is hiked up on his shoulder, the other strap completely gone, leaving frayed edges in its wake. It's the most unkempt thing about my brother beside the curls that touch his chin. He somehow manages to make the rest of our second-hand wardrobe look presentable enough to keep a different girl on his arm every other week.

"Hey Macaroni. Anyone give you any shit today?"

I shrug. "Doesn't matter." I flop the tickets around in front of his face, my grin growing. "I got them!"

His blue-green eyes go wide, and he snags the paper from my grip. "Shut up." Rex stares at the print on the fancy matte paper, his face falling when his eyes meet mine again. "You *didn't*."

I nod, my lips pressed into a thin line. "I … did. Drummy is gone, bro."

My twin shakes his head, a curse falling from his lips when he looks back at the tickets in his possession. "But you loved that thing."

Taking a deep breath, I try to shrug off the sludge of guilt working its way into my gut. "I've got the bass at school. It's okay."

Rex shakes his head, his eyes crest fallen as he hands the tickets back. "We'll get you another one, Mac. I fucking promise."

I believe him.

"It's going to be worth it, bro." I clear the lump from my throat and blink back the moisture that wants to collect in my eyes.

I did love Drummy.

Is it weird to miss an inanimate object with your whole heart?

"Then let's go. I don't wanna miss a single second of the show you sold your drum to get us into."

We're the first ones in the general admission line for the bar turned venue, armed with the fake ID's Rex found for us a few months back, and I cannot contain the nerves vibrating me to my bones.

My thumb taps out the beat of the song playing over the shitty speakers as my twin talks up the ladies standing in line just behind us.

"You guys are *twins*? That's so crazy."

I roll my eyes. It's the same shit I hear all the fucking time from girls like this one, with her bleached out hair and her manicured nails.

At least it's better than asking if we share.

People are so fucking weird when it comes to brothers born at the same time.

Even if she was my type, that's a giant *no thanks*. My brother is fucking gross.

I, on the other hand, would prefer to have privacy *and* someone with the same junk as me.

Ya feel?

The first guy I ever had a crush on punched me in the nose during study hall. I wasn't even trying to necessarily hit on him but in my defense, I was fourteen. Horny. With no clue what to do with my hands.

His hair just looked so damn soft.

He had sneered at me, called me all the derogatory names every gay man has already heard, and never talked to me in a nice way again.

It only took Rex threatening him once for him to leave me the fuck alone.

I've kept to myself for the most part since. Learning the hard way was enough for me to wait for them to come to me when they get curious about dick.

Everyone knows I'm the gay twin already anyway.

The rest of the time they steer clear and for a band geek that loves getting the D, that's just fine with me.

"Keep it single file. Have those tickets and IDs ready!"

Oh, shit. Oh, fuck. This is it!

I bounce in place as I hand the two requested items to the man at the door with one hand and smack my twin's back with the other.

The bouncer looks at me, then hands back the ID, keeping the ticket.

"Oh, hey," I mutter as I pass just by him, my brother already offering up his entry requirements. "Can I keep that?"

He rips the paper in half and hands me one.

Inside, I cry a little but accept the torn paper as Rex pushes me ahead. "Here. He gave me the other half of mine."

A half smile lifts my lips. "Thanks, bro."

I stuff the two halves of the ticket in my worn-out pocket and weave my way around the people that are already packed into the small space.

VIP fuckers.

Rex grabs hold of my sleeve when I veer off to the side, the merch table catching my wide eyes.

Please be less than twenty bucks. Please be less. Pleasepleaseplease …

"*Fifty dollars for a shirt?*" I screech to my brother whose brows bunch. "How the fuck is that?"

He sighs, the weight of being the poor kids turning his lips down. "What about that square thing? It says fifteen."

Huffing, I step up to the cashier, my sights set on the thing Rex mentioned. "The bandana?"

I'm asking my brother, but the woman takes it as the order and walks away to grab one from the maze of boxes sitting open behind her. "Oh—"

"Just get it, Mac," my brother says in that tone that's on the verge of caregiver even though I'm the older one. "We can use the five for a water. We'll share."

"Goddammit, Rex."

"I'll pick up an extra shift next week and we'll go to the arcade, okay? I'll break into the claw machine if I have to to make sure you get something else. Since you did all this."

I want to argue but I also really want the souvenir that the lady comes back with and hands over. Something that says I was here with my brother. A trophy of some kind to remember the moment by.

Grumbling, I wait for her to make our change, snagging the bills quickly when a deep bassy beat echoes across the venue.

I don't wait to see if Rex follows me, I can feel that he is.

I just dive into the thick of the crowd, worming my way through hordes of already sweaty bodies as I wrap the bandana around my forehead like a band, tying it at the back of my head.

I'm gonna need my hands free for this one.

We make it to the front barricade at the center stage when the lights go down and that beat becomes the first song I ever fell in love with.

Fuck sex and screwing with dudes that don't want more than a BJ in the back of the locker room. Fuck being poor and unable to afford the damn tickets or shirts to this place. Fuck the assholes who name call and think they're better than me because their sexuality's more common than mine.

None of that matters when the drum solo breaks out and the man behind the set sets this place on fucking *fire*.

I'm dancing before I know my body is moving, completely unbothered by who all I touch. Jumping when the vocalist growls to jump. Swaying with lifted hands when the songs demand it.

All the while, my brother and best friend is at my side, and in as deep as I am.

The grin that breaks open his face when I glance over at him is almost worth having to sell my drum just to see.

He never smiles like that.

Song after song, the band rocks the house, and I don't think there's a single moment that I stay still. It just *feels* right to move around, unbound by expectations of keeping your hands and arms in the ride of life until it's socially acceptable to do otherwise.

Somewhere around the halfway point in the show, Rex disappears into the thick of the crowd and while I don't mind, I'm forced to make sure crowd surfers don't knock me the fuck out.

I came to have a great time, not get a boot to the face.

My sight trails one way, then back to the stage, and it's that moment that I finally settle. Finally still.

Eyes sliding closed in the middle of the crowd, I experience the deep bass rattling inside my ribcage. I let the guitar riff flow through my veins like a lifeforce I didn't know I was missing.

Chills race across my skin when I focus on the drumming behind it all, keeping time for each of the other members, tearing up the beat, becoming the foundation of each song.

"This is it," I mumble to myself and let my eyes spring open, my chest filled to near bursting. "Nothing is better than this."

My smile stretches my face so wide, it aches.

It's a foreign feeling, the smile, but it's one I never want to let go of.

"What a fuckin' night!" The lead singer barks with guttural vocals into his mic. "We're Clo, if you didn't know. And this is our song, 'Goodbye'."

The place erupts in a boisterous noise that has a laugh bubbling up my throat.

Is it ever really goodbye, though?

I glance around, feeling eyes on me, only to land on a guy that looks like he's about my age. He moves closer, and for a moment, I wonder if I know him from somewhere.

But then his gaze dips to my lips and I *know*.

He's like me.

For the first time ever, I rake my gaze down his band tee clad chest, and when he makes it to my side, I don't hesitate.

My hand finds the back of his neck and reels him in until our lips are crashing together, and his tongue begs for a taste.

Sighing, I kiss the man back, in public, with music filling my soul and cheers drowning out the lyrics.

And for the first time in my life, I feel *free*.

Part I

Chapter One

Mac

"Can you just forget I ever said that?" I stare expectantly at the shrink across from me, only to receive an arch of her manicured brow in response.

"That's not how this works, Mac. You know that."

My nostrils flare with my inhale, and a muscle works in my jaw just as my thumb raps a baseline on my thigh.

"But how is that night relevant to anything?"

Doc taps the cap of her pen against her chin and crosses her ankles. "It has to do with the issues you're having with your brother."

"I feel like this is a conflict of interest," I mutter with a roll to my eyes, and I pick up the beat in my head with my other hand along my knee.

"It's absolutely within your right to choose someone else to discuss these things with."

Not only does the idea of rehashing all my life's problems to yet another stranger have my stomach twisting up, so does the ease of Doc's statement.

"*That*. Right there." She points that pen in my direction. "What just happened in your mind?"

I sigh again.

It seems to be my favorite pastime every time I find myself sitting across from this woman who clearly has all of her shit together.

Which is exactly why I'm seated here, across from all four of her degrees.

And she's there, with her notepad and her head-shrinking notes.

"I don't wanna be a burden to another stranger." Her other brow wings and I roll my eyes. "Right. Watch what I say about myself." I blow out a breath and rub my palms along my jeans. "I don't want to start over."

She nods, jots something, then sets the pad aside. "Back to that night. On the bus with your brother. What happened?"

"I cried like a little bitch."

"About?" she presses, and my rubbing palms start to itch even more.

I huff. "Shit I can't have. That's it. I need to just get over it."

Doc's lips purse. "Expecting to just *get over* something you feel strongly about does not make them any less true to you. How you feel is just as important as anyone else."

"No," I half snap. "No, it is not." My jaw works and my eyes shift over the little room.

Unseeing. Unsettling.

"Tell me again."

My teeth grit and my limbs start to jitter. "*Fine*. If it'll get you to stop asking."

I just want to move. To run. To get this the fuck over with so I can go back to beating the shit out of my set and hiding in my hole of self-doubt.

It's easier.

"I'm listening."

I let loose a soft growl and open my mouth. "We'd been on the road, again. It feels like we're *always* on the road. Bouncing from city to town to plane to bus."

I lick my drying lips and dart my gaze from her waiting stare to the floor.

"We landed in a hotel, and I tend to sleepwalk from time to time. Have since I was little, I guess. It's supposedly a stress thing."

"Did you that night?"

My shoulders drop. "Yeah." I swipe my hands again. "Completely naked. Down the hall."

"That must've felt odd."

I flick my sight back up to meet hers. "Yep. Especially when you wake up, screaming mad and terrified, in the arms of your bodyguard."

Doc gives a subtle nod. "Embarrassed, too. At least I would be."

"Nope. Not even a little bit." I rub my chin. "Not until we made it back to the room and for the first time since I became an adult did someone other than my twin give a shit if I made it back to sleep."

Doc nods some more and leans forward to brace her elbows on her knees. "Then what?"

"Then—" The word cracks just like the organ behind my ribs. "Then he stayed with me. Swore he just wanted to make sure I didn't do anything stupid."

I swallow the boulder-sized lump.

"The *he* you're mentioning is Jordan, right? Your bodyguard?"

All I can do is nod.

"So, he stayed in the room with you. Made sure you rested. Took care of you."

Another nod.

"I don't need anyone to take care of me," I say on a cracked whisper to the floor.

"What happened next, Mac? What lead to the bus with Rex?"

I suck in a breath and ignore the way my eyes want to sting at the reminder.

"Jordan was still there when I woke up."

"And?"

"And every day since."

Chapter Two

MAC

"**A**RE YOU SURE THIS is a good idea?"

Swiping the back of my hand along my nose, I flag over the bartender and order another drink.

I'm raw.

Split open and sitting next to the one person that somehow makes me need the therapy sessions where I feel like I'm cutting out my heart to show the doc all my scars, and yet …

"Mac."

My jaw clenches at the way my bodyguard says my name. It's somehow like a plea, and a demand all at once.

And just one time … I want to know what it would be like to hear that tone in a different manner. Maybe lost somewhere between the sheets of the hotel bed Jordan most often chooses to share with me, the gay guy, even though he's straight.

Sighing, I turn to my bodyguard with the fresh drink in my hand. "Drinking is a Toby problem. Not me."

Jordan's dark brow wings up behind his backwards hat. "It's his coming home party. From *rehab*."

He emphasizes the words like I don't know where the bassist in my band has been for the last several months, only available via short in-person visits and a phone he managed to commandeer.

It's the longest I've ever gone without talking to him.

Growing up, Toby was always around. Him and Leo all but grew up at the house with Rex and me, my Ma as their second guardian. And then when we all found ourselves in the barely-there garage with instruments in hand, it was like the universe dropping the sign right in front of us.

Form a band.

Music has been my lifeblood for as long as I can remember. It's what controls my limbs when I play, calms my mind when it's too loud, feeds my soul when it gets dark.

It frees me.

I don't know how to *not* play. Which probably just feeds into the constant movement I find myself making whether I'm in front of my kit or not.

"It's just to chill. Have some fucking fun," I mumble into the rim of the glass just before the taste of bitter cranberry bursts on my tongue, followed by the slight burn of not-enough alcohol.

Jordan sighs something deep at my elbow, then knocks on the bar, signaling for the check.

"Sure, I'm done now," I spit and throw back the rest of what was supposed to be a vodka and cranberry.

"It was that bad, huh?" Jordan asks me, his words pulling a glance from me that I throw over my shoulder and instantly regret.

Because of *course* there's a flash of concern riding the navy blue of his irises.

I sigh and let my eyes slide close for just a moment, hoping for a reprieve.

It didn't work.

I'm still jittery, nervous, and wondering how in the fuck I managed to tell the doc about the one night I swore I'd never bring up again.

I was over it. Had stuffed it so far down that not even my twin could feel the shit rotting along inside my chest anymore.

I'd almost convinced myself.

It's been years. Literally years since I confessed to my twin that I fell in love with the straight man sitting next to me.

Hundreds of days that Jordan has shared my sleeping space, with no objection from me, without a third thought since it started.

Countless nights of feeling him watching me, protecting me. Guarding me, even from myself.

And I had to just go and fucking let it slip on my second mandatory visit with the doc that not only is my bodyguard sharing my bed—*platonically*—but I've also been harboring feelings for the man or some shit, while my brother seethes about it from afar. *Mandatory* because apparently we all need to keeps our heads right for tour.

As if any of it was Jordan's fault.

I've been out of whack since and it's had my bodyguard hovering around the edge of my vision, watching me and waiting for me to spill my guts like I normally would.

I mean, since *I'm* the one that demands he be my best friend and all.

Which, in hindsight, seems like the least logical decision I've ever made.

The dynamic has changed in my mind, yet again, and I don't know that I can shake it off as easily as I have in the past with him up my fucking ass. Toby out of the loop. My twin so far gone for the family that he started that I have no one to run to.

I don't want to burden them.

Even as a kid, loneliness had threatened me. That ever-present knowledge that I was *different* than most burrowing down in my gut as a constant reminder to keep people at a distance. But then my twin would burst in, punch anyone that *looked* like a problem, and sit with me in the dark.

Now?

Now … I have a man I want who in no way reciprocates the feeling, who is *paid* to spend his time with me, as my only defense in keeping the emptiness at bay.

And I'm having a deal biting back the void's demands.

It's demanding its debt be paid and I'm all out of cash.

"*Since when is this how we do shit?*" I snap as Jordan's fist lands on the release bar of the exit, and he rushes out first.

"Since you're in your head and not paying attention," he growls right back, grabbing a fistful of my shirt and tugging me through the threshold I'd stopped in.

He always lets me go first …

The gravel grinds beneath the soles of my Chucks as we walk, just as my jaw grinds my teeth to near dust, but as much as I want to crawl into a hole somewhere far away from all of this, I know that I can't.

Because Toby's home.

Chapter Three

Mac

"T OBY," I CALL AFTER the disappearing back of the man I consider my brother.

"Just let him—" my band's guitarist, Fin, cuts himself off when Leo takes off after the runaway bassist. I growl at the heavy hand that lands on my shoulder, keeping me in place. "Seriously?"

"Fuck off, Fin," I snap, shrugging off his grip and spinning away from the world's greatest guitarist. *Or whatever the fuck his award was for.*

I hear disappointment in his responding sigh that's aimed at my back, but it doesn't stop me from walking my ass straight out of the coming home party without a second glance.

Not even my twin brother's searing gaze can stop me.

There's a smoke perched between my lips as I blow past the band manager that's hanging in the hallway like he's lost. A lighter to the end of the rolled paper before the elevator's doors can even close me in and a tremble to my hands that I shove in my pockets.

I had a drink before coming here.

Okay, two.

So what?

Toby's not the only one with problems and the man sure as shit reminded me during every single one of our conversations that the rest of us were not supposed to change. To not hide it from him. To keep on like normal.

So maybe he smelled it on my breath when I tackled him at the door when he got here. Maybe he caught a whiff of the massive hangover I woke up with this morning that's clung to me all damn day.

Or, and this is most likely the issue, being back in the same place he finished his last bender was a terrible idea. Having his coming home party in the same fucking penthouse that held the man's intervention before he went and got all fixed up was a lapse in judgement.

Fuck that immersion therapy bullshit. Leo was way off base for that one.

Either way, I'll call Toby later and confess that I feel like shit for needing the one vice my bestie was abstaining from. I know he'll understand, or just tell me I'm being stupid because I probably am.

He said it was okay.

Sighing, I drag in a lungful and squint against the smoke that pokes at my eye as the number on the elevator ticks down to the floor my apartment shares with our resident security staff's living quarters.

"Seriously?"

I huff when the roach is plucked from my lips before I can even make it to my door and my bodyguard is snuffing out the lit cherry on the heel of his boot.

"Jesus fuck," I snap and throw my arms out. "Why are you being a fucking killjoy?"

Jordan's brow quirks when he straightens, and it disappears behind his backwards hat.

"Why are you being a little shit?" he shoots right back as he tucks the rest of my snuffed smoke into his pocket.

A frustrated groan rumbles out of my throat, and I roll my eyes as I brush right past the man into my apartment without an answer.

I don't bother locking the door. Hell, I'm not even sure it closes fully as I walk across the marbled floors, tugging my shirt off as I go. Pockets are emptied onto the counter. Shoes toed off and abandoned as I step out of them.

I'm down to my boxers when I hit the couch in my foul mood, remote in hand and a Mark Wahlberg movie primed on the screen.

Marky Mark always makes me feel better.

"You just watched this one."

I scoff and hit play anyway, ignoring the way the other end of the couch fills out with *man.*

"*Four Brothers* is top notch, and I will die on that hill, Tyro."

"You think anything with Wahlberg in it is top notch." It's like I can hear Jordan's eye roll, but I do nothing but huff in agreement. Because it is.

"He's hot *and* talented." I nod for no reason, my eyes glued to the screen. "Hard to find both."

Jordan makes some kind of hum that's neither an agreement or a denial, and by the time I tear my gaze from the screen, my bodyguard is stretched out with ankles and arms crossed, his hat pulled low to cover his eyes.

I roll mine.

"You know you can go home, right?"

He grumbles something incoherent, but doesn't move.

I let loose a sigh, shoot a text to Toby to check in before I forget, then use the remote to turn off the lights.

The room is bathed in a grey light from the gritty vibe of the movie, but even as the scenes move along and the story progresses, I find my attention slipping back to Jordan passed out on my couch more than I'll ever admit out loud.

He's all hard lines and sharp edges with a shadow of dark stubble coating his jaw, harsh and dark tattoos lining his right arm—a geometrical sleeve tat I sat with him through, though he wouldn't tell me what the soundwave around his wrist is—and rocking the shit out of his *plain clothes.* Which are really just jeans that hug him in all the right ways and a plain black tee that's ridden up juuuust enough to give me a tease of the tanned skin covering the defined V that disappears beneath the denim.

The very same denim that bunches and bulges between his pressed-to-gether thighs.

My mouth waters and I force my sight back to the TV, only to see a shirtless Marky Mark fill the screen.

Groaning, I sink farther into the couch.

This is like being in a room full of hot guys while wearing a cock cage.

It's torture.

But then my mind does this wonderful thing where I imagine *Jordan* being the one shirtless, and now I'm trying to figure out a way to make that happen without getting up from the couch.

"Go to sleep."

My eyes roll at the gravel in my bodyguard's voice and ignore the way it makes my dick jump.

"Not tired."

"You've been awake for over twenty-four hours." He says this like I didn't already feel that in my bones.

"I took a catnap when you snuck off to the gym," I answer, because I did pass out for thirty seconds when I heard him leave this morning at the ass crack of dawn but then I rolled over in the empty bed and my mind would not shut back off.

It was too empty without him.

Something in my chest pinches uncomfortably.

"Fine," Jordan huffs and pushes to his feet, his hat back on his head, and gestures to the TV. "Pick another one and I'll be right back."

I blink at his back as he leaves and then swing my lifted brow to the screen where the credits roll.

Did I seriously stare at him that long?

Chapter Four

JORDAN

THERE'S A TIGHTNESS THAT'S settled into my chest and hasn't left me.

Even as I scour the neighboring convenience store like a kid in a candy shop, including the armfuls of colorful packages as I exit, there's still something *off*. Something weird.

I don't like it.

Taking my time at the apartment across the hall from Mac's place, I change into grey sweats and an old band tee that I think may have been Mac's at one point.

Armed with my bag of snacks and my cap back on my head, I stalk across to Mac's and roll my eyes when the door opens freely.

Good thing this place is locked down like Fort Knox.

Guess that's what happens when the band owns the whole building.

All twenty-six floors of it.

"Vida!" I call into the space as I hip-check the door closed and lock it behind me. "I came prepared."

I don't bother stopping at the counter to ditch the crinkly bags when the sound of *The Other Guys* fills the room because I know damn well that as soon as my ass hits the cushion, I'm not getting up again.

But when I step over Mac's low-top Chucks and find the TV bathing the empty leather in light, I drop the goods right in his seat and wander farther into the apartment.

"Mac?"

Turning the corner into the open bedroom, I freeze for half a second when all I see is a flash of ass. It's enough to have my stomach clenching, then releasing just as quick, while my brain screams to turn back around and ignore it.

I don't.

I've seen a lot of butt-shots. Too many dicks. Lots of naked or scantily clad bodies thanks to being on a tour bus with rock stars for years.

In locker rooms even longer than that.

Waists with tan lines. Muscular, but thin arms. Tons of tattoos I've admired.

This is no different.

Instead, I cross my arms and lean against the doorjamb as Mac pulls up the athletic shorts and snaps the elastic waistband against his smooth skin.

"Are those mine?" I ask.

He scoffs and spins, a flush to his face. "And *that*—" He points to my chest as he advances, jabbing me in the pec as he brushes passed me. "Isn't mine?"

I shrug at the glance he throws over his shoulder. "Probably."

Snickering when he mumbles something, I follow the drummer back into the living room and flop into what I've designated as *my spot* on the couch while Mac fiddles with the snack bag.

The movie is restarted as Mac settles crossed-legged on the middle cushion, his bare knee grazing my thigh ever so slightly.

It's warm, tingles even, and pulls most of my attention.

Weird.

I'm so focused on the contact and scouring my mind for *why* I'm paying any attention to it when this is common for us, that I completely miss Mac's reach until a pack of candies are smacking me in the chest.

"The fuck?"

Mac snickers and picks up the pack from my lap and slaps it right to my collar bone.

"I *know* these are yours. Skittles suck."

"*Pffft*." I smack a hand over his, holding him and the candies where they are. "*You* suck. Skittles are the best."

"I mean …" Mac drags out on a half-smile that doesn't reach his eyes. "One way to find out."

The glint that flashes is full of mischief and my stomach does that weird clenching thing again.

I clear my throat and drop my grip.

"They're the best," I mutter low like a total lame ass and force myself to look away from the things I think I see swirling around in his almost green eyes.

He's just kidding, like usual.

"Lies," he mumbles right back and dives back into the snack bag on his other side.

Dragging in a silent breath, I swipe my hands down my thighs and pick up the Skittles pack for something to do.

Instead of watching the movie, I find that my attention keeps wandering, glimpses of Mac catching in my peripheral and searing into my mind like this is somehow different than any other night.

It *feels* different.

Like the last few months of being stationary with the drummer have altered the rules by which we operate.

Which makes no sense to me.

Mac and I have spent many nights just like this, holed up in tour buses or hotel rooms, with only me to keep him out of trouble. Many hours spent together in green rooms and random car rides. So much time spent within arm's reach of one another, even at every gay bar he insisted on going to.

Being close is our thing. So close that we have a fanbase. A ship name. And everyone just *assumes* things.

Some of it's true. Most of it isn't.

Mac's the closest thing I've ever had to a friend, possibly even a best friend like he claims.

I'll take it.

And yet, as we sit here together watching one of his favorite movies, he seems like he's in another timeline. Lost somewhere in the space between his ears and not even a bag full of his favorite snacks has made him crack his usual blinding smile.

Does he feel the shift, too?

"Vida," I mutter, my sight glued to the TV so he doesn't know I've been watching him.

"Huh?" he mumbles back absently and pulls his knees up to his chest, wrapping his arms around his shins.

"Best friends first," I say, and I watch as something settles over Mac that's heavy enough to bow in his shoulders. "Right?"

His breath releases through his nose when he meets my gaze over his shoulder and then he tips his chin. "Yeah."

Why don't I believe him?

Chapter Five

JORDAN

T HE SUN HAS LONG since taken over the windowpanes on the far side of the living room, the credits rolling on yet another replay of the same movie.

And yet, I haven't moved since I woke up with stubble burn prickling my shoulder.

Sometime before the day fully took over the city, I kicked back both mine and Mac's seats, his head resting on my shoulder, his cheek rubbing against my skin, even in his sleep.

I'm not even sure when I lost my shirt or my hat, but having the sleeping drummer softly snoring against me has made it impossible to give a shit.

Think this is the longest he's slept in months.

The fact that he's at peace for now has me cradling his head enough to slip my arm around him, that stubble on his cheeks settling against my pec as I wiggle some feeling back into my fingers.

He's warm when he burrows in closer, his torso plastering to my side and his leg kicking over mine.

I should give a shit, but I don't.

Do I?

In fact, when Mac slings his arm across my middle and his breath puffs across my chest, I feel myself sink deeper into the cushions.

Fuck, this couch is comfortable.

My eyes slide closed, and my lungs fill with the scent of *drummer*. It's not one I could explain, but it's inviting enough in my half-asleep state that my nose finds his hair and stays there.

Just five more minutes and I'll sneak off to the gym.

But then Mac's hand tucks underneath my opposite hip, his fingertips gripping me just tight enough to remove all space between us until I feel him from thigh to head.

At some point, my fingers weave into his hair, the digits getting caught up in his untamed curls as I scratch lightly at his scalp to keep him asleep.

I know this won't last.

Nothing this good ever does.

So … I'm accepting it as it is and hoping for just a few more seconds of it.

It's a weird thing to hope for, I know this, and yet with the chaos that is life, I find that it doesn't matter that my client is gay and I'm straight. That we're best friends with an unprofessional dynamic that bothers others and challenges societal norms.

Or that most of my life has been spent on the road, changing homes, never really settling into anything that isn't shortly ripped away from me.

I have to find the quiet moments to keep my sanity.

My boss, Ian, thinks I'm crazy to guard the way that I do. Thinks it's borderline *unprofessional* for Mac and me to be this close.

And yet, I can't find it in me to go about it any different.

He's the closest thing I have to family.

If I can help him find peace in the crazy by watching the same movie on repeat, then why the fuck not?

To me, it's no different than scheduling a reservation and ensuring the safety of the establishment or holding back masses of fans from clawing at his face.

It's my job to keep him safe, even if it's from himself.

Which makes right now no different.

The band might be on a break for the foreseeable future, but that doesn't mean that Mac is no longer in need of someone to keep the unwanted hands off him.

Especially when it's the hands of his own demons.

Normally, I only take up about a foot's worth of space on his bed, on top of the covers. Sleeping when he does so that I know when he's awake and so he can't sneak off without me or sleepwalk into the hotel hallways naked.

Except there's something clinging to him these last few weeks that makes it harder to not call out the dullness I see leaching into his vibrant eyes. The ever-present black cloud hanging above his head that follows him around and dims his sunny disposition.

It makes it impossible not to keep him in my sight.

Wondering what the hell is on his mind.

It's none of my business if he decides not to share it.

I wish he just fuckin' would, though.

I'm aware there's shit I won't be able to protect him from.

Hoping it doesn't mean I lose the only friend I have.

But being stationary for the first time in half a decade seems to be part of his problem and not being able to do a damn thing about that is rubbing me all wrong.

What if he needs something different? More?

"Stop thinking so fuckin' loud," Mac grumbles, stifling a yawn into my skin and stretching against me like a cat. "Wait—"

He jolts upright with the heel of his palm jamming into my sternum, practically peeling himself away like a wax strip that stings every inch of skin he was touching.

"*Ow.*"

Mac looks down at me, his cheek reddened from where it's been pressed against me for the last however many hours, and a wild vulnerability shining in his eyes.

"So, I wasn't dreaming," he says more to himself than me, but the room is too silent not to hear the whispered sleep-thick words.

He's even harder to ignore when his gaze darts down my body, half naked and spread out, to where his leg is still hooked around mine.

"Ohhh no," he grumbles and twists away, taking his warmth along with him.

"You were sleeping for once. It's fine."

Except it doesn't appear to be fine when he jumps from the couch without bothering to put the footrest down and practically vaults himself away, nearly tipping the whole thing in the process.

"I am *so* sorry—"

"Mac," I half snap and snag his wrist when he goes to dart past me. It takes him a long moment to look down at me, those eyes of his latching on mine with a level of nervous energy that makes my stomach twist. "You slept. It's really okay."

He huffs out a breath, then graces me with the smallest hint of a nod in what I think is understanding.

I finally release his wrist when recognition of tingling registers in my palm, right where his pulse hammered, and he darts away from me almost as fast as he dove from the couch without a second glance.

Waking up next to a man would probably offend most guys, and if it were anyone else, I probably would start questioning things myself.

But it's just Mac.

Chapter Six

Mac

*H*OLY FUCK.

My heart pounds and my stomach clenches painfully as I lean into the vanity in my ensuite bathroom and do my best not to hyperventilate.

Waking up next to Jordan was pure fucking bliss until the reality came crashing in and reminded me that we're not like *that*.

He did it for the job.

He's straight.

My insides twist all up at the reminder and I have to force myself to blink away the burning in my eyes.

It's fine. The voice in my head sounds suspiciously like Jordan's. *You slept, it's fine.*

I … did sleep. For what feels like the first time in a long fucking time, I finally found an REM cycle and stuck with it. There were no bad dreams or constant repositioning. I don't even remember leaning close enough to end up half on top of him with his skin touching mine. His arm around me. Hands in my hair.

My cock pinned between his thigh and mine.

Which only reminds me of the *other* problem currently throbbing in my shorts that's refusing to go down, even amidst the flood of cortisol currently pumping through my system.

Forcing a choppy breath through my dried throat, I dig the heel of my palm against my groin and groan.

Shitfuck.

With fingers wrapping around my length through the thin shorts, I dive for the shower.

It takes several slaps of the faucet to get the water running and I'm stumbling into the cold spray without even bothering to undress. I'm panting, shivering despite the heat that takes over the artic flow against my back, but it doesn't matter that the temperature has hit near scalding.

All it does is remind me of the heat I woke up against and I'm fumbling around for the shower lube before I even realize I've moved.

My palm is slicked, and my abs are clenched when I peel back the wet shorts to free my cock. It springs up, nearly slapping my stomach, and hangs heavy in the air.

I can't not *do this.*

The head is angry and nearing purple, the slit winking back at me with a taunting bead of precum leaking from the tip.

It's almost as if my own boner is pointing and laughing at me for having been lacking so damn bad in the sex life department that I'm pretty sure my own hand can get me off in three seconds flat.

Not to mention, if I ever end up inside anyone ever again, I'm certain I'll come on the first stroke.

Don't think about your bodyguard.

Growling, I wrap my slick fist around my shaft and pump.

My jerking is erratic, but the tingles are immediate. From my curling toes to my scalp, I feel every stroke of my palm sliding along my flesh.

Don't think about your bodyguard.

It's been so long that anyone has been close enough that I've actually felt the skin against skin contact I crave deep down. The closeness and intimate familiarity of another body slanting along mine.

Don't think about Jordan.

I've tried going back to my one-night stands.

Hell, I've even tried the gay hookup apps like Topple.

Yet every time their hands land on me, I recoil. My skin crawls. My boner deflates.

And I feel like I'm lying.

My palm twists over the crown of my cock and a gasp escapes my throat as if to remind me that it's definitely not a boner problem.

Don't think about Jordan.

Dark hair and navy-blue eyes seep their way into my subconscious anyway and instead of fighting it like I always do, I just … give in.

Just this once.

I'm too close to coming to put up much of a fight when my thoughts become languid sexy fantasies that put Jordan on his knees for me. My cockhead sitting on the tip of his tongue. His plush lips spread wide and waiting for me to feed him my cock. He looks near desperate when I hold myself back, admiring the way my fist bumps his chin with each stroke.

In my mind, he'd be antsy. Begging. Waiting for me to fill his warm mouth.

Imagination breaking wide open, I thrust into him until I'm hitting the back of his throat and he's choking on it.

In reality … I'm practically fucking my own fist and clamping down to stop the images from ending too soon.

I bet he'd be glorious on his knees.

Sinful.

Submissive.

The thought of Jordan softening beneath me is what does me in. I'm painting the shower wall with my cum, my barely contained groans filling the shower up with all the sounds I wish I could share with someone else.

My chest is heaving with the comedown, my pulse thumping in my ears.

But with each moment that the high of the orgasm fades, the more and more my chest constricts.

It'll never be real.

The rest of my shower is completed on autopilot, an aura of darkness settling in around me as I mindlessly dry off and dress for the day.

It's so heavy that my usual mask of normalcy can't even hide the entirety of the shadows I cast as I join a freshly showered bodyguard in my living room.

He might have a quirk to his lips, a simple almost smile that's fucking mesmerizing.

But I can't even look him in the eye.

Chapter Seven

MAC

"LAST TIME WE TALKED about your twin and what happened on the bus. How are you feeling about that now?"

My eyes bulge at Dr. Ivy Surah's directness.

"You remembered that?" I ask, dubiety lacing my tone. "That was six weeks ago."

Doc almost tsks, her brow lifting just the slightest amount. "It was over two *months* ago, Mac. Besides," she taps a slender finger to her temple, "I take notes."

My mouth works like a fish before I shake my head and lean back on the couch.

"I would say the same …" I trail off and drop my sight to the floor because if I really stop to think about it, I actually feel *worse*.

"What about Jordan? Is he still sharing space with you?"

I tense at the reminder of my bodyguard so soon in the conversation but manage a stiff nod.

"And," she almost drags out. "Is that something you're still okay with?"

Another stiff nod.

I know I shouldn't continue to do what I'm doing. It's unhealthy. Each day that I spend with Jordan at my side making me more unstable than I already was when I met him.

But the idea of anyone else being in his place is *unfathomable*.

It's so uncomfy that it makes my stomach roll with just the thought.

"Mac?"

My head snaps up and I do my best to squash the voice in my head that makes me feel like I just got my hand snagged in the cookie jar. "Huh?"

"I asked if you liked it." She looks at me pointedly, like I just missed a whole important scene in the movie I'll be quizzed on, and my brows meet in the middle of my bandana-clad forehead.

"Liked what?"

Doc's lips purse and she shakes her head. "Tell me where you went. In your head. Just now."

Pulling in a cleansing breath, the truth of my thoughts are off my tongue before I can reframe them in a way that doesn't out me. "I feel like I shouldn't want this."

"But you do." *Not a question.*

I nod anyways, my arms crossing over my chest as I lean back into the cushion. "I don't want anyone but him."

The truth of the words startle me more than they do her and my wide eyes drift to the floor once again.

I thought we were past this.

These deep-seated and unrequited feelings have finally surfaced all over again. I've had them stuffed down long enough to decay.

So why now?

Huffing, I set my attention back on the note-taking brain doctor.

When she finally looks up, she crosses one knee over the other and sets the notepad aside.

Having all of her attention feels almost as bad as admitting I *used to* have a crush on someone close to me and now I just feel about two feet tall.

"I want to ask you something."

My stomach drops, but I nod her on.

"Are you jealous of your brother?"

If it's possible, my stomach drops even farther.

"What? No."

"And possibly his openness about the relationship that he's in?"

Tingling takes over my fingertips and my chest gets real tight.

"Or is it Toby's stint in rehab and all the attention he's getting now that he's home?"

I bristle at that, a flood of anger rising up so fast, I jump to my feet.

"Fuck you, doc," I seethe. "Don't you dare minimize them and their efforts to be happy." She just shakes her head, calm as ever despite my elevated tone and instead of waiting for her response, I continue spitting venom in her direction. "And I sure as fuck would never take any of that away from them."

Doc holds up a hand. It's a simple gesture, one that's meant to mean surrender, and I rock back on my heels.

I'm panting when she finally speaks.

"I never meant to infer anything beyond what I see troubling you, Mac." She purses her lips and gestures for me to take my seat.

I huff, but then finally fall back into it.

"It's difficult when the dynamics of our relationships change. It's not just romantic ones that affect us in negative ways. You experiencing your twin brother creating an individual life and growing into the man he is can be a challenge."

"What about Toby, then? Why bring him up?"

The smile that pulls at the doc's lips is genuine, but small.

"He was the next best thing. One of the few people that have known you almost as long as your brother. The two people that have accepted you, been close to you, even when you were a grumpy, pimply teenager."

"I was not," I grumble, even though I definitely was at one point. We all were. It's like a rite of passage or some shit.

"But then Toby went away. For the majority of that time, you focused on your worry for him, your appreciating of his healing, and planned things for his return. Now that he's home, he's different, I'd imagine."

Sighing, I shake my head, though she is right.

"I think your head is telling you that you feel left out, and I'd bet if you just reached out to either of them, they'd happily accept you into the new versions of their lives."

I grit my jaw against the way it ticks and ignore the pinch in my chest because while she's not wrong, she's not entirely *right*, either.

I accept them in their new lives, that my role is smaller in some ways.

What I really want is for them to accept *me* in mine.

I ignore that, too.

"Fine," I breathe out, exhausted and drained. "I'll try."

"Good. It'll be good to find the new normal before you jet off on another tour. Now …" She pauses just long enough to have me dragging in a breath and drawing my sight up to hers. "Let's talk about how no one else is good enough except Jordan."

I groan and scrub my hands down my stubbly face.

My mouth opens to respond, but an alarm sounds from somewhere behind the doctor and she mutters something akin to a doctor-appropriate curse.

"I want you to come back in a few days, Mac," Doc says as she taps away the buzz of another session completed, and I slump back. "And we can go over the rest of it then."

Nodding, I let the relief I feel flood me.

I don't have to talk about him yet.

"Fine," I mutter.

I'm on my feet, though I feel dead on them despite the real sleep I managed to get, and rush from the room without another glance.

It's like the therapy is undoing all the things I've managed to use to keep myself from crashing and burning and I'm just flat out fucking *exhausted*.

But when I see Jordan, ever-present and waiting for me with a gentle tilt to his lips, all I want to do is crawl back into his arms.

Even if best friends is all it'll ever mean.

Chapter Eight

Jordan

For days, Mac has ignored me in the daylight hours almost as much as he has at night.

We've been all over the place, chasing his niblings around, accompanying Toby to AA meetings, and even hitting up Leo's office.

And by *we*, I mean that I have followed Mac like the guard dog that I am, and sat silently in the car or the corner until he's ready to move onto the next thing.

I don't hate it. This is part of what I signed up for. The reason why his nickname has become Vida.

Because my life revolves around him.

But there's something hanging heavy between us and the normal banter seems to have just … disappeared, taking the best friend energy right along with it.

It's planted me firmly in the irritated category and I'm on the verge of snapping at him, demanding he just tell me what's going on, when he ushers me to the car and denies my request to go home.

"What could you possibly want to go do now? Nothing is open."

Mac throws me a look from under the hood of his hoodie that he's wearing despite the warmth still clinging to the air, then slides a pair of aviators onto his nose.

"Cedar closed up shop."

He pulls on the hood's strings, tightening the material around his face and making the curls not held back by his bandana stick out around his forehead.

I let out a long sigh. "So, we'll be there all night?"

"Hell yeah," he responds with a grin that doesn't quite meet the rest of his face. "Tomorrow, too."

That same grin fades when he turns to the window and watches the world pass us by for the rest of the ride to the tattoo shop.

He doesn't say a single thing when I jump from the car and clear the alleyway we've parked in, and not a word when I usher him in the back door.

The building is on twenty-four-hour surveillance and yet, I still find myself breaking away when the drummer finds his ass in the chair of his sister-in-law's best friend to do a sweep of the place. Blinds are drawn, doors all locked, and the on-duty guard that gets to hang out here for the next few hours is sitting sentry at the door.

It should give me that settled feeling in my gut to know that this is probably the second safest place for Mac to be.

Instead, my stomach is still in the same knots it's been for days now.

"Hey, Jordan," Jonathon greets from his perch by the front door—the only spot with a vantage point to the outside—and juts his chin. "How's it going?"

Leaning just to the side so that I can also see what's going on outside, I shrug. "Same old. How about here? All good?"

Jon lifts a shoulder with a nod. "Had to chase off some shitty patron earlier, but otherwise quiet today." I nod. "Hey, if you wanna take five, I got him."

My gaze flicks to Jonathon's at his offer. "Nah, man. I'm all good."

"Seriously, it's no big deal. Did he eat this time?"

My brow furrows.

Mac is a grown ass man. He's already got a ton of tattoos all over his body, including plenty of places I've tried not to pay too much attention to, and knows about how well he takes getting ink. What he needs to prep beforehand. How he throws up if the pain lasts more than a few hours.

But something in the way that Jon is asking me has me questioning myself.

Should I have asked him first?

"Go," Jonathon says, interrupting the beginnings of a spiraling thought process. "I'll make sure he doesn't leave before you get back."

"Yeah … yeah, I should get him something."

It takes a literal shove and a chuckle from Jonathon to get my feet moving.

Mac's already got headphones in when I walk by, his eyes closed, his chest rising with steady breaths.

It eases something in me to see him calm, to see him getting himself in the zone and surrounded by a safety net of people that care about him.

Including the woman that's already pricking him thousands of times with a color-doused needle.

Cedar catches my eye, shoots a wink my way, then goes right back to inking over his abdomen.

It feels odd as shit to leave him here without me, but when I catch sight of the baseball bat leaned up by the back door, an airy chuckle escapes me.

And because I can't seem to make myself walk away just yet, I do an entire round of the whole building that includes Mac's sister-in-law's boutique next door and the third shop that sits mostly empty. I check all the locks and windows, including the empty apartments above, before I clamor into the car and make my way to one of Mac's favorite drive-thru joints. It takes longer than I'd hoped, the line moving slower than a snail, but the bag is filled to the brim with piping hot burgers and mac and cheese when I finally pull away.

The drive back across town seems to be taking forever. Long enough that I'm near bouncing in my seat when I glance at the clock and realize I've been gone too long.

I should have told him I was leaving.

"Shit," I mutter to the windshield as I finally pull up to the parlor and there's another car parked behind the building. I think I recognize the SUV, yet it still makes my skin tighten with nerves.

Is he okay?

Snatching the bag from my passenger seat so fast part of it rips, I jog the length of the broken alley past the dumpster and curse when the back door opens freely.

Why does no one lock fucking doors?

The stock room is a blur of bottles and boxes, my sights set on the light spilling from the shop floor, my gaze zoning in on Mac the second he's in view.

What I expected to see was my drummer propped up by a trashcan and ready to tap out.

Instead, I'm struck frozen by his glimmering smile and shirtless torso. There's a black patch taped over his left hip, all the way up to nearly his rib cage and dipping low into his jeans.

But that's not what my sight is stuck on.

No, it's his eyes.

They're brighter than when we got here, the green of them shining behind a hint of black eyeliner.

My breath catches when he laughs at something Cedar says and my brow furrows.

Am I the reason they've been dull?

The thought rocks me, though I don't understand it, and I swallow against the building lump in my throat.

"Vida," I say, and it cracks, but I ignore that with a clearing of my suddenly dry throat. "I got you food."

Mac's sight swings on me and softens the tiniest bit. "Shit yes!" He jumps up, scrambling over to me like I'm holding the answer to everything instead of just a bag of greasy shit. "I'm fucking starved. Cedar's granola bars suck."

"Hey!"

I let loose a soft chuckle at the scowl Cedar throws at Mac's back and hold the bag steady as he dives right in and takes what he knows is his.

"So, she force fed you?" I ask with a crook to my brow, and desperately hoping for a distraction against the weird flutter happening in my stomach.

Mac's gaze flips to mine over the bag and a tingling of recognition rushes over me.

"Uh-huh," he mutters, taking a bite of his now unwrapped burger. "Get her."

I roll my eyes, the break in connection taking that weird tingling along with it, and I instead offer the bag to Cedar. "Burger?"

She snorts and accepts. "Thought you weren't supposed to feed the gremlins this late."

Mac glowers over his cheeseburger at her. "You would know since you have one at home."

There's a snort that has me shaking my head, the aura around the drummer too palpable and contagious to ignore. Like getting ink has somehow reset his mind back to normal.

I missed him like this.

It's making me both warm and fucking exhausted inside.

One minute without me and he's got his light back.

That shouldn't feel as bad as it does … right?

Chapter Nine

Mac

I FEEL JORDAN RETURN more than I see him, the little hairs on the back of my neck rising when I hear the wheels of a chair creek.

"Are you painting his nails?"

It's another session with Cedar, the second day in a row of her torture by way of shading and color. We're hours into the piece, but once more ink colored my skin, she insisted on a break because apparently, I was too green.

Hence, nails.

"You got a problem with that?" Cedar asks my bodyguard without losing a bit of concentration as she swipes black across my thumb nail.

I've painted my nails before. Multiple times. And yet there's something about Jordan being here to witness it happening, that has my insides twisting up.

Does he hate it when I do shit like this?

Nerves build up, my shoulders going tense with each millisecond that passes.

"No," Jordan murmurs as he plops his ass into a chair. I watch him watch us, *me*, and that feeling in my torso loosens.

That's it. That's all he says as Cedar continues applying the paint on each of my fingers.

There's a silence that falls over the three of us, carrying with it a tinge of awkwardness that I don't recall always being there.

Fuck, I really need to shake this off. Get a lock on these feelings that make me act strange enough for even Cedar to say something the second we were alone. I know it's radiating from me like light beams, demanding the attention of anyone willing to recognize it, and poisoning the shit in my life that's also good as it is.

Jordan as my best friend is good just like this.

Which is exactly why we're going to the club as soon as my sister-in-law is back from her studio.

I need a reset.

A chance to see more of what's available to me without all the baggage and restrictions. No more worries and no more tension.

Something to get my mind out of the rut I've fallen in with these age-old feelings that'll never be reciprocated. He's my bodyguard for Chrissake. There's rules and shit against it.

Some*one* to take me straight into the rebound I never let myself have.

Even though there's hope that I'm making the right choice, I still find myself on the verge of nausea at the thought of anyone else touching me.

For so long, it's been him. Right there. At my side, on my mind, and in my heart.

Like he was supposed to be, and not just because of his job, but instead because he *chose* to be. He took the chance to be. As my best friend and partner in crime from the time he joined our crazy little family of found fuckers.

Doesn't that mean more?

To me … it means everything.

And yet it can't mean anything.

Huffing out a breath, I blow on the wet paint in half a daze, though I know it doesn't do much to speed up the drying process.

I go through the motions of changing into what my sister-in-law gives me without much thought, the rest of the room falling away like a backdrop on the stage. No one's looking at it, but it's still there. Still filling out the space in hopes of drawing attention.

My mind deep dives into introspection as we drive, a winding path of thoughts making each step feel like I'm running through water and getting nowhere fast.

I need this, I remind myself for the thousandth time when my Chucks hit the dance floor, the flashing lights and pounding base filling the club up like it's a living thing. Something breathing. Something pulsing with life, and bodies, and freedom.

The autonomy feels so foreign and far away that when I physically reach out to grab it, to hold onto it, my hand filled with a cup instead.

I smash back the contents, though I have no clue what was in it. I don't taste a thing. I don't feel shit, either. Nothing but a tingling numbness that takes over my entire body like a cage that I can't break out of.

The lights all bleed together until there's nothing but one giant bright strobe shining right on me, the beat melding each note as one, leaving nothing but one long rush of static.

Not even the music sounds the same.

My stomach rolls when I feel pressure of a hand on my hip.

An invitation I turn away from.

It's not his.

I swallow back another drink.

Step out from another's grip.

"Mac."

It's like I've left my body behind, my mind watching from a dark corner somewhere as arms that don't belong on me try to box me in. I maneuver away with bile rising up the back of my throat.

I think I'm dancing, but I probably just look like a madman as I swat against another grabby grip.

They aren't him.

I'm swaying, stepping out of embraces and away from sweaty bodies on a beeline to the bathroom when I spot the sign through the haze.

My chest is pumping double time when I all but crash into the vanity held together by stickers and duct tape.

"I need this," I say without any heat to the reflection in the spider-webbed mirror, but not even the words can change the man staring back.

It looks like me, but he's got black smudges under his dead green-blue eyes. Pale skin that's dimmed by a sheen of sweat. A bandana with curly hair spilling from the top that's weighed down by the pressure making me hunch over the sink.

I need this.

The seams are bursting, the demons held back by the strength of the fraying strings getting the better of me.

Just breathe.

Funny how the words sound just like Jordan's in my head that hangs between my stiff shoulders.

"In and out. One breath at a time."

I nod, though I'm not sure if he's real because all I hear is my own thoughts screaming.

"Just like that, Vida. One more."

Warmth floods my shoulder and it's like someone pressed play on my simulation, waking up all of my senses at once, bringing the world back into focus.

The grime-covered drain winking at me.

Sticky tiles beneath my feet.

A white-knuckled grip on the adhesive coated porcelain.

The thumping of music.

My vibrating limbs and a coldness that's seeping into every one of my bones, fought off only by the grip on my shoulder.

I suck in the first full breath like I've been hiding underwater this whole time, and with it, my lungs fill with the distinct scent of *Jordan*.

It's sweet and clean, almost like an apple and soap, and it's the last sense I need to bring my mind home.

Slowly, I straighten and release my death grip, my hands aching in protest as I force my focus on a singular sticker clinging to the mirror's upper corner.

Take the chance. It's yours.

Very fortune cookie, and yet, it feels so damn profound.

I tear my gaze away and nearly lose all the oxygen I just collected when my sight crashes with Jordan's navy blue eyes. They're laced with worry but hardened as if he's holding back anger.

"You mad, bro?" I half snap with a lift to my brow and a thin line to my lips.

His nostrils flare and he stares like he can see right through me.

"You okay?" he grits out, his arms crossing over his puffed chest I do my best to ignore.

"I …" My shoulders sag, exhaustion settling deep into my bones. "I'm fine," I lie.

Jordan sighs, his arm dropping, and just when I think he's going to either give me shit or walk off, he just … looks at me. His gaze softening on mine as he searches for all the answers in my eyes that I let scream all the things inside me.

Maybe if he could just see it for himself.

He reaches out, grabbing the same shoulder he held to calm me and does the last thing I expect.

He pulls me in until I'm practically falling into him, our chests clashing, his heat blanketing my still trembling body.

Shit, he's hugging me.

"Let me take you home, Vida," he says into my hair as I clutch at his sides, my fists clenching around his shirt. "Please."
"O-okay."

Chapter Ten

JORDAN

"**V**IDA, DON'T MAKE ME CARRY YOU."

Though I say the words, I don't mean them.

I'd carry him through Hell if it meant I got to have him back on this planet as his normal sunny self.

Mac just hums half of a response, his lids slammed closed over his eyes that I wish I could look into again and see more than just a bunch of sadness staring back at me.

I feel like I'm missing something.

"Vida."

I shake him awake enough to climb out of the car so I don't have to maneuver his lanky frame from inside it and don't wait for another response before I wrap an arm around his waist and lift.

His long legs automatically wrap around my waist, his arms clinging to my shoulders.

It's close.

Intimate to have his nose buried in my neck and his groin against my pelvis. His hooked ankles bopping over my ass.

The car beeps it's locked notification as I poke blindly at the elevator call button. Once we're secured inside, I wrap both arms around Mac's middle and just … hold him to me.

Chest to chest, the beat of his heart syncing to mine.

The weight of him feels good in my arms.

That familiar tingling sensation creeps up my neck with each floor that passes and for once, I don't fight the feeling.

Instead, I lean into it.

Turn my head into his neck.

Let my eyes slide closed and the heat of his trembling frame seep into me.

Maybe I can steal his anxiety through osmosis.

If I just grip him tight enough, will it leach out from his skin?

Dinging has my eyes snapping open, a flush rushing over my face at my lack of focus on our surroundings, and I walk us to his apartment door.

Realization has me pausing once inside and I clear my throat. "Do you … want— Are you okay? Should I—"

"Shut up and close the door. You're letting the bugs in."

I blink, letting out a weak snicker, but do exactly as he says. "Pretty sure there's no bugs out there."

"That's what Ma used to tell us when we'd hang out the door to talk to our friends and shit."

There's a twinge inside my chest and I clear my throat again.

God, I'm all over the place.

"I'm tired," Mac whispers into my neck, his words skating over my skin, and I suppress a shiver. "Will you … can we sleep on the couch again?"

"You have band practice tomorrow," I say next to his temple, my lips moving against his hair. "You should sleep in the bed."

He snorts, his breath puffing over my quickening pulse as I carry the drummer through the living room.

"You have to at least change." I lift one hand from his back to pluck at the fishnet shirt he ended up in thanks to Aria.

I didn't hate seeing him in it. Paired with his signature black holey jeans and worn-out white Chucks, he looked like a younger, happier version of himself.

Add in the eye liner and I felt like I was going to murder the owner of every set of hands that landed on him back at the club.

He clearly didn't want them on him.

But then it all went to shit in a hot second and I'm still reeling from the deep dive he took for reasons I've yet to figure out.

Though … I find that I don't hate *this*.

Him leaning on me because he needs it.

From me.

I can't remember the last time someone needed … *me*.

My chest pings yet again, that tingling on the back of my neck sticking to me like glue.

When I reach the bed, I have to practically peel him away.

"You need pj's."

Mac drops to his feet and starts stripping.

He's standing in his briefs, ones with little rainbow-printed eggplants on them, and stares longingly at the bed.

If he didn't look so lost, I'd laugh at the briefs covering his tight ass.

They're him.

And they're cute.

Sighing, I plant a hand between his shoulder blades and give him a push. He goes easily, falling face first into the mattress with a groan.

Tingly.

Mac climbs up the bed to lay the right way and tucks his feet under the covers, then looks up at me with a glint of expectance in his eye.

He lifts the blanket in invitation.

I bite the inside of my lip.

If I say yes, does this cross the line?

"You coming?" he asks, hopefulness thick in his voice and I'm nodding before my brain can catch up.

Fuck it. Can't be worse than what we've already done.

Reaching back between my shoulder blades, his eyes locked on mine, I grip my shirt and pull. It flutters to the floor as I place my radio and holster on the nightstand. Undo my belt, letting the jeans drop with a thunk around boots that I toe off.

There's a heat in the way his sight breaks from mine, dropping to the boxers still around my waist as I step up to the bed.

But then he dives into a prone position and rolls onto his side, facing away from me in the middle of the bed.

I chuckle at the ghost of an almost grin I catch before he buries his face in the pillow and climb in behind him, keeping a few inches of space between us as the blanket settles over us.

Rolling to reach for the remote he keeps on the nightstand, Mac moves with me, his ass hitting my hip.

"Oops," he deadpans, and I laugh.

"Such an accident."

"It was," he murmurs, stifling a yawn. "I was just following the heat."

As if he called the shakes up by will alone, he trembles against me.

I hum, hit play on whatever was playing last, and turn into Mac, enveloping him with my body. His legs slot against mine, the hair ticklish. The heat of his back warms my bare chest. The weight of his head on my arm …

He fits just right.

Too right.

"Good night, Vida," I rumble into his hair and wrap an arm around his ribs, my palm flattening between his pecs.

He sighs deep, sinking into me.

"Night."

It doesn't take long for the soft little snores to accompany the sound of *Brooklyn Nine-Nine* playing from the TV, and I let myself settle into it.

This is what he needed. Comfort and connection.

To be a human for once.

Mac mumbles something, and I'm about to lift my head so that I can see his face, but then his ass scoots back and slams right into my pelvis.

My cock jumps.

Heat radiates through my boxers, warming me.

It's just been a while since I've had sex.

Been even longer since I've held someone.

And still … I know I should put a little space between us, though I don't.

Because it's making Mac comfortable and that's all I've wanted.

All I've needed.

Chapter Eleven

JORDAN

"**I**S THAT ALL YOU GOT?"

My arms are on the verge of unmovable, shaking, and still I manage to get them up.

"Oh, I could go all day."

It's a lie I've been telling myself through the pure exhaustion that settled into my bones the moment I woke up in a cold sweat, with Mac still in my arms, from yet another nightmare fueled by flames. The smoke was thick enough that my throat still feels scratchy, the heat so hot that my skin still burns.

Even after twenty-two years.

And is precisely why I snuck out of bed and have been getting my ass beat by Peach, a fellow bodyguard, ever since.

"Then let's see it, big guy." The man that's smaller than me, shorter than me, and an expert in Akido or some weird shit like that, lifts his gloved hands and flexes his fingers at me in a *bring it* gesture.

Forcing a breath through my nose like a bull readying to charge, I bounce on the balls of my feet one way, and then the other in hopes of distracting my opponent before pulling an elbow back and throwing wide.

Too slow.

Peach darts inside, sinks a jab on my aching ribs, and elbows me right in the mouth.

The taste of copper coats my tongue and brings a smile to my face.

"You're all mad, I swear," Peach remarks with his own bounce and testing jabs to my forearms.

"He says with a smile."

"Boxing was your idea, genius." I snort at his comeback and tilt my head just out of his swing's reach. "And as much as I love beating you up … you wanna talk about it?"

What a loaded question.

Do I want to talk about spending the night in my client's bed, his body tucked into me like some kind of metaphorical puzzle piece, or that I dreamt of my parents dying all over again as if I haven't thought about that night every day for the last two decades?

Or maybe I should talk about how I've never felt like a single thing in my life was steady enough to trust? No home or family placement lasting more than a few months at a time, the centers even shorter. That my foster care was filled with judgmental assholes and bullies for parental figures that made sure I knew I didn't belong.

How this job is the one I've held the longest, and I think that's only because nothing here is ever the same either, that each day brings something new for me to navigate?

That I've started having … this *something* tingling down my spine, like some kind of symbolic message from the universe, except they forgot to leave me the notes on how to read it?

And I'm not even going to let myself think about how part of my panic this morning included morning wood that got *stiffer* when I remembered it was Mac in my arms. How? I still don't understand considering my heart was racing out of my chest, yet my dick kept pointing straight.

His ass and those fucking rainbow eggplants.

"No," I snap out way too fast and duck under a swing he throws out. "I mean, no thank you."

Peach snorts. "He thinks he has manners."

I shrug and we dance, rounding the ring with light taps each of us block. "I think I'm funny," I deadpan with another lift of my shoulder.

"You sound just like Mac." Peach snickers.

My stomach flips at the mention of my drummer and a whole new wave of questions roll right over me, fast and hard.

Shit I hadn't even begun to consider.

How do I know I've crossed the line between client and friend?

I pounce, using the rush to throw a punch that Peach not only deflects, but catches and twists. He holds on, his grip tight even with the gloves' smooth surface.

"I—how did you … fuck." We circle and I fight against the hold with a growl that's all frustration and nothing to do with the spar.

"Go ahead. Talk to Papa Peach." He dips and snickers when I throw an elbow with my free arm. "Not letting go until you say something."

How am I getting my ass handed to me right now?

"Don't wanna talk about it." My chest is pumping and not from the exertion of working out with the fittest person I know.

No, it's panic that's bubbling up all over again.

Caging me in and closing my throat.

It makes me act before my brain can catch up, all of my thoughts whooshing right out of my ears as my head thrusts forward and my forehead connects with Peach's nose.

The noise that escapes him is pure shock as he stumbles back, his gloved hand releasing his hold on me to go right his face, though the leather does nothing to hold back the gushing of blood that leaks out.

"*Again?* Mother*fuck.*"

His free fist flings out, the glove connecting with my jaw and splitting my lip wide open.

"Fuck," I mutter, my tongue running through the blood filling my mouth.

"A headbutt? *Seriously*?" Peach scoffs and uses his teeth to rip the Velcro back so that he can free a hand and pinch at the bridge of his nose. "You assholes and your big feelings. *Pfft.*"

"Shit, I'm—" Shaking myself from the shit in my head, I dash across the in-house gym to the paper towel dispenser on the wall and tear off a giant stream.

Wadding it, I pass it to Peach who accepts and drops to the ring, crisscrossing his legs.

Guilt washes over me and I sit with him, though I can't quite sit like he does so I let my legs stretch out in front of me and rip off my own gloves. "I'm sorry."

"Uh-huh," Peach mumbles, though it comes out nasally. "You guys *have* to stop breaking my nose. The shit hurts."

I hang my head, and he hisses.

And then something crunches, and I nearly throw up at the idea that the fucker just reset his own nose.

He lets loose a deep groan, his eyes watering when I look back up, confirming my suspicions.

"Now fucking spill, you dick."

I pull my knees up and rest my elbows on top of them. "Should I get med for that?"

"No. Stop stalling."

Huffing, I stare right into the daggers he's throwing at me with his green eyes.

And my mouth just opens.

"How did you know … y'know …" I trail off and throw a hand out, though I have no clue what I'm gesturing to.

I feel the heat creep up my face.

"Know what?"

"That you're …" I swallow hard. "Like bi or whatever."

My stomach rolls.

Peach's spine snaps straight.

"How did *you* know?"

I think I might throw up.

Peach's head tilts like a dog trying to hear me better and though he might look like a funky Pomeranian with all the ink and piercings and highlighter orange hair, he's actually more like a German Shepherd.

"I shouldn't have asked that. I'm so—"

"No, no. Don't take it back now." He drops the paper towels, unveiling his crimson grin. "It's called gaydar, boo, and clearly you got one."

I blink.

"What's that mean?"

Peach just shakes his head and tries his best to clean up his face with the already fucked wad of paper in his hands.

With a smile.

"Yes, I'm bi," he confirms.

I swallow. "How'd you figure it out?"

He shrugs like it's no big deal to suddenly have that questioning thought gnawing at the back of your mind as if you've been missing a piece to this fucking puzzle you have no clue was lost to the void of life.

Am I … Am I attracted to—

"My dick got hard in a locker room." He snickers then winces and brings a hand up to his face only to stop midair and drop it. "And then it stayed hard for the cheerleaders, too."

My mouth works like a fish, my brows meeting in the middle of my forehead.

"It was always there for me," he clarifies as if he can see the struggle written all over my face. "Not everyone is like that, especially if there's any trauma barring self-actualization." He licks his lip, then swipes it away with the back of his hand. "It's totally normal to question those ideologies later in life."

I nod, though I don't understand most of what he just said.

"It's not like I'm …"

I'm what?

Gay? No. Bi? That doesn't feel quite right either.

Broken? Probably.

I huff, push to my feet, and start pacing.

"What's Mac say?"

My chest constricts, another wave of guilt nearly stealing my breath.

"I haven't …"

"Oh. *Ohhh*," Peach drags out. "We're ignoring that. Got it."

I nod again, though I'm not really trying to ignore anything about the drummer. It's just easier to avoid thinking about how having him in my arms felt like *more*.

Didn't it?

How I want to do it all over again because I know *he* felt good about it.

Didn't he?

And that makes my dick twitch.

Shit, I'm so fucking confused.

"If a guy made your dick hard, then you're not straight." Peach pushes to his feet with a groan. "How about that?"

Biting the inside of my lip, I stare at a spot in the floor.

"But what if it wasn't just that? What if … what if it was the *feeling*?"

Peach's non-bloodied hand lands on my shoulder. "I'm gonna text you something. Look it up when you're *alone*. Give it some thought. I'm here when you're ready to talk."

I barely nod and Peach leaves me to my crisis.

Chapter Twelve

Jordan

A LL DAY, I BOTH ignored my phone, and watched it intently.

The little red dot screaming at me from a distance, like a beacon to all the answers swirling in my mind and making my chest ache.

What if I'm not straight?

My stomach flips.

Not sure if my current state is considered *alone* enough with Mac's head on my shoulder, his couch threatening to claim us both all over again after a long ass day, but I don't have it in me to wait any longer.

His soft snores tell me he's as asleep as he has been since the movie started and with gentle movements, I lay us back once again. Just like that night that led to him clinging to me in his sleep.

Maybe it's really been me that's been fucking with him.

I'm not on my a-game. I've been distracted. So focused on what's keeping Mac deep in the dumps of what I think is depression, that I never thought it could have been my fault.

No, that doesn't seem right.

Right?

Mac has his own shit going on, but if I could get my head on straight, I could help better understand his.

I lift my phone, the blank screen reflecting back at me like a barb to my already thumping heart.

Because inside the rectangle of my case is *us.*

Mac and me.

His head resting on my chest and my nose resting in his hair.

It's dark, and his bandana is missing, but I can still make out the soft lines of his sleeping face lit up by the glow of the TV.

We look like more than just best friends.

Don't we?

I silently clear my throat and unlock the phone.

Is that how we always look?

The little red bubble on my messages calls for me to press the icon and pull up the article in Peach's text thread.

Demi—

My heart thumps wildly and I flick my eyes away from the screen to draw in a deep breath.

Could I really not be straight after all this time?

I've been with women. My entire life I've been drawn to them. In relationships. Sleeping together. So why now?

Mac stirs against me, his arm flopping over my ribs, and even more panic floods my system at the idea that I've been caught.

I swipe away the article on my screen and lock the phone.

This is insane. Confusing.

Distracting.

I know who I am and what I like and there's nothing wrong with guys platonically touching. There's nothing different about seeking comfort from those that know you.

We're best friends for fucks' sake.

That's all this is.

I'm doing a job and being a best friend.

Mac's doing okay, and that's all that matters.

My sexuality has no place here.

Chapter Thirteen

Mac

"I'm gay."

The statement earns me a quirk of the brow that disappears behind the bill of my bodyguard's hat and the flick of a fry in my direction.

I swear I remember seeing a list of definitions that piqued my interest. Things about intimacy and sexuality that had me wondering if Jordan thought I was questioning myself.

Is he trying to educate himself to help me?

Maybe I was just dreaming.

"And?" he mumbles as he lets us into the back of my sister-in-law's store.

My answer dies in the flurry of chaos that surrounds us, a clothing rack nearly clipping me when I enter.

"Sorry!"

Jordan grabs me, his hand on my arm heating my skin, and puts himself in front of me.

"Stay close," he murmurs as he begins to weave us through the maze of people and wheeled displays, the back of his shirt fisted in my grip.

I've never seen this place so busy.

"No wonder Aria needed someone to come get the Hell spawn." I spot the dino-nugget-printed pj's through the throngs of people and start pushing Jordan in my niblings direction.

Aria stands when we reach their little huddle and grabs my face hard enough to smoosh my cheeks. "*Macaroni.*"

"Hey, baby girl." I offer her a grin when she pulls me down 'til her face fills my vision.

"Fucking *thank you*," she whispers, then releases me. "My assistant's hands are already full, and they *will not* leave her be."

I snort and nod, crouching next to the twins who squeal in greeting and toss away the toys in their sticky hands.

"Uncle Mackie!"

I'm sandwiched between the two tiny humans, both sets of arms threatening to strangle me when I wrap my arms around them and stand.

"Peeball, Mackie. *Peeballs*," my namesake yells into my right ear and I swing my narrowed gaze at him. "*Unckie*," he corrects, then slams his head against my shoulder and rubs his cheek against my shirt like a cat. "Pweez."

I try to hide my snicker as Elle threads little fingers into my hair from my left. "Where's your daddy?"

Elle shrugs. "Getting dressed or somefin'."

I catch Aria's nod as she tucks her phone back into her pocket with a grin. "Part of this mess, like always," she says with pride, though she pretends to be annoyed. "I'll need you back here later, once all this has calmed down."

Nodding, I tighten my grip on the beasts in my arms and turn toward Jordan. "Ready?"

"Yeah!" Makkin exclaims, fist pumping the air, his little head still on my shoulder. "Peeballs, peeballs, peeballs."

Jordan swallows and spins away, another muttered "Stay close" off his lips as he leads us back through the working mob and out into the blazing sunlight.

We walk down the alleyway, Makkin slumping in my arms with each step closer to the empty section of the building, Elle still twirling my curls.

Well, not so empty.

While the original owner of this storefront has refused to sell it to anyone, he does charge us rent to keep it that way and in turn, we provide the security.

Which means that we sometimes use this space.

Over the years, I've collected a few things that just don't move well. Things I would legit cry over if any part of it got damaged. Things that take me back to my teenage dirtbag days with my brother and all the games he lost to me. So, when we all agreed to keep our homebase closer to Ma and the town that two of my four brother's partners are from, I stashed the shit here.

And it still brings a smile to my face when Jordan drops the paper bag he's been carrying to pull the drop cloth from the first Pac-Man inspired pinball machine and plug in the actual arcade tower right next to it.

It's only the two units for now, but I've got my eye on more.

"*Peeballs,*" Makkin whispers in awe.

"Uh-huh. Pinball." I maneuver their little bodies so I can drop into one of the folding chairs and prop them on each of my knees. "But lunch first."

Jordan sits next to me and starts handing out little boxes of nuggets. Elle nibbles, while Makkin shoves an entire fistful into his mouth.

My own box is tucked into my hand, but with the little bodies against me, I can't reach to actually feed myself without squishing them.

"*Tyro,*" I mutter and throw him a look. "Feed me."

Navy eyes dart to my mouth when I drop it open, and his throat moves with a swallow. He stares for a long, charged beat, his eyes darkening.

His lips part just slightly.

His breath quickens.

And then I nearly choke when Elle shoves a half-nibbled nugget between my gaping lips.

I cough and chew, swallowing the bite nearly whole as Makkin giggles and jams another nugget against my mouth. "Eat, Unckie!"

Making a show of stealing the nugget from his tiny fingers with my teeth, Elle squeals and wiggles an escape while Makkin just laughs and does it all over again.

By the time the nugs are gone, I feel like my face is covered in grease and breading. The little heathens have retreated to the arcade games with cleaned hands, and I'm in desperate need of a shower.

"Do you want any?"

The question catches me so off guard that I double take my bodyguard. "Demons?"

Jordan's hat is pulled low, the bill covering his eyes, making him look guarded. But he nods.

Something squeezes in my chest as I swing my gaze back to the tiny curly-haired heads and matching pj's. Makkin lets loose a war cry and mashes the button on the pinball while Elle just gently guides the Pac-Man around the little map in the screen, eating away at the white dots.

"Maybe ... someday," I answer, though the doubt is strong.

As much as I want a family, my own little gaggle of Hell raisers, I know that I couldn't do it alone. Nor would I want to. Having no one to share the little moments with? Moments just like this one where the kids get to experience the same thing I did when I was young? Learning and growing together. Discovering all the things for the first time.

Just me and a kid or two?

That's more depressing than the idea that I'll never have them at all.

Because at least then ... no one would be missing out on anything.

I shrug in an attempt to dislodge the pang in my chest.

No one except me.

Chapter Fourteen

JORDAN

*I*HAD NO BUSINESS *asking him that.*

Thinking that.

Wondering that.

The organized mayhem of Aria's shop has calmed, but not considerably.

It has made it easier to step back, watch from afar as Mac hands off the twins to his brother and is swept away by Aria.

He's safe with her, I know he is.

Yet I still find his absence palpable. Like I've left my favorite hoodie behind or lost my lucky coin. Except, I've never believed in that shit. There was never anything in my life that I could attest to being a beckon of some kind of fortune or blessing. Mostly, I've been more prone to find the things that were *unlucky,* which is probably why I opened my big mouth.

I shouldn't have asked him.

He's single and has been for as long as I have known him. That wasn't fair of me to bring it up, and yet … I can't find it in me to hate his answer.

Mac wants kids … someday.

Just not today. Which only eases the guilt swimming in my chest about looking at him the way that I did. For feeling the things that I am.

For imagining what I did when his mouth dropped open.

Feed me.

I try to shake off the tingling that has taken over my skin by walking around, checking in with Jonathon, even doing another round outside.

The fresh air does nothing to ease the tightness in my chest or the churning in my stomach. But when I step back inside and see the studio has been converted into a photoshoot, my feet root in the spot.

It's not the backdrop that takes up one whole wall and drapes across the ground like the satin can mimic waves. Nor is it the lights with the umbrellas attached or even the camera taking up Aria's sister's face.

No.

It's Mac.

As always, drawing my attention right to him despite the flurry of others in the room.

With his tight black jeans and painted nails. His Chucks that are probably as old as he is. Those wild curls of his peeking out between his bandana and the hood of a brand-new hoodie.

An unzipped hoodie with the As Above emblem painted in every color of the rainbow on the left side of his chest.

But as much as the bare chest beneath it catches my sight and dares me to hold it, I don't.

No.

Instead, I flick my sight to the hardline of his jaw that hosts a ghost of a smile and the pride that shines in his lined greenish eyes.

He lifts his chin, defiant and strong, and shoves his hands in the pockets of the hoodie. The move straightens the logo, making it stand out, a stark contrast to the dark material behind it, and my chest fills.

He looks like a warrior readying for battle. A rebellious leader.

A misfit dressed in all black.

My heart thunders in my chest when he spins, the same colorful name across the expanse of his shoulders that lift when he flexes, the hoodie raising enough to flash the skin of his lower back.

But when he tips back the hood and looks over his shoulder right at me with such an intensity in his eyes, I stop breathing.

Holy fuck, he's beautiful.

His grin spreads when I continue to stare, frozen and tingling from head to toe when he turns my way, and hooks his thumbs in the waistband of his jeans, tugging them lower.

My gaze snaps to the light trail that starts at his navel and disappears into his jeans that are just on the right side of appropriate.

My mouth waters.

The tattoo is right next to it, fresh and stretching from that low waistband clear up to his ribs. It's a gorgeously rendered eagle diving for its prey, drumsticks in its talons like it just plucked them up.

Forcing myself to look up, our gazes clash and he shoots me a wink before breaking the connection and looking over his shoulder at the camera.

I force a shaking breath. Uncross my arms that I don't remember moving. Break myself from the trance Mac put me in and spin to find Peach staring at me from behind two black eyes and a cock to his head.

He mouths an *oh* and bounces his brows but then winces.

I clear my throat and flip him off.

Movement draws my sight back to the photoshoot and my fists clench against the wave of chills that overwhelm me when I see that all of Mac's brothers have joined him.

And each one of them are wearing the same logo in different Pride color combinations.

Fin's hoodie has pink, purple, and blue.

Pink, yellow, and blue make up Leo's tee.

Toby's chest totes purple, black, grey, and white.

And Rex … his is yellow, white, purple, and black.

Though I don't know what all of them stand for, I do know that my drummer stands in the middle of them with his rainbow on full display and shining, glassy eyes.

Flashes capture the moment, but there's not a damn thing that could capture the amount of pride I feel for the man Mac is in this moment. Nothing that could express the chills that rack over me at the acceptance crackling in the air.

The raw power of a moment like this.

"Fuck," Peach mutters thickly from beside me, then takes off, photo-bombing the shoot by walking right up to Fin and grabbing at the hoodie the guitarist wears. They laugh and fight over the material until it ends up on Peach's shoulders, the hood pulled tight around his face.

A face that is blotted in red like he's fighting back his emotions just as much as I am, the camera catching every bit of it.

"Hey, Jordan," Aria's words shake me from the stupor this family has put me in, and I look down at the woman that designed it all. She's holding out a folded garment, and when I take it from her, unfurling it, my breath catches all over again.

"Ari …" I breathe out, my sight darting over the rainbow print pitched inside bold bands of white and black to the woman with watering eyes.

"I didn't think I'd be so emotional …" She sputters out a thick snicker and waves a limp hand at the hoodie in my hand. "I just thought you might like to match him."

I clutch it in both hands and nod. "Thank you."

She smiles and nods back, and I catch her before she can spin away.

"Which one is … um—" I swallow thickly, "is the demi colors?"

Her smile softens and she holds up a finger before disappearing. She's only gone a moment, but it's still long enough for my stomach to flip and regret to build up.

I clear my throat.

"Here, hun." She places a smaller bundle in my grip, and my brows bunch when I notice the print is different than all the others. The colors are the same as the one Toby wears, but this one has a black triangle feeding into the purple, white, and grey stripes.

She flashes me another warm smile, pats my arm, then joins the rest of them.

My thumb grazes over the raised pattern on the T-shirt, the shine of the black catching my eye.

"Is that fucking glitter? *Aria.*"

Chapter Fifteen

Mac

"OKAY, OKAY, GOAT NADS!" I call into the huddle and swipe a finger beneath both eyes. "Who's up for pizza?" My sight lands on Toby who visibly relaxes, a green sobriety chip flipping between his fingers.

He nods, though it's shaky, smiles, and whispers a "Thank you."

I grin back and wrap my arm around his shoulders.

He relaxes even more.

A flash of guilt tempts me with its ping of familiarity, but I let the buzz of agreement around me wash it all out.

My dark cloud has no place here right now.

Because not only did Aria surprise the shit out of me with a brand-new Pride line for our merch, I can still feel Jordan's searing gaze track my movements.

I like that too much.

But I won't let that voice in my head burst my bubble.

After pizza at Georgie's, Toby takes the twins home for bedtime and the rest of us find our way to Denver's bar. It's on the smaller side for nightlife, homier, but Den is a good friend and keeps the place respectable enough that we can show up and know that we won't be bombarded with bullshit just because we're in a band.

Shots are distributed, toasts are chanted, and liquor is consumed.

We make a dance floor by pushing empty tables back, and when the lights dip low and Den flips on the twinkle lights above, Peach finds me in the mass of bodies swaying to the Electric Call boy song blaring from the speakers.

"So, what's up with the—" I point at his nose.

His brow wings and a snicker that looks like it hurts bunches up his face. "I'll give you two guesses."

"Did you walk in on Cedar and Fin again?" I can't hold back the chuckle, but he shakes his head.

"Nope, try again."

The song changes to a slower beat and Peach follows my lead. We're kind of dancing together, not touching but close enough to probably look like we are.

"Okay, I'm stumped."

Peach snorts, his hands coming up to rest on my shoulders when a stranger bobs a little too close.

"Who?" I ask again and bring my hands up to hold his ribs. It's completely platonic, triggering no need or deep-seated desire and it's actually fucking nice to dance for once without feeling like I might throw up. *I missed it.*

"One more guess. Bet you won't get it."

The song slows again, flipping before the last one is over to Sam Smith's "Dancing with a Stranger", and Peach migrates closer.

"Ehhh, but Fin doesn't get rabid fans. If it wasn't him, then my guess is you dropped your phone on your face and are playing it off like a battle wound."

Peach barks out a laugh and sways into me, his arms wrapping around my shoulders. "I don't think a phone would break my nose, but sure."

"*Broken?*"

"Yup."

My grip tightens on his ribs, stilling him. "*Why* did they break your nose?"

He snorts, his eyes darting over my shoulder. "Dunno." His sight flicks back to mine and his grin widens wickedly. "I'm sure you'll find out."

Chapter Sixteen

JORDAN

PEACH IS PUSHING HIS fucking luck.

I'm going to break his nose on purpose this time.

His arms tighten around Mac and his head lays on my drummer's shoulder, and I've got one foot planted on the makeshift dance floor before my brain finally catches up.

What am I doing?

My chest pumps with the breath I force.

What if someone like Peach won't make him seem so dull?

Everything in me freezes except my clenching fists.

What if he's meant to—

"Guys. *Guys!*"

Breaking myself out of the trance the drummer keeps pulling me into, I turn in time to catch Leo making his way to the center of the dance floor, his phone in his hand.

There's elation lining his normally stoic face, his grin huge as he grabs onto the shoulders and arms of the guys around him.

"We're going overseas, boys!"

The news rings like a hammer fist straight to the temple after a five-round match.

"Shut the fuck up," someone yells in disbelief, but Leo just shakes his head.

"It's happening, motherfuckers. We're starting in Germany."

A European tour.

My stomach turns.

New places and venues. New fans and security protocols.

New. New. New.

My throat feels thick when I watch Mac wrap his arms around Peach and swing him around. My stomach clenches painfully when his smile is light and genuine and aimed right at the other bodyguard. And then at his bandmates and manager.

It's not until his seeking sight lands on me and drops that I feel the knife sink right into the center of my chest.

It's me.

I'm the switch that kills his brightness.

He comes to me through the crowd, squeezing past bodies with a furrow in his brow and a tightness to his features.

I can't keep doing this to him.

"Tyro," he mutters, stopping just short of me, his throat bobbing with a swallow. "Did you hear Leo?"

He deserves a better friend.

I dip my chin in affirmation.

One that doesn't wake up with a stiffy in his back.

"That's cool … right? We're going abroad."

One that's not confusing friendship and sexuality with loneliness.

He forces a smile that I return and it's like he can already tell.

Someone that's gonna light him up, not tear him down.

"Yeah," I lie. "It's good."

I clear my throat, though it does nothing to loosen the muscles hellbent on choking me to death.

He deserves this. A chance. A fresh start.

Without me killing his light.

I nod even though he hasn't said anything else.

He deserves to find that.

He playfully pushes at my tense shoulder that barely moves, his hand dropping to his side.

"Yeah," I say again, though I don't feel any bit of it. "It'll be fun."

For you.

Chapter Seventeen

Mac

W ITH EVERY DAY THAT the band gets closer to us leaving, Jordan pulls away from me.

It started with having Peach take me home the night that we found out about the tour and continued with him shutting me out in every way. Even when we are in the same room, he's avoided me. He hasn't come to my apartment to check in. Hasn't slept near me. Hasn't called.

Today will be the third day in a row that I haven't even *seen him*.

Instead, Peach has been hanging out as if their assignments have changed and everyone forgot to tell me.

The ache in my chest has burrowed deeper with each moment that passes without Jordan, steadily feeding into something uglier I've done my best to tame.

But when I call him for the second time, hoping he'll pick up and tell me he'll meet us at the airport, and I get sent straight to voicemail, I lose it.

Did he figure out I'm in love with him?

The keys to my car cut into my palm with how hard I grip them. The elevator too slow. The drive too long. My pulse too high.

And when I pull up outside of Aria's shop, the blanket of a cloudy night feeling like just another added weight on my shoulders, I storm through the front entrance with purpose.

"Mac, what the hell are you doing here? Where's Peach?"

My chest pumps with my pants. "Fuck Peach. And *fuck you.*"

Jordan jolts like my words are a physical slap and stands from his little stool.

"What is your fucking deal?" I seethe, pointer finger digging into his chest and as much as I loathe the feeling, it's the first thing I have felt other than dread in days.

Does he hate me?

"*Me?*" Jordan scoffs and swats my hand away, but steps closer. "Let's go outside."

"No."

His jaw clenches.

And even though I don't want to give him anything, I spin and punch my way back outside. Black skies greet me, their weight unloading the moment my Chucks hit the sidewalk.

Convenient.

"So, what is it?" I ask over the sound of the incoming storm, the rain pelting the pavement, and throw my arms out even though my heart is beating out of my chest. "Tell me what I did."

Did I fuck this all up somehow?

Jordan shakes his head, his eyes dropping to my feet as his shoulders lift with an inhale. "You didn't do anything wrong, Mac."

"Then what is it?" I shout and drop my arms, slapping them against my wet thighs. "How? *How* can my best friend not give a shit about something so amazing?"

His shoulders just lift.

"*A second European tour,* Jordan."

His eyes snap up to mine.

"I'm proud of you, Mac. You know I am."

I let loose a growl, my hands going to my head and dig into my wet hair. "*That's not the fucking point.*"

"I know," he mutters. "But I wanted you to hear that."

It all feels so fucking *heavy*. Like he's keeping shit from me. Hiding behind a damn façade he's never, *ever,* used on me and time's running out.

I'm supposed to be on an airplane by now.

My sight goes skyward, the burn from my eyes mixing with the rain covering my face.

"Say it, Jordan."

His sigh is audible enough to draw my sight and the hurt in his eyes makes my chest ache so fucking deep.

"You deserve this." His nostrils flare, though those navy blues swim with something so deep that I can't look away. "You don't need me for it."

There's a punch of defeat that twists up my insides.

He's not coming with me.

"You need to go, Mac."

I bite my lip to keep it from wobbling.

Doesn't he know?

"Jordan," I croak into the rain when he shakes his head. "Why can't you come with me?" I whisper to the storm, too afraid to hear the answer, but unable to walk away until I do.

"It's … I—"

I do need you.

IneedyouIneedyouIneedyou.

"I'll be here when you get back, okay?" he says when I can't get the words out. His smile is the fakest thing I've ever seen, and it *hurts.* "Be the wild rockstar in Europe. Who knows, maybe you'll like it more."

He takes a step back and I'm too shocked to call out. Then another I can't stop. Another. Until he's walking back inside my sister's store, and I'm left in the wake of his destruction.

I'm out of time.

"But we're best friends ..." I whisper to the rain through numb lips, though I know it's too late. "Right?"

He's already gone.

Chapter Eighteen

Jordan

"Come on, man," Cedar calls from her chair, her hands busy packing her bags. "We're all going to meet up with them in Dublin. Ink for everyone."

I nod and keep my ass right where it has been for weeks.

"I'll be here when you get back."

Chapter Nineteen

Jordan

"We'll be home for Christmas," Mac murmurs into the phone and something akin to hope threatens to blossom in my chest.

He didn't come.

Chapter Twenty

JORDAN

Please don't kiss anyone.

Chapter Twenty-One

Jordan

"**T**his year's Skittle combo is red, orange, and white," I say into the voice memo I'm preparing to send to Mac and lean into the bare studs behind me. "Why they added orange in the Valentine's bag doesn't make sense to me, but I think they're my favorite."

Because they remind me of you.

Bright and sunny.

Chapter Twenty-Two

Mac

I LOOK AT THE timestamp on the message from Jordan and my stomach cramps so bad that I hold it.

Sixteen hours ago.

Another missed chance. A crossed timeline that never seems to settle. Thousands of miles and a single lifetime away.

If I type a hundred *I miss you's* into the little text box, will he say it back?

My thumbs hover over the screen but I can't see the letters through the water that steals my vision.

He could have been right here beside me.

He chose not to.

Locking the phone, I throw it across my empty room and turn into the pillow beneath my head and scream.

Chapter Twenty-Three

JORDAN

*T*HIS WAS A TERRIBLE *idea.*

Sweat pours down my back.

Mac's gonna freak about this.

Fatigue threats to settle into my bones, but I push on.

I know he will.

Chapter Twenty-Four

Jordan

I STARE AT THE text on my screen, unease warping my gut.

The response is almost instant, and it makes me wonder where the hell they are.

Sighing, I lock my phone and swipe away the dampness from my face with my shirt—*Mac's shirt*.

"Jorrrrdan," Makkin chirps, his voice echoing. "Do you miss Unckie?"

I glance at the scratched marks across his paper as he scribbles giant lines over what I think was supposed to be a sun.

I sigh.

He's my best friend.

"Yeah. Yeah, I do."

Of course I do.

"Me, too."

Chapter Twenty-Five

JORDAN

TWELVE-HOUR ROTATIONS SOUNDED LIKE the perfect thing to steady all the things that went wrong six months ago, but as I lay on top of Mac's bed while the sun beats in on the windows, I lose another chance at falling asleep.

It's okay. I know I deserve it.

I'm still no closer to an answer on what the hell I want in this life. What label I'm supposed to wear. What the hell any of it means. Why I'm checking my phone and hoping that Mac'll send more than just the obligatory responses for once.

I know it's not doom scrolling the internet.

Yet here I am. Swiping through videos and ending up on the thirst trap side of the web.

And as much as I can appreciate the hard work it takes to keep a body in shape, I still find that none of them call to me. None of them keep my attention.

None of them make my dick hard.

Not even the masked women with thick thighs and enough tits to smother someone.

Sighing, I flick away another video and pause when it lands on a song I could hum in my sleep.

And then I full on freeze when a tattoo I recognize fills the screen.

An eagle inked into a hip.

Drumsticks grasped in its talons.

And a golden trail of hair that runs down from the navel to the low set of his jeans.

"Fuck."

I lick my lips when his hips pop to the beat. Left. Then right. Back again. The screen jerks upwards, filling with Mac's face and I couldn't stop the groan even if I'd tried.

He looks like a god. High cheekbones and a sharp jaw. Curls spilling out of his bandana. A deeper tint to his skin that only amplifies the tan line across his waist.

A waist I've held onto.

Fuck, I miss him.

His carefree laugh. The way his excitement vibrates through him all the time. How he can never sit still. His love for arcade games and his shitty diet.

The terms of endearment masked by stupid nicknames.

The warmth of him so close to me, but not touching, that I know I'm not alone.

The video replays and I hum along to the song, my attention zeroing in on the drumbeats in the background.

Chills rack over me when I imagine Mac playing each note, his powerful arms swinging through the air without caring how hard or how loud he has to be.

How he takes up space just by existing.

Shines in a sea of darkness.

I love that about him.

Swiping away the video, I engage the music streaming app and let the notes of Mac fill the room.

It's heavy and harsh and it puts a smile on my face.

Because it's just Mac.

Chapter Twenty-Six

Mac

"**H**EY, DOC."

"Mac, it's good to hear from you."

The tiny phone speaker has nothing on the real thing, but there's something about hearing her voice that makes me want to weep.

Because if she's here, then things aren't so different after all, even if it's been six months since we spoke last.

"You know, you didn't have to run all the way to Europe to get out of our last talk."

I snicker and tip my shoulder up to swipe at the tears already escaping down my face. "I know." I roll my watering eyes. "All I had to do was hit *cancel* on the website."

She hums and eyes me through the screen. "So? How are we feeling?"

I sigh against the weight that wants to settle into my chest and pull my knees up and hug them. "Like garbage."

She nods. "Explain that, then."

My heart crawls up my throat. "Well, for starters …" I gnaw at my bottom lip. "I'm in love with my best friend."

"Mm-hm," she murmurs and arches a brow. "And?"

"And he didn't choose me." There's a choked sob that works its way up my throat. "For the first fucking time ever, he didn't come with me, and I don't understand. I don't know what to do without him." I sniff back another noise that claws up my throat. It's ugly and it hurts. "All these amazing places and moments …" I throw a hand out. "I should be happy, but all I can think about is him."

There's a softness that takes over the doctor's features. "Have you … talked to him about these feelings? Does he know you want him there?"

I slump and dig the heel of my palm into my eye socket. "And say what? Please hug me because it's the only time I feel free?"

It's heavy and desperate and completely insensitive to the fact that he would not choose me if he didn't have to.

He's straight.

See also: he's not fucking here now.

"Then what?" I mumble to the rumpled bed sheets. "Lose the friendship we do have because I can't keep my little crush to myself?"

She drags in a deep breath and leans closer to the phone. "But what if."

My bottom lip wobbles just like it did that night in the rain. *I don't know how I'll ever go back to Aria's shop.* "That sounds too much like a fantasy, doc."

"Couldn't fantasy become reality?"

I shake my head because it's just not possible. There's nothing that Jordan could say that would change the shit storm of chance we've been placed in. Even if he did … even if he admitted he was curious … I don't know that I could bear being his first guy.

No one ends up with their firsts.

Deep down, I know that my heart wouldn't be able to take the beating of having him, only to lose him when he realizes it's just a curiosity and not a reality.

"It doesn't matter," I mumble.

"It does, though. It matters a whole lot, and you won't know unless you try."

"I thought therapy was supposed to make me feel better," I grumble and swipe at my face. "Not like I'm a dumpster fire on a crash course to self-destruction."

Dr. Surah snorts and I flick my eyes to the screen that holds her face. "It's meant to identify our self-destructive ways and work through them."

"So, you're saying I *am* a fuck up. Cool. Stamp of shrink approval right here." I muster up enough of a smile that she knows I'm kidding, but only slightly.

All of this makes me feel like I really am a headcase with a broken heart. Defective. *Destructive.*

There are too many things at risk. Too many things that can break.

And I just feel so fucking fragile.

Like an already splintered pane waiting to shatter.

I'm in too deep. Aching for the one person that doesn't want me.

Not like that.

I end up stacking the extra pillows on top of the comforter and fall into a fitful sleep in a cold bed a little later.

Alone.

Chapter Twenty-Seven

Mac

Smoke burns its way down my raw throat.

My hands shake. Ribs ache. Legs scream.

And beside me, Toby breathes his cigarette like its oxygen.

"How bad is it?" I risk a glance over my shoulder.

"I am *fiendin'*. Bad."

Taking a final drag, I flick my cigarette to the cracked pavement and push off from the wall to grab his shoulders. "Look at me."

His jaw tightens, but he flicks his gaze up to meet mine.

"Count the days."

"Three hundred, fifty. Today. Three hundred and fucking fifty and that *fucker*—"

I push him back against the wall when he jolts forward, the smell of cheap beer permeating from his shirt.

"That fucker is going to be eating through a straw for a year." My knuckles throb as proof. "Okay? Now just … gimme your shirt."

He tucks another lit cigarette between his lips and grips the logo in the center of his chest. The wet material gives away freely to his anger, shredding to pieces and landing among the debris on the ground.

"Fucking metal, Broby." I snicker and steal the smoke from his mouth. "Now let's get you to a meeting."

With my arm slung over his shoulder and our steps syncing up, I pull out my phone to look up the nearest place to take a former alcoholic, only to stop short of hitting the search engine app when a text lights up the screen.

JORDAN: *Can't take you anywhere.*

My stomach rolls over itself.

There's a link, the little preview showing a tabloid picture of me and Peach going to blows with some douche that thought it was a good idea to dump his drink on one of my brothers.

My recovering alcoholic brother.

JORDAN: *Nice right hook.*

ME: *You should have been there.*

With a downturn to my lips, I swipe it away and find us a meeting for my shirtless best friend.

"I'm proud of you," I say to Toby in front of what I think is a church and he breaks away from my hold.

His nod is jerky, his focus on the doors in front of him.

"You don't have to come in," he finally says with a tightness to his features. It's private. Guarded. So, I nod and squeeze his shoulder.

"I'll be right here."

A tilt to his chin leads him into the building and leaves me standing here with nowhere to put my hands.

Another cigarette is between my lips a moment later, my back resting against the brick, a foot cocked up beneath me.

Movement across the street catches my attention, a flash of orange hair shining in the bleak darkness, and I shake my head. How that man manages to seem invisible when he looks more like a rock star than me, I still can't comprehend.

He doesn't approach and I don't call him over.

Things with Peach got weird when we left home and they haven't gotten any better with each night that I end up in the hallway, asleep but moving, and I can't blame him for keeping his distance.

He looks as tired as I feel.

Tension in my muscles has me switching to my other foot and flexing my hands, my phone digging into my thigh when I bend it so, I fish it out of my pocket.

The screen lights up some ungodly hour with an a.m. behind it and I silently curse—

It's ringing.

Well, vibrating because the sound of a ringer drives me fucking insane, but it's alerting me of the incoming call that's got my stomach dropping.

Jordan.

I accept before I can think it through.

My gut twists up.

Fuck, fuck, fuck.

Why did I do that?

"Vida, hey."

My eyes slide closed at the relief I hear in his tone. "Hey," I mutter tightly and pinch the bridge of my nose.

I was doing so good leaving him on read the last few weeks. Not responding, mostly. Keeping this distance between us that wounds me as much as it relieves me because if he's not in my face then at least I can pretend that everything is normal. That he's just off doing other bodyguard shit and not avoiding being with me.

That there isn't this awkwardness hanging heavy over the line every time he's called.

"Clips from your show are already all over the web."

That clenching in my stomach only gets worse.

Did he see my videos—

I have to stop this.

This unhealthy obsession with someone I'll never have feels like a pin popping through my chest all hours of the night and day.

This pain that keeps me awake.

The restlessness that never ends.

I'm … tired.

Of pretending like everything is fine. Like I'm not falling the fuck apart with each day that passes, and I have to act like I'm just a rock star with a bodyguard as a best friend. That I'm not desperately looking for his face in every crowded room. Or waiting for every little morsel of communication he's sparing me. As if I'm not hoping with all of my might that he'll walk through the door at any moment, just to surprise me.

Wishing he'd fly thousands of miles if only to see me.

Find me.

Dreaming that he'd wake up and be *different.*

Not straight.

He won't.

And it feels like shit to think that.

I love Jordan as he is.

I'm *in* love with who he is.

But that's all this will ever be.

Unrequited feelings. Longing. *Destruction.*

"I'm doing something."

My heart rate kicks up when his statement draws me back and the sounds of his breathing, heavier than normal, registers.

No.

Nononono.

"What," I croak out even though I know I shouldn't.

"It's a surprise. For you."

The breath punches out of me.

"What?" I ask again, though this one is more of a squeak that works past my aching throat.

"A surprise—You sound like crap, Vida. You okay?"

My heart gives a painful thump in a too-tight ribcage.

Head drops back against the rough brick at my back.

No. I'm not fucking okay.

Because he's in my ear, hearing me for the first time in weeks and asking me if I'm okay and I'm clinging to his words against my better judgement.

And I'm here. Standing on some random street in some foreign place, in the dark, with busted knuckles and a bleeding heart.

Alone.

So fucking alone.

"Yeah," I lie and my voice cracks.

My eyes start to sting, and my tongue burns with a big, fat, *why.*

Why can't you love me back?

Jordan's sigh is audible. "Mac—"

"I have to go," I rush out.

"Wait." I pause, my composure hanging by the thinnest thread. "Drink some tea. It'll help."

I squeeze my eyes shut.

"Right."

It won't help this.

Chapter Twenty-Eight

JORDAN

For days, I've ridden on a high that I can't explain.

Even through the boredom of babysitting Aria's shop and working through Mac's surprise with enough blood and sweat to keep it all together, I've managed to hang onto it.

It started when he finally answered one of my calls.

And even though he abused his voice as much as he did his drums that night, I can't stop thinking about it.

You should have been there.

But he didn't need me there.

He handled shit.

I knew he could. Knew he would.

There's just something about the way he did that's got me smiling.

I didn't break him.

There's a pang of something that knocks at my chest and threatens the feeling I've clung to, but I won't let it.

Mac's shining brighter. Just like I hoped.

Chapter Twenty-Nine

Mac

COLD.

Everything is cold. Hollow.

Damp.

I jolt, limbs jerking.

The clock says only three minutes have passed since I last looked at it.

Empty.

The darkness looms around my vision, at war with the exhaustion that won't grab onto me and pull me under.

I just want to sleep.

But it doesn't come.

I swallow another sleeping pill.

The trembles get worse. The nighttime slipping away.

But my heart, it stays right here. Pounding through its jagged edges to drown out the sound of it breaking. Speeding its way past every spiraling thought that pulls me farther and farther into this pit of hopelessness.

There is no end to this misery.

No rest for the damaged.

Only blackness.

Chapter Thirty

Peach

A DEEP, GUTTURAL SCREAM rings through the hallway and I jolt to a stop. I'm pivoting when it cuts off, sprinting when something inside Mac's room crashes.

I don't bother knocking.

But when I go to push inside, something bars the way.

"Mac!" I call out and give another push.

There's a groan from the other side, a sound that's somewhere between pain and a sob and I push harder.

It gives enough distance for me to squeeze through, and I clamor over the overturned couch in my way.

"Mac."

He's standing in the middle of the chaos, a pillow in his grip, feathers falling out with each inch that he rips it wide open.

"Okay," I murmur and ease closer. "I looked this shit up, okay?" I raise my hands and take another step. "Sleepwalking *and* trashing shit, huh? This is a new one for me."

I risk another step, only to rock back when his wild eyes swing on me. They're wide and hardened, the whites beyond bloodshot, the green–blue nearly swallowed by the dark center.

That's new.

And terrifying.

"Shit," I breathe out. "This is worse than last night, bud. What's got you fucked up?" I keep my voice low and as even as I can. His chest pumps with his rapid breaths as it has for the past three nights. His hands working apart the shit he's holding is a new development.

Normally, he just wanders around. Ends up in the bathroom, propped up and sleeping in the shower or sitting straight up on the couch like he's wide awake.

Hell, I even caught him ready to walk out into the hallway one night two weeks ago.

But it's not the torn pillow or the sweat wetting his shirt that's got me rethinking coming in here without radioing for assistance.

It's the dead look in his eyes. The tightness of his face.

The way he *sounds* like he's crying, sobbing, and yet not a tear gathers in his eyes.

Definitely new.

All of which is nothing like what has happened every other night since we've been on the road. Normally, he listens. Walks his ass back to the bed or a couch and settles down.

"Mac," I whisper, that gaze of his searing right through me. Unseeing. "Can we sit? Will you do that?"

No change.

"How about some water. Let's get some water." I have no clue if it'll do anything. I've officially hit the extent of the research I did and while I don't want to give him something to throw, I also know that trying to do anything else is basically asking for another broken nose. *Best case.*

When I turn away to find a bottle of water, he follows, trips over the bed, and falls face first into the mattress with the shredded pillow pinned beneath him.

I let out a giant breath, relief washing over me only to halt when he speaks some kind of gibberish. It gets thicker, more jumbled as I work closer, almost like a plea.

Real tears leak through his squeezed eyelids, and he lets loose the smallest, most gut-wrenching whimper that has me dialing before I can think it through.

"Peach?"

"I didn't know what else to do," I whisper, Mac's voice echoing mine with more marble-filled phrases that don't make sense except one.

"*Jordan,*" he cries softly, his frame shaking with the emotion.

Jordan's end of the line goes silent and then, "Put me on speaker."

Chills rack over me with the demanding tone and suddenly, I feel like an intruder in whatever relationship these two think they don't have. Like a man between a man and what's his.

Doing as he asks, I press the little speaker option and set the phone next to Mac's head.

"Stress makes it worse. It'll help if you get in with him—"

"No," I whisper-snap.

"—but for the love of God, keep your hands where I can *see them,*" Jordan growls–*legit growls!*–and my hands shoot up on instinct.

"This is a fucking phone call, jackass," I murmur back but again, do as he asks and climb into the bed with the sleep-talking, sleepwalking rock star.

I give them my back in hopes of some semblance of fucked up privacy as Jordan starts talking into the open space.

Mac still trembles against me, but the deep, guttural sobs have stopped.

There's a moment of silence that stretches, free of mumbles, and I turn my head the tiniest bit to see that Mac has started to unfurl from his fetal position. Legs just curled up instead of tucked into his chest, his arms laying loosely around the phone.

"Stay there," Jordan demands into the phone. "Soft snores mean he's out for the night." *Oh, he's talking to me.*

"I'm sorry I calle—"

"*Promise* me you'll stay with him," he rasps and my heart breaks at the vulnerability shining through.

"Yeah. Yeah, okay."

"I'll see you in twelve hours."

These two are idiots.

Chapter Thirty-One

Mac

"**G**OD FUCKING DAMMIT," I grumble and smack my lips to work away the shitty bitter taste left behind. "What is that?"

I push the plate back across to my laughing twin and my eyes bug out when the heat hits. My tongue burns, stomach churns, mouth on fire.

As much as I hate it, it's also a reprieve from the shit that's been rolling through my mind all damn day. A nice distraction. A different kind of pain.

I know I got up in my sleep, like I have been for months now. Peach tried to hide it, but the signs are there. Like the ache in my foggy head and the dryness to my eyes that won't go away. Still in the same clothes I wore on stage last night, though I swore I took a shower. The rolling nausea threatening my stomach and the never-ending pounding in my temples.

Not to mention the feathers in my hair.

No clue how I got them, but when I woke up, Peach was chasing off the cleaning staff and throwing a pillow at my head.

It's … embarrassing.

To know that there are moments where I have no control over what I do. What I say. *Who* I say it to.

It's never been this bad.

I thought the sleeping pills would help tamp down the effects.

If anything, I just feel fucking hungover—severely—and still exhausted. Tense and fucking nauseous.

Half out of my mind and homesick.

Heartsick.

Is that a thing? Sure as shit feels like it.

And this bullshit my twin gave me is only making the waves rolling through my stomach worse.

"Someone can have these."

Sliding the plate away, I pull out my sticks and tap them against the edge of the table in a solid rhythm.

"Bad night?" I nod to my twin, my sight not leaving the tips of the swinging drumsticks. "Wanna talk about it?"

"No."

Rex scoffs. "Liar."

Sighing, I still my hands and immediately regret looking over my shoulder at him.

He stares back at me with his brows pinched tight, his bluer eyes too bright.

What he doesn't have, though, is bags under his eyes as deeply darkened as mine. He doesn't have a few days' worth of stubble on his chin. Or lack of color across his cheeks.

It's no longer like looking in a mirror.

He looks worried in this moment, but otherwise ... *happy.*

And I hate that it's so potent I can feel it down to my bones almost as if it were my own.

Almost.

My stomach is like lead, my grip on the sticks flexing.

"I don't know what you want from me," I say just low enough for him to hear.

"To be my brother again," he shoots right back with a tightness taking over his features, and my stomach drops.

"That's stupid," I say, though I don't mean it. Not even a little bit. "I'm always right behind you." *That part I do mean.*

I'm always second to Rex. Constantly playing catch up. Getting the leftovers of life.

Literally playing behind him every night.

"But are you?"

I rock back in my seat, my heart aching for a whole other reason.

No. I'm not really. How can I be when my brother gets everything I've ever wanted without even trying?

When the universe just dumps shit in his lap, but still makes it good. Turns his shit situations into the love of his life and what do I get?

Nothing. I get nothing.

"You practically lived on my couch and now I never see you."

That ache becomes a stabbing that just gets deeper with each of my brother's words. Because while it's true … it's also partly his doing.

Rex hates my bodyguard for being my best friend, even though I'm in love with him.

It started with a deep fake that got Jordan fired, his nose broken by my dear brother, and a whole lotta proving he was with me at the time of not only the leak, but the recording's timestamp.

After I admitted to Rex I'd found feelings.

"You don't want me on your couch," I mutter instead and drop my sight back to my ticking sticks.

"More like *you* don't want to be on my couch when the twins go to bed."

I can feel the smirk in his tone. *Gag.*

But also *ache.*

Goddamn it.

My grip tightens.

I want that. I want that life so fucking bad.

Someone to come home to. Someone to call. Someone to just fucking hug me when I need it.

I blink against the burn in my eyes and swallow back the reigning disappointment, hoping like hell he won't pick up on the thickness of my words. "*Please* stop talking about your sex life. I don't wanna know."

Rex chuckles and tosses a wadded-up napkin at my chest. "Bro, you were right outside the door most nights."

Because I was waiting for him to hang out with me.

Pathetic, right?

I fake a gag and still my sticks with a tremble to my hands. "That's different."

He scoffs and rolls his eyes.

"What? I have to *see* Aria again. I never saw those ladies come back."

Someone behind my brother sputters out a laugh and I bite the inside of my lip.

Rex levels me with a look, one that sears me so deep that I nearly break right down the middle. *Just like that night on the bus all those years ago.* "We're playing cards later," he says and tips his chin. "Be there."

Sighing through clenched teeth, I nod.

"I'm serious, bro."

"Fine. *Fine.*"

Chapter Thirty-Two

JORDAN

THERE'S SOMETHING ABOUT WHAT'S supposed to be a twelve-hour flight turning into a seventeen-hour endeavor that's got me more on edge than I've ever been.

My leg bounces.

I check the time. *Again.*

The show started over two hours ago, and if the traffic is any indication, they're finishing up. Which is enough of a bummer, but also means that Mac may not be at the venue I've been trying to get to by the time I get in there.

My stomach clenches.

He needed me and I wasn't there.

It's like ants have crawled beneath my skin and are busy making my veins their new home, the center of my chest their hub.

I was so, so wrong.

The cab driver accepts the cash I throw up front when he pulls over, the door open before he can even come to a complete stop.

Maybe it wasn't me after all.

I'm sprinting through the foyer, against the wave of people trying to leave despite the bass that fills the air, with an old-fashioned paper ticket in hand.

My chest pumps as I push through more people, rounding the floor of the stadium and squeezing in between bodies until the front of the stage comes into view.

When I finally look up, I zero in on Mac behind his set. Powerful strokes making the heaviest of beats. Sweat darkening his shirt and wetting the ends of his wild curls.

I take a breath.

He's okay. He's safe.

The curve of his throat when he tips his head back and lets loose a screaming growl that's so intense, it makes the veins beneath his skin protrude. The ropes of muscle stand out. The force of it cracking his vocals.

It's like the sound crawled out of the rawest part of him. Somewhere deep and dark and fervent enough to stop time.

Freeze the Earth on its axis.

Suspend me above all that I know and all that I am.

It's like seeing the demon inside him face to face, the anxiety that hides behind the mask, and it's … fucking—

Hot?

Something in me cracks wide open at the same time the play button is pressed, and suddenly I'm being swallowed up by the mass of people around me when the view on the screens next to the stage switches to another person coming out.

I'm breathless when the guy waves. The mob goes insane in slow motion around me.

My stomach drops when he turns his smile on Mac, the vulnerability gone from my drummer and replaced with a mask of confidence, who flashes a snarky one in return.

The world around me speeds up when my drummer stands from his set.

I don't belong here.

Roars past when the stranger leans in, presses a kiss to the Mac's cheek, and takes the drumsticks from his hands.

And Mac lets him.

He never lets anyone but the road crew touch his drums, and yet—

Mac let him.

And now the stranger is sitting where my drummer is supposed to be, smacking out sounds that don't feel right, and I'm just …

Sinking.

Stepping backward.

Holy shit, what am I doing?

Turning away from the smile that laces my dreams.

He never needed me.

And running like my life depends on it.

Chapter Thirty-Three

JORDAN

*T*HREE GRAND IN CHANGE *fees.*

The unforgiving plastic beneath my ass creaks with each bounce of my leg.

Another eighteen hours before I'm home.

I swipe my palms down my pant leg.

Why does this hurt so bad?

Licking my dry lips, I clear my throat. Tip off my hat and slap it onto my knee.

He didn't ask me to come.

My jaw clenches at how wrong I've been. How wrong I am.

These feelings, big and raw, grow with each passing moment that I sit in this airport, my ticket home like a burning coal in my pocket.

With a last-ditch effort to prove that shitty side of my brain correct, I pull out my phone.

He didn't need me.

It takes three tries to get it unlocked with the shake in my hands.

As Above's accounts are the first to pop up in the highlights of each social media platform I'm on.

And each one is like a finger digging into my chest, breaking skin, wiggling through bone. Each picture of Mac with someone else a successful stab. Every caption and comment an eradication of what once was. Overlayed by what now is.

Mac and Dare.

As Above and Banger together. The addition of Dare as Mac's touring backup.

The rivals to friends story of a lifetime.

Announced *today* and I had no idea.

Why didn't he tell me?

Did he replace me as his best friend that easily?

My throat constricts as I swipe away the apps and squeeze my eyes closed.

This can't be true.

I'm dialing without looking, placing the phone to the side of my head on instinct.

It rings twice.

Two times before cutting to the voicemail greeting that used to make me smile.

Now, it just feels like another knife.

"Hey." My voice shakes. "Just wanted to check in," I lie. "Tell you the show was good—"

"Now boarding for—"

"—I'll see you when you get home," I rush out before my voice cracks and hang up with a blur to my vision.

Chapter Thirty-Four

MAC

"MR. THOMPSON, THANK YOU for joining us on *Tonight Live!*"

The half-smile I give the host of this show Leo put me on is not a genuine one, but neither is the sickly-sweet flash of pearly whites on her face.

It's showbiz.

"Thanks for having me." My knee bounces in my dark slacks that match the black button-down Leo put me in before I got up here. The top few buttons are undone, giving me room to breathe, but the material is itchy against my blisteringly hot skin. My black bandana is stiff against my forehead, which feels unbearably wrong considering how often I wear the things, and makes my brain hurt in ways I don't understand.

The crowd applauds our exchange with no clue how uncomfortable this shit really is, they're just happy to be here near someone from a band, someone famous with the possibility of getting two seconds on TV. Just like the fans that pay the extra money to get backstage only to find that we're normal fucking people who just happen to be good at playing an instrument.

They don't see the long hours on tour, sleeping in a tiny bunk or shitty hotel bed, being in strange places for months or even years. Unable to live an actual life without being plastered all over the fucking media for having a best friend that's not even the person I want it to be.

They don't see the way my heart's racing. Or how bad my chest hurts. The sacrifices I've made to do what we do. Who we had to leave behind just to be here.

What they really see is my back relaxed into the chair, my legs spread wide, one ankle propped up on the opposite knee and a fake grin for our host that I know doesn't reach my bagged eyes.

She sits across from me, her pencil skirt tight enough to keep her torso stick-straight in her seat, her blouse way too loud for the personality I've yet to find, with her eyes stuck on me. She's too bubbly for this hour of the night. Too needy. Too demandingly rude to the staff off set the second the cameras were off.

Shit, I don't even remember her name.

"You've come straight from a show, right? The Resurrection tour?" I nod, watching as she taps her cue cards on her crossed thigh and smiles for the camera.

"Yeah, it's been great being back on the road." I lie, my thumb finding a rhythm against my thigh.

Not anymore.

Not without Jordan.

Fuck, I miss him so much.

My breath catches on that last thought, sending me into a blinking fit to bring the hostess back in focus.

"Tell me about the rumor. You're going to be working with Banger on their new album? Alongside Dare?"

Clearing my throat, I fiddle with my pant leg. "There's something in the works for sure. Not much I can say about that until the ink dries."

Fake, fake, fake a smile.

"I see that you've got a new security detail."

Jesus, she's giving whiplash.

She flips her hair over her shoulder, looking over mine to where I know I left Paul, my greener than green temp bodyguard, standing before I stepped foot on the stage.

I didn't ask for him. I was plenty accepting of the idea that I had to share Peach with Fin.

But then Fin found himself in a jam with no security around, and I was assigned a brand-new asshole without my consent.

Here we go.

"Yeah. Paul," I say, glancing back to see him standing proud just off the stage, but a few feet from where I left him, and I internally roll my eyes. *He's right in her line of sight.* "He's green, but so far so good."

That was petty. Oops.

"Interesting that you ended up with someone new after all this time. Any comments on that, Mr. Thompson?"

I shake my head, keeping a slight smile plastered to my lips even though my eyes are tired, my arms ache from the show, my feet beyond done with the dress shoes I was politely told I must wear.

They're constricting and I just want to go.

Be anywhere but here.

I haven't had to talk about Jordan since we left, except with Dr. Surah. But it's been so long that fans are losing their minds about Dare being so close to me, and now Paul following behind like the lost puppy he is.

"We've had to make a few personnel changes to cover some gaps." I pick at my nail when her smile falters and Leo's advice rolls around in my brain. *Don't walk into saying something you're not prepared to say.* "That happens sometimes."

"But your former bodyguard will be back, right? You guys have been everywhere together. Like best friends."

Former?

The thought shoots straight through my chest and makes my jaw clench.

With aching fingers, I bring my hands up to steeple the tips against my chin. There's an ache in my chest and a forced lift to my lips behind the spasming digits as I speak the words I was told to come here and say.

"Jordan is still with the security team, and still very much a part of this family. He always will be." I adjust forward in my seat with a clearing of my throat, leaning into my elbows on my knees, and tug at the shirt to get it to sit right again against my torso. "But, now, so is Dare."

There. PR stunt completed.

My stomach rolls.

Oxygen leaves the studio, suffocation settling in when I feel the attention of the entire room focused on me. Even the host lady leans closer to me, her eyes unmoving from my profile as I swing my hardened gaze directly into the camera.

"And I can't wait to get back on the same side of the planet as him."

Him, who? They'll speculate.

I clear my throat, feeling my Adam's apple bobbing against the lump that builds.

I want my bodyguard back.

I want my best friend back.

I want my freedom back.

Fuck, I miss him even though this is all his damn fault.

Severing the contact with the lens when the room breaks out in gasps and applause, I glance over to our host and cover the mic pinned to my collar. "You good?"

She's flustered, her words refusing to come, her cheeks flushed beneath the layers of makeup as she fans herself with the cue cards she's yet to look at. As if gaining her composure and remembering the lines preset for her, she checks the words written, her brown eyes shooting between them and me.

She clears her throat, but still does not speak any words.

Her subtle nod is all I catch. It's all I need to stand and rip the cords from my neck. I leave the shit laying on the table set between the chairs and stomp off the stage without another glance at the host, the crowd, or the camera.

Eyes follow me as I leave the entire live shoot behind, my abandonment of the interview on every television set, the shock and awe of the staff burning at my back almost as much as the heat from the body that sticks too fucking close to my ass.

I bob and I weave around people that begin begging for my attention once the shock wears off, demanding my exclusive interview after a show such as that—*walking off stage, how dare I?*—in hopes that I don't get too far and leave the scene.

"You think I'm green?" Paul's words break my concentration, and I glance over my shoulder at the man I would have thought was cute in another life.

He's not Jordan.

"Yeah," I mutter, my attention going back out in front of me when I nearly run over an assistant carrying a stack of files and books. "The fact that you have to ask that ..." I trail off as I maneuver around the girl and reach for the exit, only to have Paul brush around me and snag the handle from my grip.

Mother fucker.

I growl when he clips my shoulder and wait for him to push the metal wide enough for me to clear while he checks the alleyway that I step into anyway.

"*Don't* grab the door from me like that," I snarl when he steps back up to me with the intent to walk in front. I whip my arm out and stop him with a blockade across his chest. "And do *not* lead me."

"Oh." He pauses at my side, his step faltering. "That's the rules, though, Mac."

"No." My headshake is stiff, my tone gruff as my hand falls away from him. "It's my fucking life."

I knew it'd be a difficult transition.

Because there's not supposed to be one.

"But Mac," Paul tries, his steps spinning him until he's walking backwards so that he can face me—just the same way that Jordan used to—and I have to swallow back the bile that threatens to rise. "It's my ass if something happens."

"Goddammit." I freeze on the spot. "I'm still a fucking *person*." I growl the words out, my fists clenching at my sides, desperate to make contact with his nose.

"And I have a job to do." Paul's resolve is palpable, almost choking, as the collar plants its place right back around my neck for him to tug the leash on.

Fuck him for ruining this for me.

I growl at my security, tear my gaze away from him, and move forward without another word.

"I could back off, if you'd like," he offers, his gait catching back up to me easily. "I just thought we'd get along."

I spin on him, his chest slamming into mine and stealing his breath with the gravel skidding beneath our shoes.

"Why's that?" I sneer, my nose only an inch from his face, a pointer finger poking into his thick chest. "Because I'm the cool one?" I snap, my venom flying all over his face, but I don't care. "Or because I like *anything* with a dick? Looking to just replace my last one?"

That rumor hurt a little.

I'm tired of the labels people put on me.

The hate they spew at me when they don't know the truth.

"No, I just …" Paul takes a timid step back but meets my flaming gaze. "I idolized you, man." He swipes the back of his hand over his jaw. "It's not often people are open in the media like you are."

I smirk, one that has absolutely no humor, and turn on my heel to walk away from him.

"I'm sure you've heard all about idols." I toss over my shoulder like a royal asshole and stalk my miserable ass down the alleyway.

It's not my fault you're not supposed to meet them.

I shake the thought as I reach the blacked-out SUV and nearly yank the handle off to open it.

Climbing up into the vehicle, I slam the door behind me with a loud thud that shakes the car.

I just wanna be left alone.

But I know that's not going to happen anytime soon, thanks to the driver's side door opening and Paul climbing in to move us to the next location.

The cityscape passes quickly, the streetlamps passing us at a whirl. The roads become highways and I can't help the mashing of my teeth when Paul's silence ends up pissing me off even more.

Jordan knew I hated the quiet.

My knee bounces out of control in the passenger seat of the SUV as we pass yet another convenience shop that reminds me of him.

My chest aches enough that I pull my legs up to circle my arms around them in hopes to ease the pressure, or at least hold back the memories that flood me.

But I wouldn't be so damn lucky.

Part II

Chapter Thirty-Five

Mac

Six months later

"T HEY FINALLY BROUGHT ME ON full time."

After enough silence to drive even a monk mad, my temp bodyguard decides now is the time to share *this* with me, as if I'd be as ecstatic about the news as he is.

Spoiler alert: I'm fucking not.

"I thought the roster was full." I manage to ask him over the rim of my glass, a roach hanging by a thread from my lips to keep it from burning my skin.

Paul shrugs and helps himself to the bottle sitting by my elbow. "Guess they canned someone or something." He speaks as he pours, completely ignoring the judgement clearly painted on my face when he shoots the alcohol back.

"Um." Plucking the roach from my lips, I point at him with the two fingers that I pinch it between. "You're on fucking duty."

His repeated shrug sets my blood to boil, because while I might not like life right now, I'd still like to keep it in case it gets fucking better.

"I can't celebrate?"

"Fuck no." I swipe the bottle from his grasp when he attempts to pour another. "Not at the expense of *my* fucking life." Slamming the glass against the table, I pin him with a glare that bows his shoulders in.

"Shit, Mac, I'm—"

"Sorry?" I fish my phone from my pocket as the words leave my lips. "You better not say you're fucking *sorry*." Hitting dial on the head of our security team's number, I put the device to my ear, and pin the disobedient child of a bodyguard who slumps.

Slumps!

"What." The clipped response begs for a smartass comment that I would have normally fallen into but I scoff into the phone.

"You know who didn't drink on the job?"

"Jesus." Ian's string of curses that follow pull at the corner of my lips.

"Seriously?" I ask into the phone and blindly reach out for the bottle my fingers find and wrap around the neck of. "You leave me with this one? What the fuck?" I pin the remorseful guard with a stare that has his eyes shooting to the floor.

"I'm on my fucking way up." Nodding when the line cuts off, I set my phone back on the high-top table I long ago took residence at and take a swig directly from the bottle.

Still, I keep my sight trained on my bodyguard who doesn't bother to look up long enough to canvas the surrounding patrons. They've all been vetted, but that doesn't mean his job is done. He doesn't bring his gaze up from the fucking marble floor, even when the door at my back opens and Ian comes striding through the VIP section with a burning rage flexing his fists.

"Go back to the hotel." Simple, yet powerful, Ian's way of communicating is always clear and direct. Like a pissed dad to an unruly teenager, he lays down the law with the new guy.

So when my new bodyguard decides it's the time to argue, it's just fuel to the already lit fire.

"Get the fuck out of my sight." In a rare form, with a red-faced and using his hands to speak, Ian gestures to the door, just in case Paul forgot the way in is the same way out.

Like a lost puppy, the newbie tucks his tail along with his head and does the walk of shame across the mostly quiet floor. When I watch his back finally disappear through the door and into the crowd of partygoers, I ask my questions to the leader of their group.

"What the fuck, Ian?"

"I can't discuss this with you, Mac."

"Bullshit. You can. And you fucking will." Blue eyes set under a buzzcut stare down at me like I'm the one out of my mind.

"*Fine*," Ian growls when I don't waiver and slams his ass into the chair next to me, his eyes floating over the crowd behind me for a moment, then coming back to me. "We need more fucking hands."

I scoff and take another sip from the bottle only to hiss when the roach finally burns down enough to burn my fingers.

Ian snatches the mini fire and puts it out with a boot to the floor.

"And that fucker is it?" I say when his eyes come back to mine. "It's been *years*, Ian. Literal years that Jordan had my back."

He shakes his head, his hand coming up to run across his short hair. "How can you..." His voice trails off when another patron walks close to the table but keeps moving past us. "Mac, you're going to have to let me permanently assign you someone that isn't Jordan."

But I'm not in love with anyone else.

I don't say that, though, because that's almost as bad to tell his boss.

So, I settle with the other truths. "We knew each other. He got it. He didn't fuck up once."

"Except he *has*." Ian scoffs and flags the bartender over to order a soda with no ice like a real fucking weirdo. "And Jordan's the one that opted out of this."

"You don't know him, Ian. He would have come if you'd told him to."

"And you fuckin do?" *Fuck, maybe he's right.* I shake my head as Ian's beverage is placed on the table in front of him and the man takes a hike.

"I know enough," I murmur with my heart in my throat.

Thinking back, Jordan never wanted to share about his past. He said his family were good people, but then always took the first opportunity to change the subject whenever it came up. There's always been an air of mystery around it—*them*. The holidays, and the fact that Jordan never takes leave.

But I know that Ian knows more than that. More than what I know based on my internet sleuthing.

Jordan's biological parents died in a house fire when he was fourteen—the very same age I came out to Ma as gay—and there wasn't any extended family left to take him.

He ended up in the system, got in trouble a time or two, but nothing much past age seventeen was online. At least not that a *civilian* could find.

It was me; I was the civilian, for fucking once.

"It's more than you, Mac." Ian sips his soda and nibbles the droplets from his bottom lip in thought. Eyes trailing slowly from the table back to me, he shakes his head.

"You mean Rex," I correct and snag the bottle from the table.

My goddamn brother.

When Ian doesn't respond, I know I'm spot on. I can *feel it.*

"Rex does not get final say in what happens here," I growl, because while I love my twin, I'm also sick of his holier than thou attitude.

His butting in when I asked him to stay the fuck out of it.

Like getting us into this club with a basically empty VIP room for me to sulk in.

Okay, I do appreciate the privacy while still being able to be in public.

"It's not that easy."

"Bullshit!" I slam the bottle to the table, even though I've yet to take another drink. "It's the *band's* decision. Not Mac all by himself. Not Rex. Or Toby." I growl and lean closer to the leader of the security team whose spine straightens him up taller than me. "The only one with any power to do anything without the consent of the whole group is fucking *Leo*."

Ian's jaw firms, his eyes turning to grey stone as his words cement the things I already knew would be true. "Except when it comes to security measures and the safety of this team."

Gone is the sliver of understanding the man displayed. Gone is any warmth he allowed past his tough exterior.

"You mean you." I sneer, my lip pulling up from my teeth.

"Damn right I do." His chuckle is stark and holds no humor when it passes his lips. "Music wise, it's all you." His pointer comes out and pokes me in my adrenaline pumped chest. "Security is on me." His thumb jabs back into his solid pec.

"*Fuck* you, Ian."

Pushing up from the table, I can't help the sway to my step. Or the way I grip the table to prevent myself from meeting the ground with my face instead of my shoes. Ian reaches out to steady me, but I growl over my shoulder and shake off his hold. "Have a good fuckin' day, *sir*."

"You can't leave without me, Mac."

I scoff.

"Bet," I spit the challenge in his direction and swagger my ass to the door that leads out into the chaos.

Slipping through the threshold, I slam the thing in Ian's face. He rips it right back open, scanning the crowd when I step into a dancing horde of sweaty bodies. I move to blend, allowing the sway of the music to guide my hips into a rhythm that the woman in front of me leans back against.

She bumps back into me, matching my glides and glances over her bare shoulder. She grins, sly and full of shit she'll find me disappointing at, her ass grinding into my groin and her arms come up around the back of my neck.

Leaning into the disguise with my face to her neck, I put my hands on her hips and guide her so that she's more swing and less dry humping. Purrs fill my ear when my hands slip and her ass slams back into my hips.

Ow.

Chuckling, I plant a kiss on her cheek when I see Ian move further into the crowd opposite me and turn her into another group of grabby hands. She gets lost in the horde after only a moment of eye contact and a wink that sends her on her way.

Rotating my body away from where Ian disappeared, I bump into a man close to my height and grin when he doesn't immediately push away. The backwards hat reminds me of a specific someone I'd appreciate forgetting, even if for just a moment, but my chest aches with the scent of a particular musk filling my nose as our hips fall in sync.

Clean, like a fresh shower, fills my senses the same way that my former bodyguard used to, making my hands tingle to touch and tease my cock to life for the first time in what feels like forever.

He never knew.

He never knew that I stopped sleeping with anyone the moment he strolled in like he owned the fucking place. Never knew I looked when I shouldn't have. Touched as 'just friends' more than any friend I've ever had.

But I did.

The laser lights flash like strobes against the darkness of the room, fucking with my eyes and making me feel even more intoxicated than

I am. But my dance partner keeps my pace and doesn't run for the hills when I slide my hands down his torso and grip his waist.

In fact, his ass pushes back into me and his arms go up to sway along with the beat. He opens himself up to me, pulling a satisfied growl from the base of my throat.

A rebound sounds nice right about now.

Even more when I recall the fucking hiatus my cock decided to go on without my consent.

I guess even he knows it's fucking over.

Falling all in, I grind against my dancing partner's ass and delight when their purr finds its way to my ear. Leaning back until my chest warms his skin, his arms snake around my neck and hold on for dear life when the beat changes, the remix of an As Above song kicking up the tempo.

Groaning when the song filters through the mix of club music, I think of Jordan as the lyrics tickle my ears and the dancer spins to face me.

Arms wrap around my shoulders, his head down, his face buried in my neck. Hands grab at my ass, his hard cock grinding into my pelvis, while mine sits limp behind my zipper.

People jump in unison to our music, bringing a lift to the corner of my lips until feet land on mine and elbows smash my shoulders.

My partner breaks away from me, the chaos of the floor too much to keep a hold. I reach out, catching just the tips of his fingers when the wave consumes him only to lose it all over again.

Lost, I search the crowd around me, pushing by bouncing bodies as I try to reconnect with the only person that's made me feel a morsal of something since Jordan walked into my life and left me wrecked.

But he's gone, just like Jordan.

And in his place is Ian.

Chapter Thirty-Six

JORDAN

"Three whole dayssss," Makkin sings from his Little Tykes chair beside me as he flies his tiny stuffed dinosaurs through the air with the occasional blown raspberry. "Daddy and Unckie. Uncle Broby and Uncle Finnnnnny."

I swallow the lump in my throat and glance down at the little guy. "Are you excited?"

"*Today*," he screeches and makes his dinos ram into each other. "*I'm so happy*! Aren't you?"

Happy?

The word is a foreign concept that tickles my subconscious and teases too many *what ifs* in a world full of unknowns. It also most likely includes a whole lot of *not* spending way too long pretending.

Acting as if I wasn't waiting for every message I sent Mac to bounce back, to tell me my number's been blocked.

Or worse.

I kept on as if nothing had happened. That I wasn't there that night that Dare came out on stage. I knew from all the social media coverage. Cringed at all the comments asking about Mac's *real best friend*.

That I hadn't flown thousands of miles just to see him.

I don't spend every moment I'm awake thinking about him. Wondering. Questioning if the shit online about him and Dare is real.

Hoping it's not.

Wondering how the fuck I gave up the chance to be there with him.

Did he really replace me?

If I really was the cause of all the shit that kept him up at night. Peach tells me he's gotten some help with that, some kind of meds that seem to help. That he's better now. Though, I don't know how much I believe it or if Peach is just protecting him.

Hell, maybe the bodyguard is protecting me, too.

Dragging in a deep breath through my nose, I force a nod for the kid who goes back to slamming his dinosaurs together.

But then he throws them on the floor, clamors to a stand on his chair, and fists my shirt.

His eyes are wide and bright and remind me so much of his precious *unckie* that my chest clenches.

"Don't you love my Unckie?"

That familiar stabbing in the center of my chest kicks in.

"Of course I do," I answer, and my breath catches at the way it spills from my mouth so easily.

Do I?

Of … course I do. Care about him. Adore him. Admire him. Miss him.

He's the closest person to me since I was younger. My best friend. The only person I've let in since my parents—

I clear my throat.

How do I explain that to a kid?

That feelings are complicated, and the admission is even more so.

That I do have love for Mac?

But can I be *in* love with him?

Is there even a difference when it comes to him?

Would he fucking believe me if I did?

Makkin makes a grunting noise, then stretches up to flatten his little palms against my cheeks, squishing my face so that all I see is him.

Just like his mother does to them.

Then, in the most serious tone I've ever heard from a kid, he asks "Why I never see you kiss him?"

My stomach drops.

"Mommy says a-dults who love each other kiss. How else will Unckie know you love him if you don't?"

I blink, my throat too tight to answer.

Because it doesn't matter to Makkin that his uncle and I are the same gender. Or that I've been stuck in some endless questioning loop of somehow *not straight* with no answer to what that actually means. That I've spent my whole life assuming I'd never—

But then there was Mac.

Blowing out a breath I nod and force a small placating smile for the kid. "That's all I gotta do?"

"Uh-huh! Easy."

I wish.

Chapter Thirty-Seven

Mac

*T*HREE DAYS.

My stomach lurches along with the plane as the wheels make contact with the tarmac.

I can fake it for three days, right?

Protect myself and my dignity?

Who the fuck am I kidding; I can barely fucking *breathe*.

The collar of my shirt is already toting a tear, but I yank on it anyway, desperate to rid myself of this choking feeling wrapped around my throat.

Every day, I've heard from Jordan. And every day, I clung to those words like a sermon of my religion. Stowing away all the little details he's sent me like I'll need them for eternity.

Every night, wished he was there.

Yet it's been too long since I saw his face up close. Felt his presence warm my side. Known that if I just turned around, he'd be there.

He hasn't been there.

The fist with a death grip on my heart tightens when I do just that, turning to my right, and see the seat next to me empty.

It's always empty.

How poetic.

I flatten my lips, thinning them against the rush of hurt, and turn to the front where Leo's directing us off the airplane.

This is it. This is the moment.

Drawing in a deep breath, I snag my bag and stand.

Chapter Thirty-Eight

JORDAN

The first crown of curls to exit the plane has my stomach dropping and my fingers fiddling with the shit in my pockets as Rex all but runs across the tarmac to his wife and kids. They collide, her jumping into his arms, the twins' tiny bodies hooking onto each of his legs.

Pang.

Next is Fin and his brooding that's no match for when his partner tucks herself under his arm and they share sly, knowing smiles with each other.

Pang.

Then Anna's ass as Toby carries her over his shoulder off the plane, her laughter trailing them.

Pang.

Leo talking to Peach over his shoulder with a friendly grin. The rest of security piling out behind them.

Pang.

"C'mon," I mutter under my breath, my pounding heart in my throat as I step closer to the stairs leading from the belly of the aircraft.

Please be alone. Please be alone.

My mouth moves like the words are a prayer.

Mac. Mac. Mac.

He's here. *Home.* So close that I feel the ghost of a burn left behind by his stubble heating my pec. The way his curls capture my wandering fingers in their sleepy tangles. Hearing his puffing breath when he's truly asleep …

Three days.

It's not nearly enough time to convince him, to hold him. To be near him.

But I plan to use every second of it as if it's the only chance I'll get.

If he'd just get off the damn airplane.

C'mon. C'mon.

Something bright explodes in my chest when he finally, *finally*, ducks through the opening into the midday sun, his searching eyes landing on me.

Two things happen at once and both have my heart leaping to my throat.

First, I register the black eye.

And second …

He blanches.

Then a third that absolutely blindsides me.

He steps back when I advance.

"Mac …"

Chapter Thirty-Nine

Mac

HE CROAKS MY NAME like a plea that nearly breaks me and that's when I know.

Tipping my chin in a weak greeting, the strap of my duffel digs into my already fucked palm with how hard I grip it, and I force myself to step around him.

Give him a wide berth.

Square my shoulders and hope that he gets the message.

He's the one that chose this for us. Placated me by sending messages and voice memos. Kept me on his hook with his texted thoughts and random pictures.

All while I have loved him from afar.

I can't fake it anymore.

Seeing him now … wanting him still … it only proves that I will never *not* have feelings for the man that didn't choose me.

"*Vida,*" he growls out and grips my elbow, spinning me away from my disappearing bandmates until I'm crashing into his fluttering chest.

Our eyes collide and it takes every ounce of me to keep from crumbling. To keep my gaze hard and my body tense.

"Gimme three days," he mutters, those navy blues of his swirling with so much depth that I might get lost in them. "Please."

Chapter Forty

JORDAN

"For what?" he whispers and my pulse hammers.

"For—just—"

The words stick to my tongue, thick and life-changing.

What am *I asking for?*

Could it be that simple?

His tug on my grip has me grasping at air and chasing after him when he walks away from me.

What if?

I shake my head and match his stride.

He speeds up.

"Mac."

He spins on me, stiff-arming me with his bandaged palm to the center of my chest, his eyes glassy.

"No."

I recoil. "No?"

He throws his hands up, his sight going skyward.

For a beat, he's quiet, though I can see his mind running. He's still, though I can see the tremble of his frame.

But when his hardened sight lands on me, I'm struck frozen at its intensity.

"If you can't tell me why …" He shakes his head, his nostrils flaring. "Just, no, Jordan."

Him using my real name unfurls something deep inside me and I know that I won't ever be able to let it go until I *know*.

"You've never asked me *why* before," I mutter.

His jaw ticks and it's like the damn breaks, the walls slowly chipping away until it all comes flowing in waves of shit.

"Because!" he shouts. "I've never had to pretend so fucking hard with you. Never felt like I needed to protect myself *from* you. The *one* fucking person I thought was in it for me. No matter what."

"But I am—"

"*You didn't choose me*," he all but screams with wild eyes and a pumping chest.

I rock back.

"You never chose *me*. You chose your fucking job and your goddamn pride and your fucking *normal*."

A piece of me breaks when a tear crests his lashes, streaking down his splotched cheek.

"That's what you think?"

His chin juts out, his shoulders squared. "You followed me through fucking hell and back." Another tear. "Until you *didn't*."

I swallow against the ball of guilt growing larger with each truth he slaps in my face.

He's right.

I left his detail for what I thought was *his* benefit. I didn't go to Europe with the band because I thought it was what was best for *him*. That I was his problem. That I was in my client's way.

Wasn't I?

My already sinking stomach settles into the darkening pit of my gut.

"Mac."

"So, tell me." He sniffs, his jaw tight. "If you didn't choose me, then why the *fuck* would I keep choosing you?"

Chapter Forty-One

Mac

T HE HELLfiRE TEMPERATURE DOES nothing to ease the tension radiating through my body. It's like this living, festering thing that has grown wider, darker, with each day.

Give me three days …

The heel of my tender palm digs into my sternum, yet it does nothing to ease the ache behind it.

Tell me why, I beg the universe. *Tell me why and I will.*

Fuck, I would.

Even if he'd told me it was because he was curious. Needed to feel things out.

As his best friend … I could do that. Even after all this time, I would do that for him. It would break me, but I'm already fucking broken.

Could I really make this any worse?

It's a weak excuse and I know it. I'd just be choosing him all over again with no regard to my own lost sanity.

So why not let him use me?

I dip my head into the water and let it seep through my hair, straighten the curls until they hang limp in my tear-tracked face.

I stay like that until I'm numb enough that the scent of my soap fades into something else.

Even longer when I hear a thud.

Goddammit, Rex.

Slapping the water off, I wrap a towel around my waist and push my hair back from my eyes.

Thud.

Growling, I pad through my room, the cold air biting at each droplet on my skin as I all but storm in the direction of the noise.

I love my brother. I swear I do. And yet, I want to murder him for his newfound obsession with creeping into my space when I didn't ask him to be there and demanding my attention. His happy is too much to deal with when mine refuses to let me touch it. When it keeps its distance. Bares its teeth when I get too close.

"Rex, I fuckin' swear—"

I freeze when I see a broad set of shoulders that do *not* belong to my brother flex as the man reaches for another cabinet he lets slam closed with a thud.

"You hungry, Vida?" All I can do is blink at the backward cap. "When's the last time you ate?"

My jaw clenches.

My heart pinches as I watch Jordan work his way around my kitchen as if I didn't leave him dumbfounded on the tarmac only a few hours ago with tears in my eyes and an ache so damn deep. It pangs as he fills my dead apartment with life, with the scent of something that makes my mouth water as much as he does.

Gimme three days.

And it damn near stops when he turns around, his eyes landing on my bare chest and flaring.

"What the fuck are you doing here?" I growl out before just the sight of him kills me and cross my arms.

"Uhm—" He swallows, his cheeks coloring with a slight pink that I swear will not become my new favorite as his eyes snap to mine.

It's hard to replace navy blue.

"What is this?" I sweep my arm out, gesturing to the paper bag on my counter and the mess of pans on the stove. *Him* being here as if there's nothing wrong between us.

He follows the movement, his throat bobbing with another swallow and when he finds my eyes again, his are hardened.

But that does nothing to hide the heat in them.

"Answer mine first, Vida," he says as he rounds the counter, approaching me slowly enough that each step kicks up my heart rate until it's pounding behind my ribs.

I step back.

He rushes forward, catching me with a hand to the back of my neck.

I swat it away.

"Fuck you," I snarl.

He steps in close again, forcing me back, back, back until my ass hits the couch.

My palms slam against his chest and I hiss.

"Back off."

Those eyes of his are molten orbs staring right through me before they narrow then drop to the hands barring him from coming closer.

I'm so focused on watching his bent head, waiting for that gaze to swing back up, that I startle when his grip wraps around my wrists. It's tender. Gentle.

Give me three days.

My heart leaps into my throat when he tugs, turning them to see the calluses split open and just as raw as the organ in my chest.

"Mac," he sighs and looks up at me through his dark lashes.

"Don't," I choke out, my stomach clenching.

Jordan shakes his head. "Don't what, Vida?"

I lick my drying lips, and his gaze drops to the movement.

Give me three days.

Blatantly, hotly, he trails back up.

But then he migrates his hold to an elbow and spins away, pulling me all the way to the kitchen sink where my brother made me keep a first aid kit.

He drops the red plastic on the counter next to me, pops it open and digs through it.

His grip finds my hand, his touch light as he smears the clear goop onto each break in the skin with so much care that my eyes burn. I sniff when he adds one of those giant sterile pads and wraps gauze across it until it covers most of my hand and part of my wrist.

"Why?" I whisper to the top of his head, his clean apple scent filling my chest and breaking my heart all over again.

"Because." He rips a piece of tape from the roll with his teeth and secures the gauze. "I choose you."

I stop breathing.

His thumbs swipe over his handiwork, his gaze slowly rising to mine.

"I've always chosen you."

Jordan fucking shrugs like he didn't just ruin my life with one fucking sentence that not even my fantasies dared to dream up.

"Someone reminded me it could be that simple," he mutters softly, one corner of his mouth tipped up in a stupid almost smile that keeps my lungs from inflating.

What if?

Whatifwhatifwhatif.

"But you're str—"

Chapter Forty-Two

JORDAN

I SLAM MY LIPS to his, silencing him.

And when he remains stock still, I grip his face, pressing the pads of my thumbs into his chin until he drops it open.

God, fuck—yes.

He tastes like my last fucking meal.

Mac. Mac. Mac.

Chapter Forty-Three

MAC

I'M ROCKETED BETWEEN THE dimensions of time and space, where no mere mortal can exist.

I no longer exist.

I am just a mass of floating stardust left in the wake of what was.

Jordan swipes his tongue along mine, his hold on my face, his body pressing in so close that I feel him shoulder to thigh.

Three days.

He deepens the kiss impossibly so, like he's starving for me, as his hands find my hair and grip me tightly. His fingers tangle in the still wet mess, the tug stinging as he tilts my head to the side.

This is a dream. It has to be.

It's the only way I can explain the gasping breath that explodes from him when I break away.

"J-Jordan," I stammer out when he dives back in, his swollen lips trailing down my stubble-covered jaw to my throat.

His hands smooth over my chest. Lower. Scratch their way through the trail of hair leading into my towel, then take hold of my hips.

Each touch sears into me, leaving layers of goosebumps in their wake.

Don't wake me up.

A whimper escapes me when he yanks me forward at the same time his teeth sink into my hammering pulse point and my head falls back.

"Damn, Vida," he murmurs hotly against my neck and a chill races straight down my spine. "You get me so fucking hard."

He grinds against me and my flaring gaze drops.

When I can't see it for myself, I knock his hat off his head and fist his hair, pulling him away from the mark I know he's leaving on my neck. He hisses, his back arching away from me, his hips digging into mine.

There's no mistaking the bulge of his jeans pressing into me.

Just as there's no misreading the pink tinting his cheeks. The smirk tugging up the side of his mouth. The molten way his navy blues stare back at me.

"You're gonna regret this in the morning," I rasp out and release his hair.

His features darken as he steps back.

My stomach plummets.

He takes another step back.

My jaw grinds.

Does he already regret it?

He reaches for the stove without looking and it beeps.

"Give me three days, Mac. I'll regret it if you *don't.*"

Chapter Forty-Four

JORDAN

I WATCH HIS JAW tick with uncertainty.

His nostrils flare.

The hard set of his features.

Including his cock.

Goddamn, I've never wanted to see another man naked as bad as I do right now. Never wanted to touch. Never salivated over just the thought of how he might taste. Not even my dreams could have prepared me for this. For him.

For tasting his tongue and wanting *more.*

Mac. Mac. Mac.

It's like that kiss has finally released some part of me that I never plan on reining back in.

"Three days," I repeat, my voice shot.

He trembles.

I reach back and tug my shirt off one-handed.

His gaze clashes with mine, loaded and hard, and he lifts his chin defiantly. "I won't be your first."

I shake my head, some of my hair falling into my eyes, and start to empty my pockets.

"I'm serious," he strains. "Find someone else."

My tongue curls around my lip, wetting it as I tip my head. "Who says I haven't already tried that?"

His eyes flare, then narrow. "Bullshit."

I reach for my belt, and he watches the movement so intently that my already solid length gets harder.

The leather makes a snap when I tug it free from the loops and let it drop to the floor.

"Vida," I murmur, stalking closer until he's backed up against the counter. His chest pumps with his breath, his spine arching away from me, his grip on the counter's edge so tight that I see his knuckles go white. "I'll always choose you."

Reaching for him, I ghost my lips over his as I work my way around the towel still clinging to his waist.

"Jordan," he warns.

Tugging on the terrycloth, I pop free its tuck.

"*Mac*," I growl right back and wrap my fist around his hard cock. It's smooth to the touch, yet all solid steel beneath the soft skin.

His head tips, his eyes rolling back as a breath burst past his lips and rushes over my face.

"*Fuck*," he grinds out to the ceiling.

I ignore the way my cock pulses and instead focus on running the pad of my thumb over the root of him, my grip solid along his length.

"You can still take it back," he murmurs on a tremble, the cords of his neck taut. "You don't have to do this."

His throat bobs with a swallow that I lean in and lick.

"Yeah. I do."

Giving him one long stroke pulls a glorious sound from deep in his chest, but when I twist my fist over his plush crown, he covers my palm in precum.

"Jordan," he rasps out in another warning. "I won't be able to go back if you don't stop."

"*Then don't.*"

A growl rips out past his lips, and he lunges.

Hands fisting my hair, his cock punches through my fist as he walks me back until it's my ass hitting the counter hard enough that the shit behind me clatters over.

All the while, his sight sears into mine with liquid heat and enough desire to make my cock keep pulsing.

"Kiss me, Jordan," he demands. "Stroke me. *Shitfuck*, just goddamn *touch me.*"

I grab the back of his neck and yank him in until our chests clash and his breath rushes out. "As you wish."

Pushing off from the counter, our mouths crash together, tongues tangling as I pin him back.

His whimpers feed right down my throat, fueling me to release his neck and fumble around behind him.

When the round container hits my fingers, I sink my teeth into his bottom lip.

He hisses.

Suckling on the bite grants me another glorious groan and a punch of his hips.

"I want to see you," he pants out, tugging on my hair to bring my sight to his. "Fuck, lemme see you."

My chuckle is deep and dark as I free my hands and reach for my fly.

He's panting as his head dips, watching as I pop the button. Trembling as I lower the zipper. Near vibrating when I hook a thumb in the waistband of my boxers and tug until my cock springs free and slaps right into his abs.

It leaves a trail of precum in its wake, and I shiver.

"Don't wake me up," he whispers, his head falling to my shoulder, his skin hot against me.

"I wouldn't dare," I murmur back, turning into him to press a kiss on his stubbled cheek. It tickles something deep inside me to be this close to him. This open.

Mac. Mac. Mac.

"Where's your boundary?" he croaks out on a pant, his hands hanging in the air near my hips, fingers ticking like he's desperate to reach out but too reserved to. I feel the ghost of them dance over my skin, and it's enough to raise goosebumps along their path. "*Jordan.*"

Do I even have one?

I answer him with a shake of my head.

The sounds that responds are shaky, but deep as his stiff grip finds my waist. His fingers dig in, his nails biting into the skin.

"Fuck, baby, I'm not gonna be able to stop."

Two fingers beneath his chin lift his darkened sight to mine. His eyes swirl, his forehead lined with the tension he's holding back.

I lean in, my stomach clenches, and I feather my lips over his. "Then don't stop."

With a growl, Mac seals his lips to mine at the same time, his fist wraps us both up in its grip.

His lips capture the moan that rolls off my tongue onto his, his hand pumping, our lengths pressed together.

The feel of his skin smoothing over mine is like an electric shock, the callouses on his palm like a scratch to an itch I never knew I had. The perfect balance of rough and soft.

All man.

"Fuuuuuck, we need lube," he murmurs, his lips migrating to my chin. My jaw. My neck.

"Lube?" Part of me stiffens. Uncertainty straightening my spine.

Will I be good at … that?

Fuck, I should have done more research. All of the porn I watched and articles I read pretty much started with shit like this. Hand jobs. BJ's. Rimming and fingering.

Licking treats from skin.

I was fully prepared to work up to more, but skipping straight there?

Was everything I saw wrong?

"Jordan."

"Huh?" I blink, Mac coming back into focus, and my chest pinches at the apprehension tightening his features.

"Shit, this was a bad idea." His hold on us drops and he steps back, stark naked and tense. His sight trailing over me keeps me in place, like he's committing the scene to memory before he turns and picks up his towel.

"Wait, Mac—"

He doesn't stop.

I catch up to him by the couch, stopping him with a hold on his elbow. He's still solid when he spins on me, his cock pointing straight at me.

But it's the look on his face that pauses me.

"I can't do this," he chokes out, his features guarded. "Don't ask me to do this."

My mouth works but I'm struck.

I don't know what to say.

Does he really think I don't want this?

It's all I've fucking thought about for *months*.

Does he not want this?

Mac nods, his face falling, his towel-wielding hand coming up to cover himself.

"Forget it."

Chapter Forty-Five

Mac

W*HAT IF.*

I'll always choose you.

The same bullshit rolls around in my head, over and over, only broken up by the occasional knock on my bedroom door.

"*Fuck off*," I call out and pull the extra pillow over my head to block out Jordan's voice.

Except … it smells just like him.

My whole fucking bed smells like him and it's choking me.

"Vida."

I press the pillow down farther over my face.

"At least let me explain."

I growl when he tugs on the pillow, stealing the only barrier between my crumbling heart and his stupidly handsome face.

"Explain what," I grind out through a ticking jaw as the man lays down beside me, shoving my pillow beneath his head.

"That I got nervous," he answers as if it's that easy. As if all he needs to do is flash his twinkling eyes at me and I'll crumble.

That things will go back to normal.

Problem is … we're so fucking far away from normal that there doesn't seem to be a way back. That old version of us doesn't exist anymore. That version of *us* just gone.

We're not even friends.

"Get out," I say without heat.

"No," he says back with just as little emphasis.

"I'm fucking tired, Jordan." My eyes burn, my chest caving in. "So tired."

"I know, Vida," he murmurs back and scoots closer.

I nearly break when he palms the back of my head and pulls until I meet his chest. It's still bare and warm and hard beneath my cheek.

"I can't keep doing this with you," I whisper past the thickness in my throat.

His arm cinches around my shoulders, holding me close enough that a tear leaks out.

"I'm sorry." Lips press to my hair and another tear tracks down my temple. "I'm sorry that it happened like that but I'm not sorry I did it."

My breath hitches.

"I'd kiss you all over again, Mac. Touch you. More."

His fingers curl around my ribs, his other hand getting tangled in my hair.

"More, if you'd let me."

"Jordan," I whisper, my throat too clogged with emotion.

What if.

Just once. Just to see what it was like.

"Just rest for now, Vida. I'll be here until you kick me out for real."

Would I be able to survive it?

Chapter Forty-Six

Mac

I WOULD SAY THAT the twitching is what woke me, but that's a lie. It would've required me to have fallen asleep in the first place, and that's not at all where my mind has been.

Instead, I've been stuck in that space between. Not quite cognizant, yet nowhere near under. That place between reality and dreams where nothing, and everything, makes sense.

Just falling without the end in sight, but no bungee cord to rip me back to reality either.

I find that I don't much hate that space between, where things are easier. Lighter, even.

At least, until Jordan gives a full body jerk, the arm he had draped over me flinging out and smacking into the mattress beside him.

It's what snaps me back, making me realize he's covered in sweat, yet shaking. His skin has gone cool to the touch, his lids squeezed shut, his jaw ticking with its harsh grind.

"Jordan," I whisper as I watch his eyes fly around behind his lids, the rest of his features pinching like he's terrified of what he's seeing. "*Jordan.*"

My chest deflates when his hands grip tight on the sheet, and on me, and then he kicks at the air like he's breaking down a barrier in his way.

Fuck, what do I do?

I'm frozen with indecision as I watch the pain twist up his features even more.

The fear.

The helplessness.

"Tyro, c'mon."

With my stomach in my throat, I lean up and brace an arm next to his head, causing his hand to fall away from my hip easily.

The lack of contact seems to only make him worse, his head flinging from side to side, his breaths coming in deep and uneven.

Fuckfuckfuckfuck.

"Wake up. C'mon, wake up."

Snapping in front of his nose does nothing to bring him back.

I straddle his waist, hopeful the weight of me will bring him down.

All it does is pull the softest, yet most anguish-filled sound from somewhere deep in his psyche that my eyes start to burn.

Grabbing his shoulders, I shake him. "*Jordan!*"

Navy blue eyes pop wide and terrified, unfocused and darting around until they finally settle on me.

"*Mac,*" he croaks out on a rasp that yanks my heart strings, and he shoots upright, crushing me in his arms. "Fuck, you're okay."

He's shaking and clinging to me and my eyes burn for real when he keeps repeating the same thing.

You're here. Fuck, you're okay.

Like it's a *relief.*

"I'm here," I reassure him, my arms draping around his shoulders, my unbandaged hand finding his hair and fisting the strands. "I'm okay."

"I'm sorry," he murmurs thickly into my neck, his lips dragging over my already too-fast pulse.

His words ease into a kiss along the thick vein, his tongue sneaking out to run the line down to my collarbone.

I shiver when his path leads back up to behind my ear, his breath still rushing out of him like part of him is stuck in the dream.

"Tell me you're real, Vida," he rasps. "*Fuck*, show me you're real." His teeth clamp onto my earlobe, sending shockwaves straight to my balls, and my grip tightens.

"I'm right here," I murmur into his hair, mouth dropping open when he continues assaulting my neck.

His arms loosen their strangling hold on me, and I'm prepping myself to release him when his hands find my ass and squeeze.

"*Show me.*"

The ache inside my chest ignites when he drags my hips forward, grinding us together.

"Please."

It catches, burning hotter than orange coals at the thick plea cresting his lips.

"I need to feel you."

That feeling becomes a raging inferno that obliterates all that I am and replaces me with a version that grinds right back against my bodyguard's rigid cock.

All reservations vanished, vanquished alongside my need to reassure him.

"Tell me how," I mutter, leaning back just enough to catch his blown gaze.

"*More*," he breathes, his fingers dipping into the waistband of my shorts and tugging until my ass is free and his palms touch skin.

Gasping, I tug his hair when his fingers inch closer toward my crack, press my open mouth against his as the tips knead around my sensitive flesh, dipping closer and closer to the rim.

"More."

A tip taps my hole, and I nearly shoot from his lap.

My gasps feed down his throat, his tongue snaking out to capture them and drag them back into his mouth.

I'm half aware that I should remind him about lube for that wandering finger when he pulls away, making me whine at the sudden chill that sets in.

"Open," he demands on a pant against my mouth and before I can ask what the fuck he means, he's shoving that finger between my lips, chasing the taste of his salty skin with his tongue.

Together, we wet the digit with sloppy kisses.

I'm not prepared when he pulls back just enough to shove a second one in, fucking them both in and out of my mouth.

It's provocative and downright *dirty* enough that I nip at the pads and shiver when he pulls them free.

The chuckle that leaves his kiss-swollen lips seeps into my chest and nestles along some of the jagged edges.

But then the slippery tip presses against my hole and I jolt forward, slamming my lips to his.

I groan when he applies pressure, circling, his other hand pulling on my ass and spreading me open.

I'm so keyed up with the adrenaline and arousal coursing through my veins that it doesn't take much for the muscle to give and his finger to pop just past that first ring.

I moan.

He moans.

"So tight, Vida. *Fuck*." He drags in a shuttering breath against my open mouth and gives a testing pump. One out, then back in, and I'm already seeing stars. "Two?"

Shaking my head, I let it fall to his shoulder, my racing breath coasting over his now flushed skin. "To the knuckles and lube first, Tyro."

He hums his understanding and pulls me so that my chest is flush with his and fucks that finger in and out of me until I take him to the knuckle.

I shudder when his fist meets my ass.

"Get the lube, Vida," he murmurs against my neck, slowly easing his finger from inside me.

When I reach for the nightstand, his teeth latch onto my nipple, making me hiss. He licks away the sting, replacing it with the warmth of his lips as I coat his middle fingers.

Holy fuckhot, this is about to happen.

I'm shaking when he switches to my other nipple, giving it the same amount of attention as the first, and reaches behind me.

Wetness meets my hole at the same time his tongue soothes over his bite. Both circle around their target at the same leisurely pace, adding enough pressure to pull an audible breath from my lungs.

I'm two seconds from begging when his lips pop free, only to find mine and claim them just the same.

And with his hand to the back of my head, his tongue owning mine, Jordan presses his slick finger inside me.

We both groan.

"So fucking hot, Vida," he rumbles, curling his tongue at the same time he curls his finger.

I wrap my arms around his neck, holding on for dear life when he adds the second lubed digit.

In and out, he fucks them into me, stretching me, driving me to the brink of insanity with just his calloused hands.

This can't be real.

"Third?"

I nod.

My head arches back when I feel the extra pressure, the almost burn, my cock leaking from the fullness of it.

"More," I pant, my nails finding purchase in his shoulders, my mind gone to anything except *this*.

Him.

More.

The telltale click of the lube bottle opening has my stomach clenching, the anticipation rolling right down my spine.

His fingers leave me, and I have only half a second to whine about it before he's yanking me closer. Lifting my hips. Bumping my hole with—

My eyes snap open, landing on the intensity raging in his.

"Tell me you don't want to go back, Mac."

My breath hitches.

Stomach flips.

Needyouneedyouneedyou.

"I couldn't," I whisper. "Even if I wanted to."

He notches against me, the plush head of his cock slowly, *slowly* pressing into me until my eyes are rolling back and my mind goes blank.

It pops past the tight muscle, and we groan deep in unison.

"Fuck, Mac. *Fuck.*"

I nod and press a little harder against his hold of me, fiending to feel the rest of him, desperate to take him as far as he'll go.

His grip tightens, stalling my movements.

"Vida, you're so goddamned tight," he all but grinds out. "If you take all of me right now, I'm going to come."

Good fucking God.

My lungs stutter and my cock jerks, adding to the wet spot growing on the front of my shorts.

"Gotta move, Tyro," I murmur and roll my hips.

Cursing, Jordan loosens his hold just enough for me to take more of him.

He shutters out a groan and releases me completely to cinch an arm around my waist and bury his face in my neck.

"You feel so fucking good," he rasps to my thrumming pulse as I rock against him, slowly stretching around his length, taking more and more of his cock.

"Jesus, *fuck*," I mumble and when my ass finally meets his lap, the breath punches out of him.

And me.

There's a whole lot of not breathing happening.

It's not until I grind down, taking him as far as I can go in this position that we both gasp.

No going back now.

My stomach clenches when Jordan's sight clashes with mine, like maybe he's thinking the same things as me, and his hands smooth down my thighs. They wander higher, dipping beneath the fabric, his callouses catching ever so slightly along the hair that dusts over my legs.

"Mac," he nearly chokes out when I clench around him, and bunches the material in his hands. He pulls and collects it in his palms until my cock springs free, the tip glistening and nearing purple with how fucking hard I am.

This is it. This is how I die.

Chapter Forty-Seven

JORDAN

THE HARD MUSCLE BENEATH my palms feels *good*.

The heat surrounding my dick un-fucking-real.

His tattoos and flat chest. His stiff cock.

Mac. Mac. Mac.

The weight of him baring down on me, tightening around me, grounding me to this bed is so unfathomably sexy that I have no idea how I ever got nervous thinking about this.

Well—that was if the roles were reversed, me taking his cock and only hoping its half as good as how well he takes mine.

But even if it is?

There's no way I'd ever deny him this, if that's his thing.

This feeling of a soul-deep connection through touch. Allowing our bodies to do all the talking our mouths can't and *fuck*.

The vehemence staring back at me has another shiver racking down my spine, the potency of it only hungering me for *more*.

"Turn around, Vida," I growl out. "I wanna watch your ass swallow my dick."

His eyes flare wide and heated, the sound escaping him only to be described as a deep whimper.

It's then that Mac pushes at my shoulders until I flop back on the mattress, his hands bracing on my abs and his hips roll against me.

He's gasping above me, beautifully flushed as his hair falls over his eyes.

I get half a groan out when he works his feet beneath him and starts to turn, twisting on me like a goddamn Sit 'n Spin. Somehow kicking off his shorts as he goes.

"*Fuck*," I bark out, shooting upright and grabbing his waist just as he slams down on my cock, impaling himself and crying out. "That's it, Vida." I guide his hips. "Look at how gorgeous you are taking my cock."

He trembles.

He.

Him.

Mac.

Something inside me uncoils and releases a rush of recognition that tingles down the back of my neck.

This. This is it.

He's the key.

Lifting him so that I can get to my knees despite his protests, I guide Mac to grip the headboard. He braces, preparing himself and arching his ass out.

I hum an approving noise and ease back inside him.

The heat of him is almost too much when my balls meet his, the resulting moan too good to my ears.

"Mac," I croak out, my thrusts measured but deep. Slow but powerful as I blanket his body with mine, a hand bracing over his.

"Y-yeah?" he stammers, his breath rushing out with each stroke of my cock inside his trembling body.

My other hand finds his chest and flattens between his pecs, right over his heart.

"I'm not wearing a condom."

He moans and my abs tighten.

"I get tested every week."

His hand flexes beneath mine, his hole clenching around me.

"Same," he rasps.

My balls draw up tight to my body as I drop my head to his shoulder and press open mouthed kisses to his salty skin.

"I haven't …" The hand on his chest trails down, down, down until the heel of my palm presses into his groin, his hard cock feeding between my spread fingers. "I haven't been with anyone."

"*Fuck*," he mumbles, his body tightening, his hand beneath mine wriggling until he threads our fingers.

"Not since I met you."

He goes completely taut, his hole gripping me so tight that I can barely move.

I glance up in time to catch him throwing his head back, his mouth spreading wide as I fist his pulsing cock and stroke him.

"*Fuuuuuuuck*, Jordan." He trembles, jerks, and shoots ropes of cum all over my palm with rolled back eyes and groaning gasps.

"That's it," I rasp, pumping my fist over his cock, milking the cum from him until those groans of his become pitchy huffs. "Fuck, I need to come."

Mac arches his ass, burying me as deep as I'll go, and I grip him with my cum-covered hand.

"Jordan," he breathes out over his shoulder, his cheeks coated in a sexy pink flush, his hips working me in shallow thrusts. "*Me, either.*"

I jolt forward with a moan, burying myself and pulsing stream after stream of cum in his ass, filling him with a piece of me that will only ever belong to him.

"Fuck," Mac whines deep. "I can feel your cock pulsing."

The sound that escapes me is half grunt and an almost chuckle. "Same."

He groans and clenches, making me drop my head back to his shoulder with a curse.

"Sensitive?"

"Ah, *yeah.*"

He wiggles and I hiss, my eyes rolling back, my cock giving another mighty jerk.

"Just go slow." I nod and nibble his skin, making him snort. "And don't worry about the sheets. I have another set."

"I know," I mumble and press a final kiss to his shoulder before leaning back and slowly easing my cock from his body.

I'm prepared for the hiss, the shock of sudden chill, the full-body aftershock that rocks me.

What I'm not prepared for?

Watching my cum leak out of his hole and trail down his taint.

I press a hand to his lower back, folding him forward so that I can spread his cheeks and see it up close.

"Holy *fuck.*"

That flush runs all the way down his back when I run my fingers through it, collecting it along the tips, and stuff it right back into his hole.

Mac moans, clenching when I work my fingers in and out of his ass.

Like maybe he wants to keep it there as much as I want it to stay there.

"So fucking sexy, Vida."

Chapter Forty-Eight

Mac

S EX DOESN'T SOLVE MUCH.

But it sure as shit feels like a number forty-two to me right about now.

I'm still in disbelief. Still in shock. Still convinced I dreamt the whole fucking thing except I'm reminded by the ache in my ass every time I move.

And it is *oh-so-good*.

"Stop wriggling so much," Jordan says absentmindedly, his focus lasered in on the towel in his grip.

"Can't help it," I mutter through a smirk and tap my forefingers along the edge of the vanity in front of me.

Even if I wanted to, I don't think I could. Because not only did we just get out of the shower—*together*—where Jordan spent time lathering my body, he's now fixing my hair exactly as I do it without a single instruction from me.

Except … he's deliberate. Meticulous.

Tender.

Taking a simple leave in conditioner routine and making it special.

While naked.

It's got my chest swelling and my eyes set to heart mode.

Not to mention, I've been sporting a half-chub since I spunked all over my pillow.

"I haven't done that since I was a teenager, you know," I say out loud as his fingers work through my strands again, this time with the leave-in shit coating them.

"What's that?"

He takes his time, running the product through, then scrunching the ends up tight to my scalp with the towel. It feels so damn good that I almost forget to answer.

"Coming on my pillow," I respond, half-dazed and all the way relaxed.

His sight flicks up in the mirror, his head giving a slight disbelieving shake. "Can't say that I ever have."

The easy smirk I was toting drops. "You never used a pillow before?"

"For *what?*"

I snort and sink back into the way his hands work over my head. Pretty sure he's just doing the same thing all over again as an excuse to keep his hands on me.

"For sex," I mutter, my hands falling to my lap, thumbs tapping a gentle rhythm on my knees.

"Ah, no."

"Shame, Tyro." My eyes fall shut. "I'll have to show you later."

His hands stutter in my hair. It's so brief that I dismiss it, my energy too zapped to do anything except follow the way they recover.

"What color?" he murmurs sometime later, his hands reluctantly leaving my head.

I hum in thought, drifting in that space between where consciousness meets fantasy and answer "Orange."

With gentle fingers, Jordan ties a bandana around my forehead, securing the ends at the back, just like I do.

Something light brushes over my cheekbone and I crack an eye open with a softening smile to find Jordan staring down at me. He's wearing that endearing as fuck almost grin tipping the corner of his lips.

My gut explodes in tingling flutters and I turn into the warmth of his touch.

"Orange suits you, Vida."

Pressing a smiling kiss to his palm, I reach for his hips and tug until he's standing between my spread knees. The height of the barstool I'm on puts his chest right in my face.

The moment feels so delicate as I wrap my arms around his ass and plant kisses along his abs, but there's a question burning into my subconscious. An answer I need to know, though I can't explain *why*, considering all the things I *should* be asking him after what has happened in the last few hours.

Things like: *How would you rate your experience here today,* and more importantly, *where the fuck do we go from here?*

I sigh against his skin when my mind threatens to shatter the bubble we've planted ourselves in and rest my chin on his sternum to look up at him.

"Can I ask you something?"

He tips his chin and cups my face, his calloused thumbs brushing over my cheeks. "Sure."

"What … were you dreaming about?"

He stiffens against me, his features hardening.

"I … my …"

His throat bobs with a swallow and my chest tightens as his eyes glaze over.

"Never mind," I rush out and squeeze him to me, flattening my cheek against him. "You don't have to say anything."

Hands to my shoulders, he gives me a squeeze right back. "You deserve an explanation."

A lump forms in my throat.

Is this where the bubble pops?

Please tell me I didn't just fuck everything up.

He sighs something deep and pulls back, taking the tranquility of the moment with him as my hold breaks.

That peace I held onto snaps when Jordan steps back.

"Mac," he mutters, and I shake my head.

"Forget I said anything."

What have I done?

Heat rises in my chest, curling up in a ball of regret and hurt and just when I think he's going to leave …

He kneels in front of me.

"Vida."

I can't look at him. My heart too heavy, my love too deep for a rejection to come so soon.

I slept with him. Fucking fuck, what did I do?

"Hey, hey, hey, look at me."

Jordan cups my face again and draws my sight up, up, up until it crashes with his.

"I've been having nightmares," he answers and my stomach twists up. "That's all."

It doesn't feel like it's that simple.

I swallow.

"And, uh … you were in it."

My heart sinks and my stomach twists all up. "Me?"

A single dip of his chin is his answer and judging by the resounding silence after it, it's all the answer I'm going to get.

"That … sucks," I murmur and pull back, pushing to my feet.

I don't know what else to say or how else to transition from something that feels so fucking heavy. Something that's his to know and mine to not.

Even though it's big enough that he … fuck, he needed me after.

Slept with me. Another man.

Has that even sunk in for him?

A wave of anxiety rolls right over me and plants its ugly head right in my sternum.

What happens when it does?

"Mac."

I turn to find him, still on his knees where I left him—fuck, he's a sight—with a grit to my jaw.

"It's just a nightmare, okay?"

Shaking my head, I walk away.

Because with us … it's never that damn simple.

Chapter Forty-Nine

JORDAN

T HE SPACE BETWEEN MAC and me hurts.

He doesn't trust me.

The thought runs through my head like it's a marathon, circling and circling, with no end in sight.

It's another layer to the shitstorm that has my hands shaking and my stomach in a permanent knot.

Which has made being at his Ma's house, surrounded by not only his band but all of security, such a hard place to pretend at.

To act like I'm not waiting for every glance of his to land on mine from across the room, or each pass of his to stop by me.

But why would he when he's spent so long without me?

Having sex with him once won't change that.

God, I just want to fucking touch him. Hold him. Tell him this isn't just a—

I shake my head.

Just a phase? Was I really about to say that to myself?

The thing about phases is that you never really know it's not permanent until one day you wake up and realize you're still listening to the same type of angsty music, or wearing all black, even decades later.

I tip off my hat—its worn out nature an icon of my exact thought pattern with its faded black tint and the missing Trapt logo from the front—and run a hand through my hair.

I'm infatuated with the drummer of a band not too different than the very one that made me love rock music.

I mean, what teenager *didn't* envy all the musicians of every band they listened to?

A tingling sensation runs down my neck and I blink myself back to the room.

Except it's full of people that are already busy entertaining each other.

"I'm gonna do a walk," I say to no one in particular and spin back to the door.

The boards underfoot creak the moment I step out it, the scent of fresh outdoors filling my lungs with each step that leads me around the back of the house.

Toby's on the patio with Ma, their heads scrunched together.

"Ma, I need a favor, and you can't say no." I hear him say as I pass and shake my head.

"If that's how you're asking, then the answer should probably be *no*," the woman answers and I snort to myself and keep walking.

Before I realize it, I'm standing in a clearing with only one tree breaking up the grass, staring at the bottom of a treehouse built into its sturdy trunk, a ladder leading up into the belly of it beckoning me.

It's already open, a glow illuminating the inside as I climb up.

The first thing to hit me is the haze of smoke, then the scent of burning weed as I breach the floor and vault myself up to sit with my legs dangling through the opening.

"You shouldn't be in here."

"Hey to you, too, Vida."

Mac snorts and blows a plume of smoke through his nose. "I'm smoking. Get out."

I shake my head. "When did you even come out here?"

"You were too zoned out to see me walk right past you."

My jaw grits.

Shit.

"Has it hit you yet?" he asks me from his perch on a beanbag and sucks in another hit from the joint pinched between his lips. It makes the cherry flare bright orange under the twinkle lights that cast shadows on his face.

"Where's the black eye from?"

"Dare," he answers easily, too easily, and I stiffen.

"What?" I snap out with a heat I can't explain taking over my chest.

"Got too close while he was wailing on his set. *Your turn.*"

He takes another hit, and my jaw remains clenched at the prospect of Mac being anywhere near the other person, especially close enough to get hit. The very same person that stepped out on the stage that night I flew thousands of miles just to see Mac with my own two eyes and shattered the reality I thought I knew. The one I've ignored the existence of, if only in hopes that he's not real. Not close to my drummer. Just a pawn in the game of promo and reputation.

"That sounds like bullshit," I force out.

"And that sounds like deflection. *Has. It. Hit. You.*"

Growling, I push to my feet and stomp closer to his beanbag. "We're not talking about me." I snatch the joint right from between his lips and snuff it out on the sole of my boot. "Why did he hit you?"

Mac huffs and pulls out a fresh joint.

"Like I said, got too close during practice."

"Bullshit. I've never seen you share your set."

He flicks a flame to a lighter and burns the end of the joint. "You haven't seen me do *shit* for months, Jordan."

I flinch, a red-hot feeling burning my chest wide open.

Actually … make that green.

"Did you sleep with him?" It tumbles out of my stiff jaw before I can stop it, my heart racing too fast.

He rocks back, his brows flying up behind the bandana I fucking tied on his head and pinches his smoke between his fingers.

"Did I?" His smoke-holding hand goes to his chest, and he lets loose a laugh that's bordering on hysterical. "Did *I*." He pushes to his feet and plants a hand right between my stiff pecs. "Did I? No, the only thing I did was fuck a straight man with a God. Damn. *Complex*."

My stomach twists violently and I growl. "This isn't about *me*."

Mac nods and works his jaw. Takes his time pulling in a puff of smoke that flows through his nose, before his hard as fuck sight lands back on mine.

"Then tell me what you wanted three days for."

My tongue sticks to my teeth.

"Tell me what your nightmare was about. Better yet—" He pulls in a puff and points two fingers in my face, "—tell me why the fuck you couldn't come to Europe with me."

Me ... not us.

Insides burning, hands itching, I flex my fingers and will them to stick to my sides despite how badly I want to just grab him. Kiss him. Show him why none of that matters now.

Show *myself* why none of that matters.

But I don't touch him. I don't reach for him until he's scoffing and brushing past me.

"Vida."

"Do you regret it?" he asks the wall, a tick to his jaw and a redness to his eyes that has nothing to do with the weed.

"I don't have regrets," I lie and swallow hard.

I didn't ... until you.

"I'm glad *you* don't."

A piece of my heart chips off and shatters at his feet when he jerks from my grasp, his comment hanging so fucking heavy in the air that it grows and grows with each second that I don't stop his retreat.

Stop him, something warns me. *Stop him before it's too late.*

But my tongue is too thick for words, my brain too foggy to clarify *how* to stop him, my heart begging for him to just give me a moment, when he pauses at the ladder's opening.

"Would you take it back?"

I shake my head at his back. "No."

He scoffs and puts the joint between his lips, dipping to get the latter under his feet.

"Mac," I rush out and he pauses halfway through the opening, though he still won't look at me. "I …" My hands shake and my chest feels like it might explode. "I wouldn't take any of it back."

"Why?"

"Because … I …"

"Jordan."

"Because I like you."

Chapter Fifty

Mac

"**L**IKE ME?" I scoff though my eyes are *burning*, my heart pulverized in the blender that is my chest. "Jordan, I *love you*." I let my gaze collide with his shock-wide eyes and it takes everything in me to hold myself back. To stop my lip from wobbling. To keep the tears at bay. To keep myself from going to him.

Because as much as he keeps protesting … this *is* about him.

It's his life. His sexuality. His closet to find his way out of, or not.

Even if it's killing me.

"Mac," he rasps out and steps closer.

He leans down, kneeling in front of me for the second time today.

I have to stop this. Him. Before there's nothing left of me.

His hands are on my face before I can escape him, his lips crashing into mine.

I let him kiss me and I lean in, giving it everything I have as his tongue sweeps along mine. Licking right back, I ignore the way my eyes leak and my chest rips wide open.

This is it. This is all it will ever be.

Stolen kisses and secret fucks. Forever behind closed doors. Hidden away in the closet that I swore I'd never step the fuck back into.

A gasp rushes past his lips when I pull back and cup his face.

"I'm fucking sick of giving you the chance to catch up. You won't, and that's okay."

A pain-filled noise escapes his nose, and I shake my head. "Can't y—"

"It's okay, baby," I murmur through the thickness in my throat to his red-rimmed and glassy eyes. "One day you'll figure it out, or you won't." I lift a shoulder though it feels like the weight of the world has settled on them and force a shaky smile. "But I can't let you use me to do it. Not anymore."

"But Mac …"

He sniffs and I go numb.

"I'll see you when we get back."

Chapter Fifty-One

Jordan

R ain pelts the pavement just outside the glass I'm perched in front of for what feels like the thousandth hour and does nothing to dispel the crease in my brow or the burn in my chest.

All I see is Mac. Standing there with the tears in his eyes mixing with the moisture from the sky. All I hear is his voice begging me over the sound of the storm.

This one is worse than that day, but it's still there. Clinging to my subconscious as a reminder of what I fucked up.

It hit me square in the chest the next morning when Mac didn't come home, to his own apartment. I waited for the pain to be about sleeping with a man for the first time, for the panic to sink in, but all I felt was the emptiness Mac left behind. A hole shaped just like him that was left gaping.

But then my mind flashes to the opening of a treehouse where he yet again begged me to open up and I just … couldn't.

So here I sit, counting down the hours until my shift is over, while he's out there being his exuberant self somewhere overseas. With someone else as his protector on another continent. Someone else watching his back.

Someone else having movie nights in and greasy midnight drive through.

It's better this way. For him to find something better, somewhere far away from me and the dark cloud that has followed me since that night my parents, my house, blazed beneath the night sky.

At least that's what I keep telling myself. Maybe one day I'll finally believe it.

I check my watch and frown.

Less than an hour until I can go.

The closer it gets, though, the more that burn in my sternum becomes a full-on stab right to the center of my chest.

Because what I plan to do when I leave here feels like a betrayal of everything Mac and I had.

Like I'm breaking all the promises I made him along the way.

I'll be here when you get back—

Except I won't. I can't.

For two and half weeks I have waited. And each day since I gave that up, I have reached out.

All but begged him myself.

Only to be completely ghosted.

Texts and calls not responded to.

Comments and voicemails left unchecked.

I can't let you use me. Not anymore.

It *hurts* to know that's all he thought it was.

But to me, our connection is what drove me. That invisible tether stringing between us that kept us closer than anyone else I've ever known.

Did it though?

I shake my head and push to my feet.

"I'm going to do a walk," I say to Aria in passing. I feel her watch me warily more than I see it but I don't let it stop me. "Call me if you need me."

"Jordan," she calls after me and it's only when I hear the pattering of her feet that I stop.

"Yeah?"

She's much closer when she speaks next, yet that does nothing to prepare me for what comes out of her mouth.

"He does love you, y'know," she says gently.

I stiffen, that stabbing pain becoming a gaping wound, festering inside me.

Other people can see it?

"I know," I mutter back through my clenched jaw. "He … told me that much."

"Then …" When she pauses, I let my heavy sight meet hers. "Can I give you some advice?"

I swallow, and lift a shoulder.

What other choice do I have?

"Love him back—" she grabs my arm with a reassuring squeeze. "Or let him go."

My chest pinches painfully.

I already care about him and look where that's gotten us. Me. *Him.*

So why does the idea of letting go hurt so much worse?

Eyes burning, I nod.

"I know."

Chapter Fifty-Two

Mac

OUT OF RESPECT FOR Toby, I've managed to not drink away my heartache until I'm passed out in a slop of meat and bones.

Instead, I've eaten my weight in sugary confections and enough deep-fried carbs to stop my heart.

Maybe then it'll stop aching.

But the one thing I refused to give up for the rest of the night is the joint I found stashed in my pocket. And the second one I found hidden under the couch cushion when Toby passed out.

Breathing smoke in deep, I hold then release it out into the freshness of the nighttime air. It's gotta be closing in on morning at this point and after another long inhale, I finally start to feel the fuzz filling around the edges just as the grey sky begins to blend into the black horizon of night.

"Dude. Pass."

Joint pinched between my thumb and middle finger, I offer it up to Dare.

I'm not sure when he ended up here, how long we've been here, in some empty parking lot but I'm glad to not be alone. It makes it easier to ignore the pressure currently crushing my sternum.

"Didn't work out with the lady friends?"

Dare snorts on his exhale and coughs out the rest of the grey haze. "I fucked them both, bro. Duh."

He holds the joint out in offer for me to take it back. I hesitate.

"Were they at least clean?"

"You saying you don't want to put your mouth where mine has been? Too late for that, Thompson."

Dare shrugs and takes another toke, holding it long enough that he's nearly gasping when he pushes it back out.

"I definitely fucked that guy before you did. Besides." I gesture in his general direction. "That was before *this*."

Dare laughs, tokes, then offers it once again.

"I'm pretty sure you just said metalgod looks good on me." His smirk is languid and smug. "I'll take it."

Rolling my eyes, I snatch the joint back from him before he can smoke it all. "I said that you got second rate dick from an amateur in high school and *that's* what you've been bragging about all these years."

"Uh-huh." Dare's arms cross over his thick chest. "So, he learned it all from you, then."

I snort and nearly choke on the burn of smoke through my nose. "Those weren't my best days."

"You mean you're not still there?"

I tag Dare's shoulder with my knuckles and grin when he hisses. "It's gonna kill you to never know, isn't it?"

The stretch of Dare's lips is too wide. "All you gotta do is ask."

I fake a gag. "Over my dead body."

"Hey, I'll try anything once."

I sputter out a laugh and pass back the joint. "You need more of this so the hallucinations make sense."

"Dude, it's just weed," he says, but takes the offer and speaks through the smoke rolling from his mouth. "I've been meaning to ask where's your bestie? I thought he followed you like a dog."

The anvil sitting on my chest tilts and digs further in. "Doing … bodyguard shit."

The raised brow Dare throws in my direction tells me he doesn't buy my bullshit. And to be honest, I wish *I* bought it.

"People are still going nuts online about him not being around."

It's all so much bullshit.

I push out a sigh. "Mind ya bizness."

"Bizness minded." Dare holds his hands up in surrender. "All's I'm saying is that it's been cool to be real for once. Thought you'd want the favor."

Perfect opening to redirect the spotlight.

"For once? You mean you *still* haven't told your band that you like dick sometimes?"

Dare's jaw snaps shut, his teeth making an audible clank. "Mind ya bizness."

I mimic his earlier pose and let it go. "Fine. Suffocate." *Mostly.*

"*Fine,*" he snaps. "Die alone."

I throw my hands up in the form of *what the fuck* that Dare shrugs off.

"I knew I never liked you," I mumble and snatch the near roach from his lips just as he's relighting it.

Pulling in deep, I let the fuzz try to outweigh the jagged edges of my mind, though it does nothing to ease the turmoil coiling inside my chest.

Hurt and anger merge in my veins all over again, making it feel like thousands of bees are stinging their way through my blood instead of the soft peach noise I was going after.

He's just processing. No way he meant a single thing in those messages.

The shudder that racks me has nothing to do with the early morning chill and every bit to do with the waves that roll over my stomach.

"*Fuuuck*, you really are in love with him, aren't you?"

Startled out of my spiraling of despair, I swing my gaze from the cement at my feet to Dare.

Who looks lost as shit.

"Nah, batballs," I mutter too softly. *Pretend, pretend, pretend.* "That's not for me."

Some people get to have their love in the lifetime they find them in.

Those people *aren't* me, like I wish they were.

God, I fucking wish I was one of them.

I swallow down the truth thickening in my throat and deflect. "You really are seeing someone, aren't you?"

Dare wheels back like I slapped him.

Bingo.

If my heart didn't feel like it might burst, I'd celebrate. Pump my fists up in the air and poke all of the fun at him.

But I do none of that because none of this feels … *real.*

"We're both fucked, aren't we?" Dare asks the cement with downcast eyes and a downturn to his lips.

I sputter out a macabre laugh and lean back into the tour bus's fiberglass side. "Yeah. Pretty much."

Dare mimics my pose and shoves his hands in his pockets. "Is it Jordan though, right?" My brows shoot up past my bandana. "How the hell does this work?"

If it's possible, my brows jump higher.

Deflect it!

"Oh shit, Darius. I know it's bad when you're asking *me* for advice."

Dare smacks his lips but doesn't deny it as his gaze travels back out to the parking lot surrounding us.

But then his head falls back against the tour bus, and I can see the indecision warring across his pinched features.

Pretend. Pretend. Pretend.

"Are we really doing this?" I ask, tilting my head and begging my heart to not leap out at the first chance to say how it feels out loud. As if sharing the load with someone else might lighten it just the tiniest bit.

That maybe, and I mean *maybe*, some of this will make more sense to someone else.

Because, fuck, I wish this was easier.

What feels like hours but is probably only seconds later, Dare's head lulls in my direction and a single dip of his chin is all the answer I get before he opens his big mouth.

"You're stupid for not admitting it to yourself."

I scoff, though my heart thumps angrily inside my chest. "And you're stupid for pretending to not like guys even though you're clearly seeing one."

"Burn."

Shaking my head, I let my weight slide down the side of the tour bus to the cement parking lot. I'm pretty sure that if all my feelings weren't trapped inside my sternum it'd be uncomfortable, but it seems to be all I can focus on. This ball inside me that festers and rolls and collects debris the longer I try to hold it back. Growing larger until I feel it buried just behind my tonsils.

"You're right," Dare murmurs as he slides down the side of the bus to join me. "I don't know that it's quite what you have with Jordan, but I'm seeing a guy, and I definitely did *not* fuck those chicks back at the penthouse."

I shrug and ignore the ping of jealousy for what Dare *thinks* Jordan and I share. "You don't have to justify shit to me. You do you."

"It's been rocky as fuck." He sighs. "We never agreed to exclusive, and I never expected that he *would* be."

My brow furrows some more. "But no one knows about you two."

"Nah. Well, everyone suspects something's up, but no one has asked outright."

I nod, an understanding washing over me at his words.

"So, you're dating your lead singer, and I'm … fucked."

I'd laugh if it weren't so fucking pathetic.

Dare chuckles, still not denying it, as I mumble, "Aren't we a perfect bunch."

"So, what are you going to do?"

I sigh out a heavy breath. "Well apparently I'm stupid, if I'm listening to *you*."

"You should." I wing a brow at him only to find his sincerity lining his stony features. "Listen to me, that is."

I twirl a finger in the air, encouraging Dare to get to his point.

"Because in my situation, *I'm* the runaway. Just like you."

Me?

No.

No.

No?

Chapter Fifty-Three

JORDAN

"**H**ERE ARE THE KEYS, Mr. Kauffman."

I swallow hard as the cool metal drops into my waiting palm. The realtor's back retreats after a mumbled thanks and I just stand there next to the reception desk with my hand in the air for way too long.

This is it.

The foundation on which I plan to build the next chapter of my life laid out before me on mat-covered hardwood.

Three sturdy floors.

A hefty brick exterior.

Original stained glass windows set into the side.

Enough equipment to keep the gym rat side of my brain occupied, and several repairs that will need my attention between that.

It's my fresh start. The one I needed so that I could leave all the old things in the past.

A rush of something almost warm and familiar breaks through the fog as I wander the floor, run my fingers over the ropes to the boxing ring, then hoist myself up to just sit on the raised platform and stare.

I did it. I did something for me.

So why does it feel like I've made yet another bad decision?

Pushing out a sigh, I fish my phone from my pocket and dial the one number I've been dreading.

"What?" my boss snaps over the line on the second ring, his gruffness out in full force.

It makes my palms slick over, even though I know it's just a cover for how much he cares, and swallow.

"You got a second?"

His deep sigh echoes over the line and when he remains silent, I take it as my cue to go ahead.

"I … this is—"

"Spit it out, kid. I gotta get this crowd cleaned up."

I lick my lips and drop my gaze to the floor.

"I quit," I rush out before I can stop myself and knock the fucking wind out of my own lungs.

"Come again?"

"I … I'm giving you my notice, Ian. I'll stay long enough for you to find my replacement, then I need out."

He huffs out a grunt.

"Call Mac."

I bristle at the mention of the drummer and scowl. "What? What's he got to do with—"

"I don't rehire, Jordan," Ian grinds out.

The room suddenly feels too small, the ropes at my back too stiff.

"I don't understand."

"The night the video leaked, I fired you."

I swallow, something deep and heavy settling in my chest at the reminder of the spoof video that got me canned, only to be brought back. There was a guy that looked an awful lot like me getting what looked like head, inside Mac's hotel room. Except it wasn't real. None of it was, except for the footage of the room itself. "That was years ago."

"Uh-huh."

Popping to my feet, I tug on the collar of my Sentry Security shirt when my throat feels too tight. "What are you—"

"I wasn't the one that brought you back after that fucking fiasco. Mac did."

All I hear is wooshing in my ears. All I feel is that festering wound in my chest spreading.

Mac did?

I look down, if only to see the logo printed on the shirt, confirming its mark over my left pec.

"Call Mac," Ian repeats but all I hear is …

Let him go.

Chapter Fifty-Four

JORDAN

TENSION LINES MY SHOULDERS as I push, push, push until the bar finally clinks against the rack and settles in the hooks.

I'm covered in sweat and in desperate need of a drink. Something to help me forget the last twenty-four hours.

Hell, something strong enough to wipe out the last five *years.*

The last two fucking decades.

I take my time showering in my new studio apartment two floors up, doing my best to wash away the heaviness of the day. But when I stand in the middle of it in nothing but a towel, trails of water still clinging to my skin, my feet root to the spot.

There's not much here, not much I own.

A single couch.

Bare walls.

I can't see the glasses in the cabinet, but I know that there's four sitting on a shelf by themselves.

If I could have bought only one, I would have.

There's something absolutely crushing in the fact that you can't. That not even the glassware in my kitchen is as alone as I am.

The bowls. The plates. All in fours.

But me?

It's just me.

Yet all I can think about … is what Mac would think of the place. Would he like the swirl of orange in the tumblers I found? Would he crash onto the couch and complain that one side is too lumpy to sleep on?

Would he fall into my bed instead and use me as a pillow even though I'm less comforting than the shitty cushions?

My jaw grits as I move to the dresser and jerkily shove my limbs through fabric.

Even the drawer is half empty, devoid of the fullness that I'm used to when I've borrowed Mac's clothes or grabbed something for him.

No color or stupid prints, just my plain black briefs.

The tick in my jaw jumps into overdrive, my sights swinging around the room and pinging off of all the memories I'll never have here.

All the things Mac will never see. Never be a part of or be able to comment on.

The things we'll never do together …

I fucked us up.

With burning eyes and a tremble to my fingers, I swipe my phone from the armrest and pull up the clock app, its list of different time zones flashing back at me by the second. I scroll past all the previous entries, their time already into the morning light of tomorrow and when I get to the bottom, I pause.

One p.m.

He'd be awake.

The tight knuckled grip I have on the phone makes it creak.

It's the time I've been waiting for, a moment where I know he's available and I'm in the sanctuary of my own place instead of driving away from his sister's shop or sitting inside his apartment where I've been staying until now.

None of it felt right—feels right—and yet I'm dialing. Waiting for the inevitable voicemail greeting when he ignores the call.

Just let him go.

I fall back onto the couch, my hat staring at me from its perch on the little coffee table with its ghost of an emblem missing as it has been for years. The song that it triggers twists up my stomach.

Is this me running from him?

The greeting picks up.

I'm still locked on the faded black when the beep knocks me out of my head, my tongue too tied to speak at first.

"Mac," I rasp finally and clear my throat when it cracks. "I'm …"

All of my muscles go taut when I attempt to force out the words I've been preparing myself to say, the same ones I told Ian two nights ago.

The same two words that would set us both free, finally, to move on.

I quit.

Yet I can't say them to his inbox.

My eyes wander around the room, desperate to find the answer hiding somewhere among the solitude, only to land on the cabinet that houses those damn glasses and their colored swirl.

To the barely used dresser and the lumpy cushion beside me.

Then they drop to the designs inked into the skin of my arm, the geometric style bleeding from bold at my shoulder to nearly faded and hiding the line of a gradient soundwave around my wrist.

Foundation and balance.

Stability through music.

My fingers curl into a fist when the voicemail prompts me to end the call.

Instead, I delete the message and hang up.

Chapter Fifty-Five

Mac

Tʜᴇ ʙʟᴀᴄᴋ X ᴏɴ my palm smears all over my drumstick, smudging it until there's nothing but a blob left as it does every night that As Above plays on stage.

Tonight, I added eye black above my cheekbones because I was feeling particularly dark just before we took the stage.

Not even my twin's spiel to the masses about lifting yourself out of the darkness is getting me anywhere near the light and when the set ends, all I can think is *finally*.

I do my duty by running to the front of the stage, pose with my brothers, and toss my sticks into the grabby hands of fans.

Ignoring the way I want to linger, to watch security pull the final confetti speckled bodies down from the wave in hopes that maybe, *maybe* Jordan's hidden in the line that protects us from the mob, I pluck the final pick from Fin's mic stand. I run it over my fingers, then toss it, pinging it off Peach's head on accident, and nearly grin when a fan all but bulldozes over the bodyguard to get to it.

He scowls back at me.

I flip him off and saunter backstage.

"Take me for a drink, Thompson."

Scrunching my nose up at Dare like his statement smells as bad as it sounds, I shake my head. "The fuck would I do that for?"

"Because you've been avoiding me since the other night."

"I've always avoided you," I mutter and push passed him in search of a water.

"Not like this."

"Bull shit," I snap back and take a pull from the cold bottle placed into my hand. "Just because we had that one conversation does not make us pals."

No, he thinks I'm *the runaway.*

Fuck him.

And he thinks I didn't see him running comments about Jordan online, but I did.

So double fuck him.

"Don't forget," he murmurs with too much mirth for my sour mood and points in my face. "We also swapped spit."

I make a show of guzzling some of my water, swishing it around in my mouth, then spitting the shit right at his Vans-clad feet.

"*Dude.*"

Shrugging, I brush passed the other drummer once again, but before I let the growing crowd of roadies swallow me up, I throw a middle finger over my shoulder.

Smoking the same joint does not constitute swapping spit.

"Bro, hey, we're gonna—"

"Nope," I pop out to my twin and pat his shoulder as I pass. "Not losing to you again tonight. Ask Toby."

I don't stop moving until I catch the flash of orange hair and the new barbell through the bridge of Peach's nose.

"Can we go?"

"Let me check in with Ian." His green eyes bounce between mine for only a moment before his gaze drops to my chest. "You plan on taking that shit home?"

I want to tell him that home doesn't exist. That there is no place left for me to belong, in peace, without this mind of mine wandering. This heart of mine aching. And though I don't really want to go back to an empty hotel bed … I also don't have it in me to be around all this … *happy*. These feelings. The giddiness of the after-show energy that my brothers all get. This weird sense of comradery and *let's spend even more time together.*

Instead, I follow his line of sight and sigh at the earpiece and wires hanging down the front of my shirt.

He's already waving down an audio tech when I look back up.

Once I'm less a battery pack and earpiece, Peach and I swiftly make our way through the crowd and out into the night air.

He radios our departure to the rest of security before we pull away in a blacked-out sedan.

"Hell of a show, Mac."

I grumble a thankful response and slide farther into the seat.

"You wanna talk about it?"

My teeth clamp together as I watch the city pass by.

"No," I finally mumble to the fogging glass.

There's a rumble of understanding and a stretch of silence that falls over the car so long that I'm tapping out a beat against my thighs with stiff thumbs when he finally speaks again.

"He called you earlier."

I sink farther under the weight of the reminder. "I know."

More silence stretches, yet it does nothing to quiet my spiraling mind.

"Can I ask why you're avoiding him now?"

I love him and it hurts too much to bear.

My exhale is shaky, my chest too tight.

Yet every morning I wake up without him in my bed is like a knife to my already bleeding heart.

"He's annoying." It's what I settle on, but what I really mean is that Jordan Kauffman is a confused man with nowhere to put his curiosities except on me and I can't carry them anymore.

But have I?

Peach snorts and guides the car into the hotel parking lot. "Sure is. But keep lying to me."

He parks and kills the engine, turning to me in his seat instead of scanning the surroundings and I huff. "Aren't you supposed to do bodyguard shit?"

"Sixteen cars in the lot, a couple sneaking into the side entrance that probably have a key and are staying here but drank a little much judging by her laugh, and an empty bus under the overhang. Red sedan has someone smoking inside," he says without breaking his sight from mine. I blink, then turn to see the couple laughing as they stumble through the glass door. The bus. The red car with a window cracked and a lit cherry flaring red. I don't count the cars, but I trust that there's as many as he suggested.

"Shit, Peach."

"Thanks," he mutters smugly and props his elbow on the back of his seat. "Now lie to me again."

Groaning, I roll my eyes. "There's nothing I can tell you."

He hums. "Acceptable answer."

With a pat on my shoulder, he grabs the handle and clamors out of the car. I follow close behind as he leads me inside and up to the floor that As Above has for the next few days. It takes a second tap of the key card to let us off the elevator and another to open my door, but then he's rushing back out of the suite and I'm left standing in the living space between the two bedrooms all alone.

Now that I'm here, I don't know what to do with myself.

My hand goes to the back of my neck as I take in the white walls and tan couch. The TV boasting the hotel's in-room features on a continuous scroll. There's a balcony beyond the French doors on the opposite side of the room, but I honestly don't trust myself to be out there.

A closed door to the room I'm using.

Kitchenette with a stocked minibar including snacks.

I step closer when it beckons me, something seemingly misplaced atop the small fridge.

My brow furrows over the mixed nuts and pretzel bags still in place where they were when I looked this afternoon.

Wasn't there a pack of Skittles?

Shaking myself, I slip my drumsticks from my back pocket and twirl them between my fingers as a distraction when I force myself to step away.

"Probably Rex stealing my shit," I say under my breath as I cross the room. My plan of showering off this day before collapsing in bed sounds better with each step.

But when I push open my bedroom door, my entire body locks up on the spot.

A warmth crackles in my chest only seconds before it's taken over by a red-hot rage that makes my fingers tingle and my spine snap straight.

"*Jordan?*"

"Hey, Vida."

Chapter Fifty-Six

JORDAN

H E'S STARING AT ME.

Mouth working.

Muscles taut.

Face contorting as every emotion slides over his features.

A weariness makes his movements hesitant as he takes one step into the room and then just stands there gawking through the haze of black that's around his eyes and on his hands.

He can wear all the black in the world. Smudge his eyes in the darkest colors. Paint his goddamn nails with ink.

Yet none of that does anything to snub out the lightness of him.

His golden curls lifting from his bandana like a halo. The almost tan tint to his skin. Colorful tattoos peek out from around the deconstructed jeans and holey shirt.

A freckle poking out from behind the mask of makeup high on his cheek, slightly larger than the rest, calling to me like a beacon.

I never noticed that before.

The way he cares for those around him, so deeply that he hurts more than he'll ever admit. His nicknames and antics. The wild jokes.

I'm on my feet before I realize I've moved.

"What are you doing here?" he asks, the words shaking from his lips as I come to a stop right in front of him.

His features harden as if anger is the armor he's settled on.

And it's a bright goddamn thing to see in him.

Where there's anger, there's still hope.

If there's hope … there's a connection that's salvageable.

What the fuck am I doing? I came here to quit.

To his face.

And yet …

Seeing him after all this time is like being revived while being underwater. A jolt to my too-dead heart. Like I've finally found the thing I've been looking for and it's still just out of reach.

"You ghosted me," I settle on instead because my tongue feels too thick to say the rest.

A scoff forces from him, his arms thrown up at his sides.

"I told you to stop using me," he growls out. "But here you are, and for what? *More?*"

I shake my head. "No—" *Yes.* "—I needed to see you."

"Well, douche nugget, you saw me. Now get the fuck out and leave me alone."

He goes to brush passed me when I force out, "no."

His head hangs for a long beat, hands on his hips, breath coming in choppy.

When he looks back up at me, his eyes shine but his words are a solid slap to the face.

"Stop hurting me like this."

Doesn't he know this hurts me, too?

Chapter Fifty-Seven

Mac

A fire rages in his molten navy blues.

Just say it.

Just fucking say it.

"I'm a goddamned fool."

I blink.

And *blink*.

Because with that chance statement from Jordan's lips comes a softening to his features I wasn't expecting, but watch nonetheless as his jaw unclenches and the crease between his brows smooth out.

Like he's melting into the moment while I stand here on edge with pins and needles taking up residence in my veins.

This is where he lets me know it never should have happened.

That it was a phase. A curiosity.

That we'll be better friends, and he hopes that I can get past it.

"You motherfucker," I snarl on the shake of my head, my skin growing hot and tight. "I can't fucking believe you. Coming all this way just to tell me—"

I cut off when gentle, yet rough, fingers graze my elbow and for a second … I let myself hope. It's a dangerous thing to allow when I feel so damn raw, but I can't *not*.

Not when he's goddamn touching me.

My gaze drops, zeroing in on the touch before jerking away from him.

"Just go, Jordan. It's fine. I don't need the spiel I've already heard."

The bathroom is in my sights, it's glow calling to me like a ship lost to the turbulent sea and welcoming me to the shores if only my feet could move across the carpet.

But Jordan's words freeze me on the spot once again.

"What spiel have you already heard?"

My eyes slide closed, and I force a breath that does nothing to calm the tremble taking over my limbs and threatening to strangle my insides.

"Fucking name it and I've heard it before," I murmur through the clench in my jaw as my head falls back and I stare at the ceiling. "*My wife can't find out.*" My stomach rolls and my chest gets tighter. "And *I don't normally do this, but you're* you." My sight drops to Jordan, my voice cracking with each excuse I've ever heard off my lips. "*I swear I'm not gay. Or this will never work with a man.*" My eyes sting and my throat goes raw. "*Men can't love each other so this is what I can give you. This is blasphemy. You're the reason I'm going to hell.*"

I swallow against the way my voice shakes.

"So fucking *excuse* me for not falling for that shit all over again."

His grip is on my jaw before I realize there's tears tracking down my face and I grab him right back, yanking him off me.

"Jordan," I warn when he lands a hand on the back of my neck.

When I smack that hand away, he darts back in, wrapping me up in a bear hug that shouldn't make me feel like I'm fucking crumbling, but it does.

"Get off," I snarl, though my eyes leak.

"No."

I wiggle and jerk, a growl ripping from my gut when he only coils tighter around me, holding me together when all I want to do is break.

"I swear to fuck all, Jordan. *Get the fuck off me.*"

My fingers dig into his hips, anchoring into the muscle there, making him hiss. When that doesn't loosen him, I aim a knee for his thigh that he somehow blocks.

The momentum knocks us off kilter and we meet the mattress with a grunting thud.

Struggling against him, I shove until he's on his back and my knees are digging into his thighs, and still he doesn't release the band around my arms and chest.

"*Fuck you.*"

An animalistic noise rips from my throat and I wedge my arms beneath him, pushing until he's forced to let go or cling to me as I lift. His upper body slams to the mattress when his hold finally breaks and I plant my hands on his pecs to shove him further back.

He bucks his hips up, and just when I think he's going to throw me off, his hands land on my thighs and bring me back down with a grunt.

Right on his stiff cock.

Blood running hot, I blame the groan that escapes me on the anger and drive the heels of my palms into his solid chest.

"I'm not like them," he growls and lifts again, pushing me forward, making me brace next to his head or go flying.

Still, his grip is steady when it migrates to my waist, holding me in place when I jerk from him.

"But you *are!*" I yell back and drop my weight, sitting fully across his groin. "Yet you were just about to be like everyone else. Readying the fucking excuses. Reasons *why not.*"

My heart squeezes in my chest, more tears spilling over my lashes as I drag my hips over his bulge.

"You've dangled yourself in front of me for *years.*" I press down. "Pretending to be my best friend. Pretending to give a fuck. Well you got that last part."

He pushes up, his fingers digging in with bruising force when another groan rips out of me.

"I've been with two people, Mac." He pants. "And then there was *you*."

I growl and give in to the movements, grinding against him unabashedly as something inside me snaps.

"Don't you get it?" I pant out when his fingers find skin and trail up, pulling my shirt along with them and leaving goosebumps in their wake. "That makes you no different."

"Feel me anyway."

The shirt is pulled over my head, leaving it banded around my biceps as his hands fall to my fly and pop the button.

Leaning back with my heart in my throat, I toss the shirt somewhere.

Fingers dragging down my zipper, the back of his hand grazes my raging hard cockhead beneath the denim, and I almost choke on air.

"I don't believe you," I pant, though my hips work over his matching hardness, his digits dipping passed the elastic of my boxers and tugging.

My cock pops free and his fist wraps around me, jerking me fast and hard.

"Fuck, fuck—"

My back meets the mattress half a second before Jordan rips my pants from my legs.

I'm panting when he leans over me, his lips crashing to mine and stealing what little breath I could muster with each stroke of his tongue.

He gasps when he pops free, his sight clashing with mine, his nostrils flaring.

"I'm not like them."

His head dips before I can make sense of that, lips meeting my neck and suckling over my hammering pulse. Lower. He trails kisses across my collarbone and down to a nipple he latches onto.

I'm aching with need when he makes it to the other one. Writhing beneath him when he goes lower.

His tongue dances around my belly button.

Lower.

"Jordan," I rasp, his exploration leading him right to the trail of hair beneath my navel.

"Vida," he murmurs right back with just as much rasp as his nose trails through the patch of hair, his breath tickling my skin.

Lower.

My cock pulses.

"*Jordan.*"

Is he really going to—

Without warning, he wraps his lips around the head of my cock.

"*Fuuuuuuuck.*"

Chapter Fifty-Eight

JORDAN

THE CHOKING CURSE THAT escapes Mac is all the answer I need to know that I'm doing the right thing.

Because it shoots electricity straight to my cock. Tingles down the back of my neck. Elicits an itch in my fingers to touch, to roam over his body and feel the hard muscle beneath hair-dusted skin.

Mac. Mac. Mac.

The heady flavor coats my tongue as I tentatively swirl it around the head of him, slipping over the slit and tasting the precum leaking from him.

It clings to my tastebuds and my mouth fucking waters because it's …

Savory.

Almost salty.

All Mac.

And enough to have my tongue lapping at the tip in search of more.

"*Fuckshit—*"

I look up just in time—passed that fucking trail of tantalizing hair from his navel over his flat chest—to catch his neck arching back, his chest laboring with his breaths.

It has a need like I've never felt before pulsing through my veins and landing right in my groin.

A need to ignore the recognition tickling my mind about thinking with the wrong head.

And as I lick a long stripe down the underside of his cock and his hips punch up, I shut it off completely.

Settling between his legs, I spread him wide enough to accommodate my width and dance my tongue back down the length of his straining erection.

He's hard … for me.

I trail down his sac, nip at the junction where his thigh meets his groin.

Lower.

Over his taint.

There's no nightmare this time to justify my actions. But there is this burning need for connection settling deep inside. To be as close as possible.

To make him feel good.

Nothing else even registers as I splay him wide open and dive between his cheeks, teasing at first. Tasting. Testing the boundaries.

Tattooed fingers wrap up in the sheets, knuckles gone white, unintelligible sounds slipping from his lips.

It drives me to add pressure to his rim and a startled moan slips from my throat when he loosens enough to let me in.

"Ah, fuck," Mac groans out, hands finding my hair and pushing.

For the briefest moment, I wonder if anyone has ever done this to him before. If another has been face first in my drummer's ass.

Did they care about him or was it just to get off?

What if I was the first?

An uninvited growl rips from my throat, and I spear my tongue inside him, licking his hole until a sheen of sweat breaks out on his skin.

"J-Jordan," he rasps out, all breathy roughness, and it shoots straight to my tight core.

He yanks on my hair, and I hiss at the sting in my scalp.

That … shoots straight to my balls.

"I'm gonna goddamn come if you don't stop."

My spine tingles.

I want that.

Except … I want it to happen while I'm inside him.

I want inside him.

Him.

Mac.

"Two?"

His nod is immediate.

Working in both my middle digits slowly, stretching him, I fight for the same space with my tongue.

"Curl your—"

He nearly shoots off the bed when I crook a finger.

"*Godfuckyes,*" he barks out and I find myself chuckling.

"Three?" I ask, swirling my tongue around the digits.

"Lube," he pants and lets loose another sound that I could only describe as *pleasured* when I hit that spot again. "*Lube.*"

Reluctantly, I pull back, withdrawing my fingers from his heat and chuckle again when he whines.

"Hurry," he murmurs, wrapping those inked fingers around his shaft and languidly working them down the length.

I climb off the bed with a painfully stiff cock in search of his pants, shucking off my shirt as I go. As suspected, there's a packet and a condom inside his pocket.

"How old is this?" I ask, dangling my find in his direction, but when I glance at him, he's staring at my clearly bulged zipper.

"Fresh," he nearly whispers back when I drop my pants and boxers, his fingers tightening around his length and stroking.

My steps back to the bed studder.

Why did he need to replace it?

"The other one was expired," he adds as if hearing my thoughts out loud and I resume my climb onto the bed with an uncurling feeling in my chest.

Leaning over him, I tear open the pack and empty the contents on my fingers. My cock. His hole.

There's not much, but it's enough to aid the glide of three stretching fingers.

"*More*," he pants, and it tingles.

How am I supposed to say no to that?

Knee-walking between his spread thighs, I dip low enough to run my tongue over that same leaking slit and hum at the rush of flavor.

But Mac doesn't let me savor it. No. He's grabbing my hips and wrapping his calves behind me to yank me closer.

"More."

Growling, I notch my cock against his entrance and push my way inside his hot hole.

With no barrier between us, I feel every goddamn inch of his body taking me. Matched with his shuddering breath, and wispy moans.

It feels like a goddamn wet dream come to life.

And I've had a few of those since the last time I was inside him.

Except this time feels more urgent.

I ease out a fraction, then back in a little farther than the last stroke and watch raptly as Mac's eyes roll back.

"Pillow."

Blindly, he reaches around above his head until fingers meet fluffed cotton, and he flings it in my direction.

I oof when it smacks me in the face and lands on his leaking cock, but I don't care that it's getting messy already because it's going under his ass as soon as I bottom out.

Another choked curse slips from his parted lips when I do, and that tingling spread from my neck down to my chest.

"Lift."

Planting his heels, Mac lifts up enough for me to shove the pillow beneath his lower back, then drops back onto my cock at the perfect angle that has us both groaning.

"Shit, you were right," I breathe out and cant my hips, reaching that spot that makes him gasp with shallow thrusts.

"Fuckfuckfuck."

His gasps settle into the gaping space that's been inside my chest until they are all I can think about. All I want to keep hearing.

This can't be the last time.

The thought stalls my movements, flipping my insides, and I stare down at the drummer.

His eyes are closed and shrouded in dark smudges, bandana askew on his forehead, fingers lost in their grip of the sheets.

Pink nipples standing out amongst the colored ink, small and lickable.

That golden trail.

His length, hard enough to follow that line up his abdomen.

"Don't stop," he murmurs to the ceiling, the cords in his neck pulled tight.

My stomach flips.

"Look at me."

There's a slight shake to his head, blown pupils trained above us.

Growling, I drive forward, burying to the hilt and leaning over him.

"Look at me," I force out and grind against him, that ass of his sitting right on my groin, his stiffness rubbing against my abs.

Eyes clashing to mine, glassy and blown, I see everything I feel screaming back at me in the almost green color. They soften for the briefest moment before rolling back.

His lips pop open. Hips meeting mine.

"I'm gonna—"

He tightens, his body clamping down, and I grab his chin to guide his sight back to mine.

And with our eyes locked, he comes, warmth bathing my stomach and chest as his lips let loose the harshest of guttural vocals.

It's enough to set me off, his body milking mine with each deep stroke as I find my release inside him.

Love him back.

"Mac," I croak out with shaking limbs, the aftershocks racking me so hard that my arms give in.

My chest crashes to his, the stickiness of his cum spreading between us.

And for a moment … we just breathe.

Long enough that my cock begins to soften and slide from him. Even then, I don't want to move. But then Mac hisses and I lean back enough to see the glassiness of his eyes.

"Jordan … why are you here?"

Chapter Fifty-Nine

Mac

Tʜᴇʀᴇ's ᴛᴏᴏ ᴍᴜᴄʜ sᴛᴀʀɪɴɢ back at me when I ask that question.

Yet … Jordan leans back wordlessly, fully withdraws from me, and flops into a sitting position next to me.

My chest caves in, the emotions and implications settling in deep and too fucking heavy.

Its got me sitting up too fast with a spinning head, ass leaking *him* as I spin to plant my feet on the floor.

"Vida," he rumbles in that beautiful deep voice of his and I ignore the chills that race down my spine at the sound.

Throwing a glance over my shoulder, seeing him lounged about in *my* bed, the sheet draped over his still wet cock, has my chest caving in even more.

He'll never be mine.

The thought chokes me and I face front.

"What?" I whisper to the wall, my heart in the blender and set on demolish.

Get it over with.

Rip the band aid off.

It's all I can think of as I sit there with chilling skin and that same sinking feeling that has plagued me as long as I can remember.

This is how it always went. Get to the fucking part only to skip right on to the line where letdowns come and shit you can't take back is said.

I can already hear it in my head, all the things he'll say to get out of this. To get away from me and my life. All the ways he'll talk about being friends, but everyone knows you can't be friends with someone you've slept with. Someone you love.

Especially when only one of you is in *love.*

Pushing to my feet, I square my shoulders and face him.

Because if he thinks I'm going to make it easy on him to reject me by keeping my back to him, he's wrong.

"Say it," I demand stronger than I feel.

Please don't say it.

Jordan's chin lifts, his own shoulders tight and straight as he looks right at me, almost through me like he can see that little thought tumbling around inside my head.

His throat moves with a swallow and his jaw flexes.

And then he knocks the fucking wind right out of me with two simple as fuck words.

"I quit."

The world tilts.

An all too familiar whooshing sound takes over my ears and the darkness descends around the edges of my vision.

I was right all along.

Chapter Sixty

JORDAN

THE WAY THE COLOR drains from Mac's face has that festering wound inside my chest breaking wide open.

Fucking fuck, this is all messed the hell up.

Why didn't I talk to him first?

"Mac," I croak out and stand, pulling the sheet with me as he jabs his feet into his pants and zips. "Just listen to me."

"No," he says with enough vehemence to have me pausing. "I have listened to you for too long."

Everything in me freezes. "What?"

"And every fucking time, I end up breaking my own heart."

Stalking to the door, he whips it open so hard that it bounces off the backstop and into the smack of his palm.

"Now get the fuck out of my life," he all but growls and my head spins.

The tick in his jaw, the intensity staring back at me, all settles in my gut like a punch.

I knew better.

It was too good, Mac and me. We had it right when we were friends. I guess they were right when they say that sex ruins things.

Shit, I … I have nothing to give him. No way to convince him.

How can I when—

When I don't even know what the hell I'm doing here.

I intended to let him go. To release him to whatever the hell else will make him happy.

I thought he'd be okay with that. I was sure he would.

Seeing him … made it impossible to not feel like I've failed him completely.

Scooping up my clothes and boots, I pause beside him at the door.

He won't look at me.

"I didn't mean for it to go like this, Vida."

"Yeah?" His nostrils flare. "*Me, either.*"

I swallow down the hurt at the venom in his voice and lift my chin. "I may not be able to explain shit, but I hope one day you'll let me try."

Still as stone, Mac says nothing.

I don't blame him.

Shit, I came here with the sole purpose of quitting, to put a stop to this shit, and hoping for things to make more sense after.

Now … nothing does.

Nodding, resigned to the stance we've fallen into, I leave his bedroom.

My eyes slide closed when the slam of his door echoes around in the crater of my chest and I force a breath. I can still smell him on my skin. Feel the ghost of lips against mine. The stickiness of my groin wrapping me up like a vice.

Forcing a swallow, I clear my throat and bend to shove my legs into my pants only to freeze at the sight of argyle socks.

Heart rate shooting to the sky, I tuck my dick away and meet the bodyguard's hard gaze.

Except Peach won't look at me either. Instead, he's trained in on the white square tucked between his offered fingers hanging in the air between us.

My stomach twists at the familiar sight, the knowledge of the typed words inside that little note like a brand to my organs.

"You have to," he mutters almost soundlessly.

I know this.

There's no denying what went on in that room with a rock star that I no longer work for. No contesting the walk of shame he caught me in the middle of.

Yet it doesn't stop the lump from forming when I snatch the paper and unfold it. The edges crinkle and show enough wear to tell me it's been in his pocket long enough.

I know because I have the same thing burning inside my own pocket.

Mac was right. This makes me no different.

Heart in my throat, I take Peach's offered pen with a wince when my tacky fingers touch the plastic, and I sign the nondisclosure agreement just like every other one-night stand.

I don't bother looking when I shove the page back in Peach's direction and stab my feet in my boots.

This is it. It's over.

Pen in my pocket, I jab my shirt over my head before reaching the exit with the heaviest of weights settling down on me.

I'm at the elevators when my vision clouds.

In the lobby when my throat closes up, hurt coiling its way around the broken organ in my chest.

Closing the car door when a sob works its way out of my gut.

Slam the heel of my palm against the steering wheel.

And for the first time in two decades, tears cascade down my cheeks.

Part III

Chapter Sixty-One

JORDAN

One year later

"**W**HAT'S THE DAMAGE IF we close early?"

I barely manage to get the browser I've been staring at minimized when I feel the sting of a slap on my ass and the heat of a body sidle up on my right side.

It's borderline sexual harassment in the workplace but there's no one here. It's just Lemon. And unless I wanna fire my second in command and wingman, I'm shit out of luck.

He touches when he's excited. I'm used to it by now.

It's actually how we met.

In a moment of confusion and desperation about ten months ago, I went to a bar that's LGBTQIA friendly and when a shitty patron kept harassing the tiny bartender that flew over the bar at him, I stepped in. Made a friend. Then offered him a job at my shiny new gym.

I'd just quit Sentry.

Bought a building two blocks away from Aria's boutique.

And saw the tabloids all continuously boasting about the infusion of not just As Above with Banger, but the friendship that blossomed between the drummers of each band.

Mac and Dare.

Rumors of more between the two circulated like wildfire when a picture of them leaked. They were just outside of a tour bus, sharing a smoke, but the looks on their faces were enough to burn into my subconscious.

I'd flown halfway across the planet to see Mac and that picture …. it was taken just after I'd gotten there the first time.

And then I did it all over again, only to ruin everything a second time.

I tried to hang on. To wait for Mac to come home. Ignore the ache that spread and do what I'd promised.

Avoid the voice in my head that screamed I'd never be good enough.

But I got nothing in return.

I was ghosted. Ignored.

Left.

And he never said a word back.

I'd had enough of watching my role be filled by someone else.

My heart was too broken—*still is.*

So, I found my own place. Cut ties with the guys from Sentry. Poured myself into this gym.

I was celebrating alone. Sad and desperate when that guy antagonized Lemon enough to go at him.

We made out that night—proved my face is at least bisexual, even if my dick is hung up elsewhere—and have been good friends ever since.

He swears we're too similar, but I don't see it.

There was never anything between us, but Lemon is hellbent on getting *something* to happen for me.

Forever the wingman.

One night a few months ago, I told him who I was. That I'd been harboring feelings or something for Mac when I walked away. My tail tucked. My mind muddled and my heart in pieces.

Hindsight is a bitch.

"We should stay open," I argue and click around on the screen like I'm busy.

"*Come on,*" Lemon whines and wraps his bony arms around my bent elbow. "They're having that block party tonight."

I spare enough of a glance that I catch his bouncing brows and roll my eyes.

"No."

"Shut up." He releases one hand to steal the mouse and click right on the browser I was hiding from him. "Like you don't wanna know." He points a painted nail at the screen filled with the banner announcing As Above's return stateside, signifying the end of their European tour.

The same one I've been staring at all day.

Mac's home.

My heart flutters around an ache and I shake my head. "Nope." I close the browser and power down the computer.

"Yes."

I sigh.

Turn to him with intensions of shutting him down and immediately regret it.

Because he's throwing me those big brown puppy eyes. Has his hands clasped together in a plea. Pokes out his bottom lip in a pout and I roll my eyes.

I palm his face and push him out of my way. "You can go."

"You know I'll just call you every two seconds."

"I'll turn off my phone," I mutter as I walk the mats, turning off lights as I go.

I may not wanna go to the party As Above is throwing literally two blocks away, but Lemon has a point. This place is dead today. No one is gonna fight the masses to come to the gym tonight.

"Then I'll show up at your door and pound until you answer."

I spin into him and have to look all the way down my chest with how close he is. "You think I couldn't stop you from breaking down my door?"

He shivers. "Sure you could—"

"*Don't.*"

"*—daddy.*"

I growl and walk away to hide my snicker.

"You're ridiculous."

"*Come on,*" he whines, following me and slapping lights I miss. "Introduce me to your beefy friends then. The old security buddies." He puffs up his tiny chest as he walks, his arms lifted up like he's got muscles. "Be my wingman for once."

"I don't think—"

I pause.

Were any of the other guys bent like me?

I scrub a hand over the five o'clock shadow I've let grow in and shake my head.

"No way."

"There can't have been just you, Jay. Get real."

There wasn't.

But that's not up to me to tell people.

My stomach rolls over at the reminder.

Peach is the only one that knew about any of it.

"Uh-oh. Where'd we go?" I blink and rear back when Lemon waves a hand in my face. We've made it back to the front of the house where the storefront windows let the sunlight in, casting little rainbows across the floor.

I sigh.

"Will you shut up if—"

He squeals and hops, clapping.

"You didn't even hear my *if.*"

"You said yes! Doesn't matter." He's pulling on my arm before he even gets the words out. "Let's go get your man back."

"Nooooo, no."

I grab his bony shoulders and pull him to a stop.

"I will only go *if* you steer clear of the band. *And* security," I add the last part when his eyes glitter with mischief. "Okay? I see any of them and I'm leaving."

"You're no fun."

"I'm serious, Lemon."

It's been almost a year since I saw my former coworkers. Longer since I saw the band.

And it's been too long to go back now.

My heart won't be able to take it.

Chapter Sixty-Two

Mac

T HE SECOND WE STEPPED off the plane, I started looking for him.

When we piled out of the bus. Joined the party thrown in our honor.

I haven't stopped looking for him in every crowd, in every stranger that has passed me by, for over a fucking year.

Years.

In my head, I've ran through every conversation I want to have with him should I ever see him again. And in the darkness of a desperate night, I hoped that he'd apologize. That it was genuine enough for me to believe it and I'd find it in me to forgive him for shutting me out. For not fighting for what he seemed so desperate to want that night. *He got it, what he wanted.* In those weak moments, those dark nights, we'd fall into bed. Finally … finally hold each other. Kiss like it means more than just appeasing a curiosity.

I'd show him what it was like to be with the right person, and he'd show me what it was like to be loved by Jordan Kauffman.

But those instances got fewer and farther between with each day that went by.

Fantasies never meant to see the light of day once his ass hightailed it out of my hotel room for the last time.

He was just fucking *gone.*

Quit.

Left.

Supposedly, no one could find him, not even the security crew. Which I don't believe for a minute. *They know shit.*

They just didn't have it in them to tell me his choice was final, despite his parting words to me.

He chose to leave me.

"*Try* to fucking smile," Dare murmurs into my ear. His hand tightens on my ribs and my skin crawls.

My smile is mostly a sneer aimed in his direction. "We aren't friends, dipshit."

Cameras flash in my face, capturing the two of us together, leaving spots behind. I pull away from him before they even fade.

Yells are directed toward me, but I don't stop weaving through the crowd until the storefront comes into view and I stop dead.

It's like I can feel the rain all over again.

Cold and pelting me in the face. Soaking into my clothes and seeping all the way to my bones until the fate of us was etched into them like cave markings, telling the story of where a friendship ended, for all of time.

Except no one knows the story but me.

That of those friends … one lost more than the other.

That a piece of me shriveled up and died beneath the storm clouds. Another piece gone the night he begged me for three days. And the last gone the night he showed up, pumped me full of so much hope for him, for *us*, only to quit.

To not pick me.

That had done me in; to have him quit after everything.

I don't blame myself. I don't. But if I could go back to that night … before it all went to shit … I'd at least tell him how much his friendship means—*meant*—to me.

That I'd take him as that over losing him completely any fucking day. How I always have.

And that just … makes the churning of my gut even worse.

Because I *have* to let him fucking go.

Squaring my shoulders, I force a breath into frozen lungs and light a joint.

Take a step.

Fake a smile.

And hope like hell I can forget.

Chapter Sixty-Three

JORDAN

MY FRIEND IS TINY. Easily picked up and carried away despite his raging flair and gargantuan attitude.

So, I wait just outside, my back against the brick and my phone in my hand as a distraction.

Staring at As Above's socials yet again like a lost puppy hoping for their arrival.

And if the pic of Mac and Dare is any indication … they arrived two hours ago.

"Ready?"

"To leave? Yes." I push off from the wall and step back in the direction of the gym. Lemon snags my arm in protest and yanks me back.

Then steals my phone and types in my passcode with quick thumbs. His brow swings on me and I sag. "I have a problem, okay?"

He snickers and swipes away the app, locking the phone, and stuffs it into my jeans pocket. "Let's go shopping."

"You *just* did the thing back there." I point at the building he's pulling me away from and cringe. "That can't be normal."

"Oh, c'mon." He throws out his free hand. "All we did was make out. I got his number."

I wing a brow back at him as he wraps both hands around my bent elbow, leading me into the thick of the crowd. "Bullshit."

"What? Maybe baby wants someone to come home with him, huh?"

"Stop calling yourself that."

"Reverse psychology, Jay."

I shake my head and laugh. "That is not how that works. Not even a little bit."

"Besides," he goes on, ignoring me. "This is almost like Pride. There's dick everywhere."

I snort. "Wouldn't know. Never been."

Lemon halts. Turns his head to me in slow motion. "Say that to my face."

I shake my head.

His gasp is dramatic enough to pull the attention of others around us. "You mean to say that you were following around *the* gay drum—"

I slap a hand over his mouth.

"Shut up or I'm gonna carry your ass back to the gym."

His brows bounce.

I roll my eyes and wrap my arm wound his shoulders, keeping my palm against his mouth to keep it shut.

"Shop with your eyes, Lemon, and stop talking."

He looks at me pointedly.

I level him with one right back until he's cackling behind my hand.

"Okay," he finally mumbles and taps the back of his hand to my abs. "Okay."

I release him and wipe the left-over moisture on my palm down his arm. He squeals and darts away, running right into someone that—

Face tattoos. Piercings. Bent nose.

Oh fuck.

Highlighter orange hair.

Fuckfuckfuck.

"Hey handsome," I hear Lemon coo, and I spin away. Rip my hat off my head.

Shiiiiiiiit.

I'm stuffing my hat into my pocket when I look down at the band's logo on my chest and curse again.

I wore it to blend in, even paired it with the holey jeans Lemon made me buy, but now …

It just feels like a billboard.

A giant neon sign.

With fucking glitter.

Chapter Sixty-Four

Mac

A PULL LIKE NOTHING I've ever felt before has my sight sliding away from the conversation I'm having with Makkin to the motion on the other side of the window.

My stomach drops completely through my asshole at the scene on the other side, unaware of their audience as hands are wrapped around arms and a smile is thrown up at the taller of the two guys.

All I see is his back, but I know.

It's him.

Right there.

Tilting his head away from the store.

The two exchange words and it's clear that the short guy hanging off Jordan is perturbed about leaving the area but happy to listen to whatever justification Jordan's giving him.

It's like watching a version of what could have been my life on a goddamn TV screen as they turn, and shorty tucks his hand in the crook of Jordan's arm.

He glances this way, and I'd swear I could see a widening of his eyes through the glass, though I know you can't see inside from the out. He has no clue I'm here.

And it should stay that way.

But my feet are moving toward the exit before my brain can catch up. The heart in my throat leading the way.

I'm in the throng of bodies just as fast, as if I'm moving on autopilot. Following the pull of the metaphorical string I tried so desperately to cut.

He's right fucking there.

And my chest is *aching*.

Calling after its other half, desperate to be whole once again.

Who was I kidding?

It'll only ever be him.

"Jordan!"

A hand lands on my shoulder and spins me away, engulfing me in the group of fans requesting autographs and pictures.

When I come up for air, he's gone.

Taking my heart along with him.

Chapter Sixty-Five

Jordan

Sixteen … Seventeen …

The gym might be closed for the night, but that doesn't mean I'm not in it.

Eighteen … Nineteen …

Clinking of weight resting on metal with each rep keeps me counting them over the sound of the music pumping through the speakers.

It's become like a sort of meditation that helps bring me down.

Twenty.

And after damn near running into Peach earlier, I hightailed it right back here for just that kind of peace. Lemon claims I'm hiding, but I disagree.

Avoiding, maybe.

Letting the bar drop back on the shoulder press with a thud, I lean forward and let the song wash over me as Dave Grohl rasps about having a confession.

Is he giving his best to someone else?

"Here."

I don't get a chance to react before a towel is thrown in my face.

"Thanks," I mutter and wipe the sweat from my brow.

But when I look up, it's not the tiny wingman on the other side of the toss like I expected.

Everything in me locks up. Breath leaving audibly.

When I swallow, it clicks.

"A gym?" Mac asks, brow raised. "How very Tyro of you."

It takes what feels like minutes of staring at the drummer for my body to thaw and my muscles to move.

I'm up off the seat, closing the distance in a heartbeat.

Mac. Mac. Mac.

He holds up a hand, but I don't stop until that palm is touching my damp chest.

He's here.

"Who's the little guy?"

The corner of my lip tips up. "Little guy?"

"Yeah." His lips thin. "The tiny man."

I snort. "Don't let him hear you say that."

He schools his features, but even after all this time, he can't hide the sharpness in his eyes.

I lick my lips. "He's a friend," I answer honestly because the last thing I want is for him being here to go sideways. I like that he's here, even if it's just a fleeting thing.

We could be friends.

Right?

Something twists in my gut.

"Look, as much as I love seeing you … why are you here?" I ask, unable to hide the thickness from my words. It comes out almost standoffish, even though that's the last thing I'm going for, but I don't have it in me to fight all over again. I'd rather have it out on the table at the beginning instead of finding out later, like last time I saw him.

Mac nods, his features softening briefly before sliding behind a guarded mask. The same one I've seen him wear in every goddamn photo for years. Toted around in front of those he didn't like.

The one he uses on people he doesn't know.

I know it's to protect himself.

But that he feels he has to use that shit with me hurts more than I'd like to acknowledge.

"I … don't know," he admits and after a beat, some of that armor slips. "Y'know, I had this whole conversation planned out if I ever saw you again and now …"

If I ever saw you again.

If. Not when.

That hits like a train to my torso.

He's shaking his head, his thumbs fiddling a beat along his thighs. It matches the new one filtering through the speakers.

Trapt.

I bite my lip and step closer.

"Vida." His breath hitches. "I'm glad you found me."

He blinks rapidly and meets my gaze. "I'm sorry I tol—"

"Don't." I shake my head and brush the back of my hand over his cheek. His lashes fall closed over his freckle-specked skin and he shudders. "I don't need an apology."

"What do you need?" he whispers to my chest.

You. I need you.

"You're here and that's enough," I say instead, though I mean it just as much.

It's then that he dives forward, crashing into my chest and wrapping his arms around me so hard that it's difficult to breathe.

I welcome it as my arms find their home snaking around his rib cage and his shoulders, my palm to the back of his neck.

His head is on my shoulder and his grip is tight enough to squeeze my swelling heart. It might be bruised and neglected, the muscle beating in my chest, but right now … it feels whole as it beats alongside his.

"Tell me what *you* need, Mac," I mutter in his hair.

He trembles against me, and I hold him tighter.

"This," he answers.

I hum, though it's thick.

And even though there are a million and one questions rolling through my mind at his appearance, I pull back just enough to look into his eyes and ask, "Did you eat?"

Chapter Sixty-Six

MAC

"W**HAT THE FUCK IS** this?"

Hands up and eyes wide, I stare at the sudden jabs in my thighs that belong to the curling creature now taking up my lap.

"Oh, shit. Sorry," Jordan murmurs distractedly.

He's behind me, at the stove I could see if I turned around but refuse to look at, while the black and white cat circles over my legs.

The thing sniffs my knee, then flops unceremoniously across me and *purrs.*

I think I just fell in love.

Burying my fingers in the soft fur, the corner of my lips lift when the cat looks at me with brilliant green eyes and slow blinks.

Definitely in love.

Shit, this was a mistake.

I swallow hard and get my hands under the creature with every intention of displacing the animal, but then those eyes meet mine and I slump.

"I don't know what I'm doing here, cat," I whisper thickly. "I was supposed to be mad at him. One look at him, and now I'm here. What do I do?"

Nothing but the sound of Jordan clanging around in the kitchen responds.

"Right. I'm talking to a fucking cat." I blow out a breath. "I've lost it for sure."

"I talk to her all the time," Jordan admits, and I jump at the sound of his voice near my ear. "She can be a good conversationalist when she wants to be."

Biting my lip, I nod and scratch behind her ear. She lets loose an appreciative noise and lays her head down on a paw.

Shit, that's cute.

I clear my throat and risk a glance next to me where Jordan leans over the back of the couch and reaches to pat the cat's head lightly.

My heart nearly stops at the adoration softening his face. The closeness of his person. How, if he'd redirect by like an inch, he'd be touching my leg.

Goddammit, this was a terrible fucking idea.

"I should go."

"Food's almost done. At least eat first," Jordan says almost like he's *happy*, then backs up, wafting his clean apple scent as he moves.

I inhale deep, letting the smell absorb into my blood like oxygen.

God, I've fucking missed him.

"Her name's Cookie, by the way." I look down at the ball of fur and huff out a short-lived chuckle. "I think she's two."

"Was Oreo already taken?"

Jordan snorts. "Too obvious. Everyone names tuxedo cats Oreo."

"Cuz you know so many people with cats."

Reality slaps me like a cold-water bath.

He might know lots of people with animals now.

But he chuckles as he works and says "There were a few when I was younger, but you're right. I don't know anyone else with a cat."

My hands freeze, fingers lost in the fur of his companion.

It's slow, but when I turn to glance over my shoulder, he's completely unfazed by the admission of something from his childhood and my heart gives a patter inside my chest.

He's never volunteered that before.

"You had a cat?"

"No." His head shakes, dislodging a few strands of his hair. It's a little longer now and I let myself imagine for the briefest of moments what it would feel like in my hands. Would it be as soft as the fur already curling around my fingers? "They were alley cats. Ones that the whole neighborhood took care of, or the older ladies, depending on where I was."

That last bit has me furrowing my brow.

I want to ask what he means—where was he?—but I don't.

He shared something on his own and I don't want to minimize that.

"So, Cookie, then." I shift back to the sleeping feline and blink against the sudden burn in the backs of my eyes.

"Here."

A bowl with a spoon already in it is shoved beneath my chin, the scent of cheesy-rich noodles filling my nose and making my eyes water even more.

"Thanks," I mutter and accept the dish of my favorite meal with both hands.

"It's nothing fancy," he mumbles as he slumps into the cushion beside me. "Just a box."

I clear my throat. "You know I don't care."

My jaw clenches, stomach in knots when I risk a glance at the man that knows me better than anyone. Even after all this time, he's got me.

Only … he's holding a fork over the bowl beneath his chin, the tines lined with green leaves.

Those knots in my stomach tighten.

"I know, Vida," he murmurs around his fork, chewing.

Do I watch his Adam's apple bob with his swallow? *Yes.*

Should I? *Clearly not.*

It's sexy and thoughtful and—

Tearing my sight away from him, I stare into the bowl and have to will myself not to fucking cry over mac and cheese. That Jordan cooked. Just for me. While he eats rabbit food.

It might be a simple box of noodles and flavored packet. Something as easy as boiling some water and making sure the pasta part doesn't turn to mush. Yet, I can't help but feel like my heart is ready to burst out of my chest and present itself to him right here on the couch.

"This is the first homecooked meal I've had in over a year," I mutter, and it comes out thick as shit.

I think he nods, but I'm too afraid to look.

Blinking hard, I finish the whole bowl.

It's the best fucking mac and cheese I've ever had.

And when I scrape the last bit of cheese sauce from the sides of the ceramic, Jordan offers to get me more.

Sniffing, I let him take the bowl and set both on the coffee table next to his hat when I shake my head.

He scoots close enough that his knee grazes mine.

"All it took was a hotdog."

When I swing my furrowed brow on him, he nods to the curled-up creature in my lap.

"She was hanging around outside and I was worried she'd get hit by a damn car. So, I coaxed her with a hotdog."

If I wasn't worried I'd scare the shit out of the cat, I'd let the laugh that bubbles up out.

"Sometimes it's that simple," I murmur, and it cracks.

"She doesn't normally like other people," he half blurts out and I'm not sure why, but that makes me feel good. Like I've been chosen or some shit. "She only tolerates me because I feed her."

His chuckle is all air.

And it sends a spike of warmth down my spine.

"I'm only tolerating you because you fed me, too."

The responding laugh is deep and reaches somewhere in the depth of my soul and pets it like I'm petting his cat.

"Are you … Do you want to watch a movie?"

Chapter Sixty-Seven

Mac

The new Mark Wahlberg movie is queued up before I can ratio-nalize *not* watching one with him and I don't have it in me to walk out now that it's started.

I also have no clue how the fuck I managed to get here to begin with, but there's something in me that's latching onto the feeling swirling in my gut the longer I sit here. It's confusing, yet warming. Terrifying, but not. Like I'm somehow making the right decision about something I didn't even know needed deciding.

Is it intuition or am I just crazy?

And suddenly, I feel like I'm staring into a cracked bathroom mirror with a single phrase rolling through my head.

Take the chance. It's yours.

"I don't have any snacks. Sorry."

"S'okay," I manage and force myself to watch the action on the screen. It's a good movie, one I didn't have the heart to tell him I already watched, but it isn't keeping my attention like the films with the hot actor normally do.

I blame the cat. Yep. It's definitely Cookie's fault for being so damn *soft*.

My thrumming fingers gently wander over her back and hind legs, the places I know are semi-safe zones on a cat, and I try really hard to keep my gaze on her black and white spots instead of looking at her dad.

He's a fucking cat dad now!

A new ache blossoms inside my chest at all the things that I've missed, all the newness of everything in Jordan's life, things I would have never known if I didn't walk through that door, and yet … here he is. Right fucking next to me. Making it seem like things are the same as they have always been. As if there were never a thousand miles separating us. That this is just another movie night between rock star and bodyguard turned best friends.

I thought he hated it.

Only did the things and agreed with me to keep me appeased. To keep my ass out of trouble.

Called me his best friend because I said so.

Slept with me to ease an itch.

But now he doesn't work for Sentry, and he's made me mac and cheese and I'm petting his cat from inside *his* apartment in the damn gym that he bought and runs on his own.

"Why are you doing this?" I blurt out to the side of Jordan's face, a little too loudly, and startle the cat.

She takes off, leaving only minimal skid marks in her wake and a whole lot of fucking white hair all over my black shirt. I don't even care because I'm looking at that strong jawline and waiting.

Waiting to see those navy blues light up. Or his brow quirk.

Or that goddamned not-smile.

Jordan is slow to turn to me, to meet my gaze, with only a mild hint of a grin and some hesitation.

He's calm otherwise, to my racing breath and near panic. Stoic.

Gorgeous.

So goddamn gorgeous.

Meanwhile, I'm certain that he can *see* my heartbeat with how hard it thunders inside my chest. Maybe even hear my stomach wring up. Feel the vibration of my limbs through the couch.

"Why don't we start with why you came."

"I … needed to—" I swallow hard because I'm not sure I should admit to anything, but *fuck*, I want to. I want to tell him that I've looked for him in every person I've passed since I met him. To tell him that no one has ever gotten me like he does. That no matter how hard I fucking try, I've never been able to get him out of my head, even after all this time. Because I know things. I feel things deep in my soul that tell me I will never belong to anyone but him and I needed to know if there was ever a chance. A hope. A spark that ever existed.

That I need closure.

To end this chapter of my life once and for all.

And that I'm sorry. For the way I acted over the years, but especially for what happened when I saw him last.

He watches me, not harshly just curiously, as I get my mouth to move except no sound comes out.

I'm gearing to tell him that last bit. The one about closure, and yet I'm frozen.

Because it feels so fucking *wrong*.

Closing this thing I can still feel sparking between us … it feels impossible.

And being here with him … even as old friends falling easily back into our old habits like movie watching and sharing space … that is what feels fucking *right*.

"This couch is not comfy," I blurt instead and the bark of laughter from Jordan nearly startles me, but then settles into another one of those wide-open craters in my chest.

"I knew you'd say that." He's still laughing when he gets up and heads back to the kitchen with our dishes.

I follow because I feel like I should help and end up in the way when he sets a kettle on the stove to heat. Mugs are pulled from a bare cabinet, and I frown when the simple burnt orange-patterned ceramic is placed on the counter. He adds tea bags, sugar to mine, and props a hip on the counter to wait out the kettle. And me, I guess.

Why are there only four plain ass mugs in there?

"I've been going to counselling a lot more," I admit on an almost ramble and cross my arms over my chest. "And she helped me realize that the last time I saw you …" I bite my lip when the wave of pain takes over my chest. "Not only did you hurt me, but I hurt you, too."

He nods, an encouraging thing, so I continue.

"It's stupid to hold onto the things that I did. Things others said or did, against you. It wasn't fair." I take a deep breath and stare at his chest instead of his face. "But neither were you."

There's a slight jerk to him. Like he tried to hold back the reaction to the sting and failed.

"I felt for a long time that our friendship was conditional. Part of your job to keep me entertained. That it was only ever surface level for you and nothing more. Which terrified me, to be honest. But I …" I have to swallow back the emotion that clogs my throat.

"Mac," Jordan croaks and it's so thick that it pulls at my heart strings.

"I meant what I said that day in the treehouse."

"Which part?" he nearly whispers.

My inhale is shaky. My exhale even more so.

"That I love…d you," I whisper back to his chest, my eyes burning, my ribs aching. "And it's okay that it'll only ever be that."

His shirt rises. Falls with his deep exhale and it's almost as shaky as mine.

"You done now?" His voice is all grated husk.

The kettle lets out a rumble from its boil between us, but it's not hissing just yet.

I nod.

He stays silent for a long beat, and in the past I would push him or get upset that he's so damn quiet. But something about this whole night is just … different. So, I stay staring at his pecs and clear my throat. He'll say something or he won't and then I'll finally know for sure.

Closure and all that bullshit.

"You're not the only one—labels are fucking bullshit and people are complicated. More complex than a simple identifier and I refuse to follow the textbook because none of them make any fucking sense." My brow creases at his frustration and my glance raises from his chest to his chin, though I don't think his emotion is aimed at me. "How you love me—*loved me*—" he clears his throat "—doesn't make sense because I hid so much and I'm, *fuck,* I thought I was simple, but I'm not. I'm complicated, just like the rest of them. Us. *You.*"

I shake my head. "You're not making any sense. Of course you're complicated. You're human."

He growls and snatches the kettle, though it still hasn't whistled.

"I know," he says shakily. "I never thought—" He clears his throat and pours. "I never thought I'd get the chance to actually say this shit out loud to you."

That hurts.

Accepting the offered mug, I follow him back to the couch with trembling legs and tight knuckles.

We settled into the opposite sides, and I note this side isn't nearly as lumpy. Which is just fucking weird because the whole thing looks broken in and now I'm questioning my sanity.

I make the mistake of looking at Jordan, preparing to make a comment on the matter, only to freeze at the sight of his clenched jaw and far off stare into his mug.

No, wait … he's staring past it like it's not even there.

I follow his gaze and—

His hat?

"I'm done running."

The mug hits the coffee table harsh enough that some of his undrunk tea sloshes over the side, but he pays it no mind. Just wipes it away on his shorts and turns to me full on. When that's not good enough, he pulls his leg up, bending it along the cushion between us and stares straight into my fucking soul.

"I'm not straight."

Everything in me freezes.

"I kissed Lemon when I met him and though I didn't hate it, I didn't like it either."

I must look as struck as I feel because Jordan's gaze softens on me, and he reaches for my knee. Pulls back. Settles his warm palm against the denim anyway.

"Mac, ask me why."

I swallow. *I don't know that I can.*

Do I want to know what he felt when he kissed someone that wasn't me? I mean … I did tell him to fuck someone else, but then we fucked and—this whole thing is fucked.

My throat works and I finally croak out a rough "Why?"

The side of his lips tip up in the saddest smile I've ever seen, and it *hurts*.

"Because I kept wishing it was you."

All of the breath leaves me on a choked sound I try to reign in, but can't.

"I kept just feeling for you. Waiting for you. Wanting you. Wishing … it was you."

There's no holding back the sob that creeps up this time, deep and soul-crushing.

"Our friendship was never fake, Mac. It was the foundation for everything I feel for you now."

My eyes are screaming, and my heart is aching, and can this be true?

When the shake to my hands is too much, Jordan takes the mug from me and replaces it with his own. It's warm and scratchy against mine, yet it feels like so much more than just a comforting gesture between friends with the tingles it brings. It feels like home in a grip.

What if?

I squeeze his fingers, and it feels *good* to hold them. Maybe a little too roughly, but he's squeezing mine right back.

"So … I—" He clears his throat and stares at the way we fit together. "I'm not straight. That's as close to a label as I got."

I nod. Wipe my face with the back of my other hand.

A beat of silence falls over us and though it's a little loaded, it's not awkward.

But then Jordan adjusts our grip and my breath hitches when he interlocks our fingers together instead of letting go.

He turns so that he's sitting facing forward, but he's stiff as he scoots closer, resting our joined hands on his thigh. Clearly, I've died and gone to heaven.

That is what this has to be. I'm dreaming or heading to the afterlife, and this is the result.

I don't ever want to wake up.

DNR me, bish.

"The closest thing I could relate to was demisexual."

I choke on air.

The realization is like a sucker punch straight to my gut with how many things suddenly file under different categories in my mind and turn into making *sense.*

Friendship. The platonic stuff.

All the times he let me be … *me* … and smiled at me anyway.

All the touching, but not sexually. All the time he spent at my side, even when he didn't have to. All the moments we shared … The connections …

His grip on my hand tightens when I open my mouth, and I quickly snap it shut.

"You weren't the only one that went to a shrink."

I nod, staring at the side of his head with wide eyes.

"Now just … hold my hand and watch this movie with me, yeah?"

Blowing out a breath, I nod again. "Yeah. Okay. Yeah."

"Okay."

It doesn't take long, once the movie is restarted, for Jordan to relax back. His shoulder brushes mine, as does his thigh where our hands still rest, and though it's a sweaty grip, I never want to let go.

He's holding my fucking hand!

There's a giddiness that's worming through my system and filling my energy tank with such high levels that I'm nearly shaking with it.

The foundation for everything I feel for you now.

Now.

What if?

Whatifwhatifwhatif?

"Here."

Wooden sticks are planted in my field of vision and my breath hitches all over again.

"Drumsticks?" I ask and it cracks. "You just have these laying around your apartment?"

The corner of his lips tip up.

"Yeah. I do."

Chapter Sixty-Eight

JORDAN

"PROMISE ME SOMETHING," I mutter, my voice sleep thick and my body drained. But Mac's head is back on my shoulder and I'm not dreaming of terrible things, and I admitted to him out loud that I'm not entirely what he thought I was, yet he's still here. Nearly asleep and leaning on me. His hand still clinging to the sticks I gave him, the other still clasped in mine though I know it has to be aching from the angle like mine is.

I don't plan on letting go though.

Not yet.

"Wha?" Mac rumbles back, his lips moving against my shoulder.

I smirk.

"Best friends first. No matter what."

He's silent long enough for me to worry he fell asleep between his response and my answer, but then his head is moving against me, his stubble creating the perfect burn on my skin.

"Me and you, Tyro." He nuzzles me just like Cookie does and something inside me settles. Eases. Relaxes into a reality I never thought I could live, however brief it's going to be.

But for tonight … I'm content to sink farther into the couch and let my drummer sleep on my shoulder and bring life into my apartment with his soft snores.

Chapter Sixty-Nine

MAC

A GYM IS THE last place I ever expected to find myself, but I have a renewed sense of hope buzzing beneath my skin as I walk the third floor.

Jordan's apartment is small, and the light was just right to watch him sleep, but then I felt like a creeper staring at him. Felt like a lovesick fool for sticking to his side all night long.

Not even a sleep adventure moved me.

Hence the walk.

Which has led me to a large room, one whole side letting in the early morning light, another covered in mirrors with a bar anchored only a few feet in front of it.

The floor is hardwood, and the ceiling is painted black to hide the duct work, but it's open and breathing and holds a shit ton of potential.

Following the buzzing energy's lead, I wander around the rest of the place, passing the clinks of metal and grunts, until there's pails and buckets and Jordan's pots all overturned along the hardwood, set up just like an extended version of my drum set.

Sticks in hand, I paradiddle and smash, the attack ringing through the open space with the perfect amount of acoustics to have me grinning.

I'm deep in making a rhythm from the everyday things when a snick registers in my mind.

He held my hand and he's not straight.

I don't know what it means. Or where this leads. But just knowing that has lifted a weight off my shoulders. Made it easier to breathe.

He thinks he's demi. Maybe.

I can work with that.

I push back all those voices in the back of my mind that threaten to remind me of every other asshole that claimed they were something they weren't, only to back out when things got real*ish*.

Jordan's different.

He has to be.

Otherwise … after all this time apart … why did he have drumsticks and macaroni? He didn't know if I'd ever be here, and yet … he was prepared for me to be. Like he *wanted* me to be.

Was waiting for me to be.

Lips turned up, I rapid fire on the bucket's bottom with both sticks, tapping the edge every offbeat and I don't stop until a shadow creeps its way closer.

Even then, I look up at the little guy Jordan called a friend but keep beating away on the pail with one hand.

"Drum lessons would make great cardio."

I blink, then snort and choke the sound by slapping the sticks sideways against the plastic.

"You the PR guy around here?"

"Me? No. I'm absolutely just pretending not to judge you."

I settle back on my ass and twirl the sticks, taking the guy in.

"Mighty blunt of you."

He snorts and flares his hands out in front of him. "*Honesty*. You should try it sometime."

Ouch.

"I see." I nod and get my feet under me, pushing to my full height.

I have to look down at him and he's staring all the way up with only a slight look of fear in his eyes betraying the boldness of his words.

"What's your name again?"

"Ooh, ouch. I know damn well Jordan told you."

He did, but Lemon doesn't need to know that.

"He kissed me, you know," he adds, a glint of something in his brown eyes.

Pursing my lips, I nod. "And?"

Lemon makes some sort of snorting chuckle and gives me a slow once over. Then another. It's almost intrusive the way he appraises me, like he's measuring me up and maybe the little spitfire *could* take me out. Bet he'd start with my knees.

"And he spent a lot of time trying his best not to think about you, yet here you are."

That one hurts, too.

I swallow and refuse to let him see me sweat. "Here I am."

And I don't plan on going away.

Arms crossing and features pinching, Lemon seems to make up his mind about me.

"What are your intentions with my guy?"

A muscle in my brow twitches at the claim I have no right to contest, yet feel like I must. He catches it and grins like the Cheshire cat that's caught his mouse.

Not today, bud.

Not after *my* guy admitted that he's not straight.

Finally opened up and let me the fuck in.

I grin.

"My intention?" My gaze flicks over his shoulder, Jordan's furrowed brow taking in the sight of the two of us from across the room. "Is *everything.*"

Slowly, I bring my sight back to the overprotective friend, my grin even wider.

Lemon throws his hands up and rolls his eyes but laughs.

"*Fine. Don'tyoudarehurtmyfriendagain.*" The last part is rushed and nearly growled beneath his breath as Jordan approaches, only replaced with a forced smile when he gets within hearing distance.

"Lemon, *manners*," Jordan all but snips, though the guy is all smiles and fluttering lashes that have me chuckling by the time Jordan stops between us.

"I have all the manners!"

"Mac, this is Lemon," Jordan adds, ignoring his friend's innocent act.

"We met." I chuckle. "I see why you like him."

Jordan's brow quirks, but so do his lips, and now all I can think about is kissing them.

Would he let me?

But even as my mind wanders over the idea, Lemon steps in close to Jordan, sneaking a thin arm around his waist.

Jordan snorts. Tugs him in for a side hug.

Then steps away from Lemon and closer to me.

"I have a thing this morning, but …" There's a slight pink flush on his cheeks and suddenly I don't give a shit that Lemon just tried to stake a claim because Jordan's looking at me with something that looks an awful lot like *hope* in his navy blues.

Fucking fuck, I missed him so goddamn much it hurts.

"What are you doing later?"

Fluttering erupts in my gut, and I do my best to tamper the resulting grin.

It doesn't work and I'm certain I look every bit the madman I feel.

"You asking me out, Tyro?"

That pink darkens the slightest bit, but then his lips tip up in an almost smile and he fucking *nods*.

I'm dying right here on the hardwood.

Send everyone my love, because I'm following the reaper into this afterlife.

"Yeah, Vida," he breathes out and steps closer, his knuckles brushing my abs and I nearly swallow my fucking tongue. "Yeah, I am."

Gawd damn.

Another burst of fluttering steals all the oxygen in my lungs.

The only answer is one word and it cracks; "Okay."

"Okay." He nods again, searches my gaze for a beat with hands wringing in front of him.

Then he leans in, steals what's left of my breath and presses his soft lips to the stubble on my cheek. It's quick. Swift. Over too soon and leaving me staring after his retreating form.

Yet ... it's everything.

Chapter Seventy

JORDAN

I TOLD MY THERAPIST.

Not that she didn't already know about Mac, but saying the words out loud only made them feel more real. Solidified them. Gave them a crackling of sunshine in the perpetual darkness.

She warned me to go slow. To take my time and make sure this is what I want. But also to be safe and enjoy myself for once.

Do the one thing I've wanted to for two and a half goddamn years.

It's a date.

Holy mother of fucking all things … I have a date with Mac Thompson.

I'm nervous.

Jittery.

Excited.

I haven't felt this high strung since … well … the last time I saw him. When I sat in his hotel room and hoped with all my being that he'd hear all the words I wasn't saying.

He didn't then.

But I think he will now.

Blowing out a breath, I reach for the shirt I hung on dresser's knob and scrunch up my nose.

Wrong choice.

It gets added to the pile already taking up my mattress and I curse for the thousandth time.

"What the fuck do I wear?"

Cookie stares at me from her patch of sun on the carpet and huffs.

"I know he won't care. Fuck, maybe I should just text him."

The cat lays her head down, ignoring me, and I take that as a yes.

> ME: *Should I sneak you into a movie or kick your ass in pinball?*

There.

His answer will answer my dilemma. Movies mean stealth mode, while pinball is right down the street from where he's known to frequent, but crawling with security that isn't me.

A flittering takes over my chest as the responding bubbles pop up almost immediately.

> VIDA: **Like you could beat me at pinball.**

An eye roll emoji pops up next and I laugh out loud.

> ME: *Bring your a-game, Vida.*

I no sooner hit send that the phone lights up, the entire screen covered in a selfie of Mac that I didn't put there.

Tingles.

It's got him half-smiling. Like he's fucking coy or some shit. While his hand is in his hair and his freckles stand out. Green-blue eyes that stare directly at me.

Something in my chest studders and I gasp when the pic disappears.

> VIDA: **Answer me.**

The picture fills my screen once again, another call, and I swipe to answer him this time.

"What are you wearing?"

His voice is deep, grated gravel that tickles right down my spine. It reminds me of mornings I spent attempting to sneak out of his bed to get to the gym only for him to draw my attention back to his sleepy mumbles.

Or late nights after a show with his voice destroyed and a mug of tea in his grip.

Movies that made him laugh so hard that he could barely talk.

The way he says *Tyro* with the roll of his tongue.

His wit and banter.

His will and strength.

He's goddamn beautiful.

"What are you thinking?" he whispers over the line and it's then that I realize there's two boxes on the screen, the majority of it black, but the smaller rectangle reflecting back the soft smile on my face.

"About tea and sleepy mumbles," I answer easily and raise the phone until the little frame fills with my head and bare shoulders. "I'm also undecided on attire."

"If you're not wearing pants, I'm coming straight over, and the date can wait."

I snort and dip the phone to show my jeans.

Mac curses, but I can hear the smile in his voice.

It makes that flittering and tingling intensify.

Was it always like this?

No. I would have recognized this shit.

Wouldn't I?

That cloud of self-doubt teeters at the edge of my subconscious, menacing and leering like it deserves the attention it's starving for.

It won't last.

I clear my throat.

Blow out a breath.

I deserve good things, I remind myself just like my therapist demanded I attempt in moments like this. *Not everything is temporary.*

Mac isn't temporary.

"Come over."

Chapter Seventy-One

MAC

I've never stolen a set of keys so damn fast in my life.

The bowl they were in rattles as the door slams behind me and I'm on the garage level before I can take a full breath.

Come over.

Yes. All the way yes.

I click the unlock button on the fob until the car it belongs to beeps—Leo's Audi—and I'm diving into the driver's side at the same time Peach runs after me.

I'm laughing my ass off as I shift to drive and the momentum is shutting Peach's door for him.

"Where's the fucking fire, Mac? Holy shit."

My pants.

Snickering, I bank the exit with a turn that leaves burnt rubber behind me and squeal right passed a line of vans and beater cars trying their best to blend in. They don't mingle at all, and I don't know why the paparazzi even try anymore. We know they're there. They get what they get. Anna, the band's media specialist, handles the rest.

Which is why I'm not at all surprised when headlights fill the rearview mirror a little too close.

"Circle the block," Peach mumbles and passes me a pair of aviators from the glove box.

"Yup," I murmur and swallow back the burn of disappointment.

I will not let this temper my mood.

Having the tailgater doesn't change the fact that not only did I fall asleep with Jordan last night, he also asked me out on a date this morning.

A fuckin' date!

The man that I have loved for nearly a decade … is waiting for me.

Come over.

I take the sharp left across traffic without a signal and nearly clip a parked car in the process. The street narrows and I have to swerve around some jackass opening their car door streetside while I'm flying past.

When I glance at the rearview and catch the thrown-up hands, I shake my head.

Only to have to swallow back a wave of dread that rolls over me.

"Take the next left."

I shake my head.

"They're back, Peach."

"Shit."

The bodyguard turns between the seats to look behind us and jerks out to grab the back of my seat when I take the crest of a cross street too fast.

"Go right," he demands. "Right now."

I tap the brakes.

Turn the wheel.

The car goes right and keeps going right until we're losing traction and spinning and it's the flash of blinding LED headlights that have me pulling the wheel and slamming the gas.

I'll always choose you.

I jerk at the reminder of Jordan's words and tap the brakes too soon.

Come over.

There's a crunch and we jolt forward.

What if?

My foot is on the brake, nearly standing on the pedal, but it does nothing to stop the momentum of both cars from skidding into oncoming traffic.

What if I don't make it?

"Mac! *Watch out!*"

Chapter Seventy-Two

JORDAN

THIRTY MINUTES HAVE BECOME forty-five.

Forty-six.

Take a breath. He's not disappearing.

I force myself to do just that and take another lap around my apartment.

I've already put away all the clothes I dug out, just in case the bed is needed. Thrown on an old Goo Goo Dolls shirt. Cleared the dishes from last night out of the sink.

Made sure there was another box of mac in the pantry.

Forty-eight minutes.

I check Cookie's food for the thousandth time, and she eyes me warily as I snatch her water bowl and end up spilling half of it because it's fuller than I realized.

Both dishes are sparkly clean and full at the fifty-nine-minute mark.

"Calm the fuck down, Jordan," I mumble aloud and suck in a breath. "He said he was coming."

Cookie comes to me when I flop on the couch and rub my hands down my thighs. They're damp and tingling and my stomach is in knots.

Why is he not here yet?

I lick my lips. Scrub my face.

"God, I'm so nervous," I tell my cat. "Am I really doing this?"

I should have picked him up like I'd planned.

The cat stares at me, which is not unusual, but then she hops up in my lap and her pupils dilate.

It's been too long.

I pet her head, but she dips out of my reach and nails me with another look.

Blinking, I watch her pupils flex again and my stomach sinks.

"Something's wrong."

My feet are already under me when she jumps away, my shaking hands grabbing at my keys and knocking them off the hook.

I curse and dip to snatch them from the floor when the ring of my phone pierces the silence.

It's loaded and heavy and I'm trembling when I look at the screen to see Peach's name flash.

There's no picture this time.

No blinding grin or gorgeous guy.

Just a scrolling name that screaming all the things I feel deep in my gut.

Nonono.

It takes two tries to swipe the answer button far enough to engage it and my apartment is immediately filled with the wail of sirens.

"Mr. Kauffman?"

Suddenly, I'm no longer in my own space, but in Mac's instead. Seeing the slump of his shoulders at the claim of best friends first with only Mark Wahlberg as my witness.

On the outside of a photoshoot where I saw Mac as something more for the first time. Something fierce. Something … devastating.

But then I'm in the rain, watching as he lets the storm hide the hurt in his eyes.

A treehouse surrounds us as he tells me he loves me, and I believe him.

I don't know how to say it back.

The hotel room where he told me to leave his life.

Then my gym. The dance studio I never found a purpose for, only to find Mac having taken up the space with his own thing. Asking him out with a flutter to my stomach and a hope brightening my chest.

Come over.

It all comes cascading down like shattered glass.

"Mr. Kauffman? This is Officer Smith. There's been an accident, and you were listed as an emergency contact."

This is all my fault.

"Where are you taking them?" I all but growl with my gut somewhere near my knees.

"Sir, they're en route to the hospital."

They.

My lungs freeze, my heart stopping, but my feet are moving and I'm running.

Driving.

Running again, this time over pavement then squeaking linoleum.

The walls are whitewashed, but all I see is a club bathroom.

Except this time … I'm the one on the verge of hyperventilating.

I should have never told him to come over.

My chest burns as I pass a nurse's station, their protests falling on ringing ears.

Carts and gurneys wing by, but I don't stop.

Room after room flashing by, the boulder in my gut gaining momentum in its sink to my feet with each one that doesn't hold my drummer.

"Mac!"

Another room. Another sickly patient that I disturb.

"*Mi Vida.*"

My steps slow like I'm rushing through cement sludge with each second that ticks by, and I don't see Mac. Or Peach. Or any-fucking-one that I recognize.

My chest *hurts.*

This can't be it.

Memories I've spent years and years building defenses against rush over me.

The burning of my skin.

The scent of charred *everything.*

The screams.

"Jordan!"

I whip around in slow motion at the sound of my name and the world tilts when another bodyguard rushes to me.

"Lugh. *Lugh.* Where are they?"

The larger man huffs through a tight jaw and pushes me back around. "Prepping for surgery."

My heart sinks even farther.

"Mac?"

He shakes his head, telling me he doesn't know, at the same time an alarm rings over the PA system.

A sound we both trained to but hoped to fucking God we'd never hear.

Someone's coding.

And we fucking run.

Chapter Seventy-Three

JORDAN

AT 8:41, PEACH'S HEART stopped.

For two minutes, the man that pulled my drummer from the burning wreckage was technically dead.

Blood loss. Shock. Complications.

There's a whole myriad of reasons why it did, but none of them matter right now.

Because I'm trading off between staring at the squiggling heartline of his monitor and the rise of his chest.

He saved Mac's life.

There's a paper cup of sludge the hospital has passed off as coffee cooling in my grip and a pack of half-eaten Skittles on the stand next to me. Neither are sitting well in my rolling gut.

It's been days.

Days since I answered Mac's call and changed the course of everything.

I was supposed to pick him up.

I was supposed to keep him safe.

It should have been me in that car, not him. Not *them.*

Instead … he's in the next room, comatose, with swelling on his brain.

And Peach is laying here with several broken ribs, bandaged burns, a maze of stiches and staples holding him together, and discoloration darkening his too-pale skin with each passing minute.

"How is he?"

I sniff at the rasp of Mac's twin and don't bother hiding the old tear tracks tightening my face when I glance up.

"He's alive," I croak out with rough, unused vocals.

My eyes burn all over again. Chest tightening.

I rub at the ache.

It only seems to spread. Deepen.

Crack wide open until the agony can swallow me whole.

Screams in Spanish.

Arms so tight I can't breathe.

Singed hair. Clothes. Skin.

Deafening roars of blistering heat.

"I'm sorry." The thickness of Rex's voice filters through a fog of crackling timber and my chest studders painfully. "I'm sorry he pushed you away."

A fissure snakes its way down the center of me and it's like I can feel every inch of bone and muscles ripping apart.

"It was my fault," I whisper to the blanket tucked around the cool packs on Peach's sides.

"No, it was—it was mine."

The outline of the bed blurs.

"He's better when he's with you."

I shake my head, and it dislodges a tear clinging to my lashes. "Don't you dare blame Peach for this."

"No. *No.*" Rex's exhale is so deep that I hear it over the sound of the machines assuring Peach is alive between us. "I don't blame him. Or Mac. Or you." I would say the addition of me jolts me, but it doesn't. "The asshole that chased them, now *that's* a different story."

Sniffing, I nod.

"But I do need you to get your head out of your ass."

The statement is slow to compute and has me furrowing a brow at red-rimmed blue eyes. "Me?"

He juts his chin. "Stop running from him. He's going to fucking need you."

Another chip breaks off from that crack widening my chest. "He doesn't need me. This is what I bring." I tip my head.

"Bullshit," Rex growls. "Don't make me break your fucking nose. *Again.*"

I scoff and shake my head. "You don't know what you're talking about."

"Except I do." He points to his chest. "I fucking *feel* it, Jordan."

Sighing, I lean back in my seat.

"He told me."

I stiffen.

"Told you what?"

"That he fell in love with a straight man." He looks around, then pins me to the spot with the intensity staring back. "How much longer are you going to make my brother wait?"

That crater inside me caves in, burying me in the rubble.

He told his brother that?

"When?" I rasp out, my vision blurring all over again. "*How long?*"

There's a hand on my shoulder even though I didn't see Rex move around the bed and I break just a little bit more.

"Six years ago, Jordan." There's a pause so loaded that I hold my ragged breath, the weight of his words pulling me so far under that I couldn't stop the sob that breaks. "When a Thompson knows, he *knows.*"

Love him back.

Love him back or let him go.

Chapter Seventy-Four

JORDAN

"**Q**uédate abajo, hijo mío."

I shake my head.

"*Hay fuego.*"

Pinch the bridge of my nose.

"*Mi hijo!*"

Scrub my hands down my face.

"*Fuego!*"

I jerk around, blinking dry eyes into focus.

Except there's nothing but the night staff watching me wearily from the station right outside Mac's room.

"You good?"

Blowing out a long breath, I turn back to Lugh, who's on hallway duty, and shake my head. "Honestly … no."

He juts his chin in understanding.

"You don't have to go in."

"I …" I swallow and it clicks. "How bad is it?"

His nostrils flare, his laser focus analyzing me. He must settle on something, some way to tell me the truth gently, because he nods once.

"He looks better than Peach," he admits on a rasp that I wasn't expecting. "But it's damn difficult to see, Jay."

The wind rushes out of me. My pulse spikes in my ears.

I have to try.

As much as I know this is all my fault, the pain of *not* seeing him has been just as difficult to breathe through. It feels like a part of me is lost. Asleep. Too far away from the rest of me.

And it's not until Mac came home, came and found me, that I realize I've been fighting that feeling since he left.

Sending an acknowledging tip of the chin to Lugh, I steel myself against my past and step into Mac's room with a racing heart and held breath.

The tube beneath his nose is the first thing to draw my attention. The bit of dried blood beneath it that someone missed. The dark coloring. The bandage taped to his temple.

My eyes well up.

"It should have been me."

I'm shaking, aching, but getting closer.

"Fuck, it should be me in that bed," I croak to his lax face. "Not you, mi Vida."

His hand is right there so I grab it. Hold it. Interlock our fingers together.

He's colder than normal and it makes my lip wobble, but I refuse to let go.

"It's just you and me, okay?" I lift our joined hands and press my lips to the tattoos on his knuckles. "And I'm so goddamned sorry." Touching my cheek to the back of his hand, I let the wounded sound trapped in my chest out. "Just … come back to me, all right? I'm not done with you."

Chapter Seventy-Five

JORDAN

"JAY, YOU NEED TO go shower. I can smell you from here."

I shake my head at Lemon and switch the cross of my ankles. They're propped up on the side of Mac's bed and ache like a mother fucker, but I refuse to move them.

"I showered this morning."

Three minutes in the tiny stall while the nurses checked Mac over hardly counts but it was good enough to clear some of the fog from my mind and the grime from my skin.

"Ugh, fine. How about some damn sunlight?"

I point at the window next to me, the blinds open and letting a few beams in.

"The gym is on fire?"

"Insurance," I mumble on a shrug and rub my thumb across the back of Mac's hand. He's a little warmer today, each day that's passed like one small as shit step closer to him waking up.

At least that's what I keep telling myself.

It's been eight days since the accident and each one of those days I've spent just like this. By his side, talking to him, holding his hand, and hoping with everything in me that I get to have more time with him.

The doctors won't tell me much since I'm not related to him and I'm not a spouse, but that hasn't stopped Rex, and their mother, from telling me every bit of information they've gotten.

Like the swelling has gone down, enough for it to no longer concern them, but that he's just … sleeping the trauma off.

That he'll wake up when he's ready.

That's the part that has me on edge.

Mac never sleeps.

So while the diagnosis tracks, the behavior doesn't.

It's kept my stomach in knots and my ass planted in the shitty hospital chair next to him every second I can possibly manage since.

"You hungry, you damn buffoon?"

My stomach clenches and rolls at the question from across the bed and I give a short nod.

I'm really not, but I know I need to eat something.

I feel Lemon's eyeroll more than I see it because I'm too busy watching Mac's chest rise and fall steadily.

"I'll be back," Lemon sighs and I nod, still not looking away from the tattoos peeking out of Mac's hospital gown. They're colorful splashes against all the drab and washed-out shit surrounding them, just like my drummer is with life, and it makes my eyes burn.

"I miss you, mi Vida. So goddamn much."

Resting my temple on our joined hands, I zone out while staring at the way his feet pitch the blanket up.

And all I can think about are his worn-down Chucks lying stranded in the middle of his hallway floor.

He loved me then.

Something in me snaps and it aches so deeply that I can't tell if it's falling into place or cracking more apart than I already feel.

Somehow … it feels like both.

How much time I've missed.

Time I'll never get back with the man that somehow stole my heart when I wasn't aware it was even up for grabs.

I'm not even convinced that *it* knew what was happening.

"Never once," I mutter to the fabric covering his toes. "Did the others feel like this." I lick my dried lips and roll my head over his knuckles. "Not even the sweetheart I had all through middle into high school. The one I was convinced was gonna last a lifetime. Once we traded V-cards, I was in it. Granted it took me three years to do it, but we did, and things were okay*ish*." I chuckle at my naivety. "She turned out to be fucking the entire football team all of junior and senior year."

Looking back at it now, I understand that my connection to her was more friendly than it ever was romantic. That my trauma-fueled and hormone-addled brain made the dots all line up enough to make it seem like more.

She was there before my parents died.

Gnawing at the inside of my cheek, I nuzzle into the warmth of Mac's hand.

"The second was right after high school. Right time, right place kinda thing. We dated for months before I could work up the nerve to make anything happen. I chalked it up to jitters. Trauma. *More* trauma. For years, we went back and forth. Being friends who dated when they weren't busy. It was good until Lugh showed up in the gym I was working at the time."

My chest clenches at the memory of the biggest guy I'd ever seen walking through the door.

Looking for a temp membership, only to leave his number behind for me to call if I wanted more out of life than cleaning equipment and taking payments.

"I loved that gym. It was part of what saved my life. But Lugh spoke to a different part of my soul that screamed for more than what I was given. The stability I'd been looking for. It felt like fate calling my name."

I sigh out a shaking breath.

"If only I'd known it would bring me here. To you."

For a long while, I fall into listening to the heart monitor's steady beep. A confirmation that Mac's heart still beats in his chest as my eyes fall closed.

As long as there's sound, there's life. His life. Brilliant and too goddamn good for this earth.

Too good for me.

Will he still be willing to go on that date with me when he wakes up? Or will this change everything all over again?

I'm not sure how long I stay like that with my heart in my throat, uncertainty nearly choking me to death, my hand long passed falling asleep.

It's so numb that not even my hair falling over my crown tickles it.

I know I should move, but I can't. My head feels too heavy to lift, my neck too stiff to tilt.

More of my hair falls over my brow and skates across my forehead, causing goosebumps to rise along my spine.

Something nudges my scalp, and I hum at what must be a dream sinking it's claws into my subconscious and attempting to pull me under.

Sighing, I let it ease me with its caress. Console me with its softness.

Gentle scrapes have my lips parting and my breath evening.

Stillness claims me, slowing my heart rate for the first time in a week.

It almost feels … too real.

"Tyro."

Warmth settles over me like a blanket at the name and I lean as far into his dream that I can.

Blunt scratching along my scalp has tingles spreading all down my back and across my cheeks.

"Baby, you're killing my fucking hand."

I shoot upright, hair falling into my widening eyes as the sight before me burns into them.

All I can do is blink at the blinding smirk aimed at me, his hand hanging in the space between us, his eyes open and staring right at me.

"Mac?"

My lip wobbles when his grin grows.

"I would say evil twin, but that title's already taken." He gives a half shrug, then drops his free hand back to the bed.

The chuckle that comes out of me is so fucking watery it might as well be a sob. "God, I'm so fucking glad to see you."

He snickers. "You act like I was in a coma or something."

My stomach drops.

"Mac … you *were*."

His brows furrow before he does a sweep of the room, then they meet in the middle with how deep his scowl becomes.

"That's fucked. All I remember is Peach yelling at me to—"

He goes stock still, blanching even more.

I swallow hard.

"Oh, my God. *Peach*."

Grabbing his wrists when he starts ripping at cords and monitors, I lean until my face is all he can see.

"He's next door, okay?" His eyes are glassy and full of pain. *Just like mine.* "But he's gonna be okay. He's busted up, but he's gonna be all right."

I swallow when Mac nods and muster all the strength I can to keep my own emotions at bay.

Peach might be alert and better than he was when I saw him last, but that doesn't change the fact that had I not been an oblivious asshole, he never would have ended up here in the first place.

But he's alive.

RAE STONE

Mac's alive.
And that's more than I deserve.

Chapter Seventy-Six

MAC

"Drive around for your total."

The little speaker crackles its reply to our order, and I can't help the lift at the corners of my mouth.

What can I say? Being in a coma puts a damper on a guy.

But now that I've been sprung free from the prison of germs, I'm feeling every bit of the feistiness that's been stored for the last however many days I've been cooped up and out of commission.

It's only made better by the tatted chauffer scowling at the road like it did him dirty.

"Wanna bet?" I ask as Jordan palms the wheel and gets us around the little curve in the lane.

"For?"

"Whether they recognize me."

Jordan sighs. "I'd rather they didn't. Can you change your face real quick?"

I mock a wounded gasp and touch a hand to my chest as we inch closer to the window. "How *dare.* You don't like my face, Tyro?"

He snickers when I tuck my arms tight across my pecs and throw him my best fake-angry face.

"You hate my face."

His eyes roll as he leans to the side and fishes his wallet from his pocket around the seatbelt. "I don't hate your face."

I scoff. "You definitely said you hate my face."

"No, I didn't."

"So did."

"I *like* your face. Now shut it."

Jordan pulls up to the window, and my stomach is growling, and I snicker. "I knew it."

"Wha?" He's distracted by my comment when the window flings open and the employee on the other side barks a total at him. "I said I liked it. I'm the one that has to look at it every day."

"*Excuse me?*"

Jordan's head snaps to the side where the window sits wide open, with an employee wearing one of those old school aprons and a dirty look is staring at us.

"No, I was talking to my—Mac." He throws a gesture my way as he attempts to juggle his card, the receipt and his wallet. "I was talking to him."

The woman leans down and catches my gaze across the car. "You *his* Mac?"

I beam. "Yes, ma'am."

"Well, I guess it's a good thing he likes your face, then, dear."

That pink flush takes over Jordan's cheeks and I laugh.

"I suppose so," I mumble through a cheeky grin and plant a hand on his thick thigh when he white knuckles the steering wheel. "He's still getting used to it."

The woman hums, a sideways glance thrown in Jordan's direction before she returns her smile on me. "He's a lucky man, honey. Don't let him forget it."

"*Never,*" I say to Jordan's frozen profile, tossing the woman a grin. "You got a pen? Marker?"

The woman snorts, throws barking orders over her shoulder into the store, then hands one through the window.

I reach across Jordan and accept it, diving into the glove box next for a leftover takeout napkin. I quickly scroll my signature on the paper and hand them both back to the woman. "I don't wanna see that for sale online—" I squint at her name tag. "*Birdie*. Okay?"

With a toothy grin she accepts and nods. "Of course, Mac. Enjoy your *face liking*." Smirking, Birdie hands out our bags of takeout burgers and Jordan can't pull away from the window fast enough.

"*That* is why," he huffs.

I throw my hands up, though I'm snickering. "Birdie was nice, Tyro!"

"You gave her an autograph." His lifted brow wings my way briefly as he makes our way through the lot and back out onto the street. "You know how much those things go for online?"

Shrugging, I dig around in the paper bag. "Even if she gets few hundred for it, I don't care."

"I don't get it." Jordan shakes his head. "Why?"

"Why not?" I mutter around a giant bite of cheeseburger. "Made her night at the least."

Jordan blows out a breath that suggests he still doesn't get it, but steals the carton of fries from my grip.

"You shouldn't give away pieces of you for free."

The words are a low rumble beneath his breath, so low that I question if I heard him right over the faint sound of the radio droning on.

And when I stare at his profile, waiting for him to repeat it for my response and all I get is that pink blush, I bite my lip to hold back my smile.

I could maybe get used to this.

Chapter Seventy-Seven

JORDAN

"Y OU HUNGRY?"

Mac aims an unamused stare my way from beneath the mound of blankets and pillows.

"Dude, you *just* fed me."

Shifting my weight, I plant my hands on my hips and nod. "Right. Yeah." I'm still nodding for no reason as I check off a list in my head of all the things he might need in the next few hours once I inevitably force myself to go home.

He needs rest. No stress. No exertion.

Which means my heart stays in this weird sense of limbo for the time being and he needs to go to sleep.

His checkup is in two weeks. *I can wait another two weeks, right?*

"Tyro, sit down."

I shake my head and clear my throat.

"I should probably …" Trailing off, I walk back to his room and steal the charging cord from his nightstand for him to use in the living room where I've set him up in front of the TV. "Marie'll be here in the morning. Lugh is across the hall with Peach."

The quirk of his brow is his only reply.

"Okay." I blow out a breath. "I'm gonna—" I thumb over my shoulder in the direction of the exit which only makes his face do this weird scowl that I feel right through the center of my chest.

"Baby, sit the fuck down."

Tingles.

It's not the first time he's used the term of endearment and every time he does, my chest warms over a little bit more. Those craters in my chest filling in inch by inch.

He's alive and home and …

"No one's ever called me that before," I admit softly without thought and bite my lip. "I don't know why that matters right now." I'm shaking my damn head like that's all I know how to do when his face softens. "I should go."

Mac reaches for me.

Fingers curling in the *gimme* gesture and all.

My stomach flips, those tingles that used to take up the back of my neck all shooting straight down my spine as I step into him.

His arms weave around my waist, chin tucked against my fluttering stomach as he stares up at me.

Just like that night in the bathroom after I was inside him for the first time.

My chest tightens up at the memory and all the lost time in between.

I want that time back. I want that so fucking bad.

"You still owe me." My brows furrow. Hands resting on his shoulders. "The rest of the date I was promised."

The thing in my chest skips an entire beat. "But Mac, you're—"

"I'm *fine*," he assures, squeezing my waist and even pinching the back of my thigh. "But it's good to know where your head's at, baby." He winks and if he wasn't already holding me up, my knees would have buckled.

"What?"

"Doc said no sex for a few days, but he didn't say no making out."

He tugs and I go willingly, my knees falling to either side of his thighs.

"*Slow*," I demand to the fire burning in his eyes, my hands wandering into the hair at the nape of his neck.

He hums some deep sound that vibrates through me like a caress, and I suppress a shiver.

When did his nose get so close?

I nudge it with mine.

"Say you agree to that, Mac," I whisper, desperate for one of us to keep some control over the flames stoking between us. It's so thick. Hot. I swear I'll let it burn me alive with a smile on my face.

"Mmm. What is it you told me before?" he asks, his lips feathering over mine in the sweetest tease. "As you wish?"

I release a breath through my nose and smirk.

"You remember that?"

Hands gripping my hips, fingertips curling into my ass, he nods. "There's not a day—a moment—spent with you that I've ever forgotten."

The organ beating in my chest sparks to life. Flies because of this man and everything he makes me feel.

I'll always choose you.

A memory slides into my subconscious and has me tightening my grip on Mac.

Because it's not the time where I told him the very same thing, but much earlier in my life that it was told to me.

Dark blue eyes just like mine had shone with fear. Terror even.

But more than that … was *admiration*.

Pride.

Faith.

Love.

"Siempre te elegiré a ti, mi vida," I whisper and press my lips to Mac's.

I will always choose you.

It takes him a split second to shake off his confusion, but then he's kissing me back and that tingling inside my chest lights like sparklers glowing orange.

The ease of it spackles over more of the cracked open bits inside me, filling in the tiny broken pieces of me with a blinding brilliance that casts out more of the darkness.

My hands are cupping his face when his tongue swipes over my lip, my stomach full of fluttering butterflies when I let him in.

Finally.

Something inside me clicks. Clearing like the sky after a storm.

And, goddamn, kissing him is like tasting the sunlight without getting burned.

"Shit," he murmurs breathlessly against my lips and my heart patters. "I could fucking kiss you all night long."

As if to prove his point, he dives right back in, licking and teasing me as his fingers dig into my ass. He pulls, dragging me over his lap and along the hardness barely contained by his shorts.

It doesn't even matter that my own cock is trapped, harder than any erection I've ever fucking had, by the confines of my jeans.

The gasp that leaks out is almost as involuntary as the groan that follows when he does it again.

"*Vida.*"

"Mmm, yeah, baby," he rumbles, and it rolls right down my spine, lighting me on fire from the inside out. He's full on palming my ass, hauling me close enough that our chests are touching, and our pants are in tandem. His breath feeds mine. His teeth trapping my lip with the faintest sting he licks away. That tongue of his trails along my jaw and down my neck where he nips and suckles at the skin, and it takes everything in me not to embarrass myself with the moan trapped in my throat.

It's like he knows all the right places. All the perfect spots to burn me up. Make me hard. Leave me panting. Aching. *Wanting.*

Pulling and pushing, he works me over his stiff cock as my head falls back.

It's never been quite like this before.

I've never wanted someone so fucking bad.

He reads me like a book, the instructions painted clearly on the page.

Him.

My missing piece.

He was right fucking there, in front of my face, just waiting for me to catch up.

"Mac," I choke out and fist his hair, pulling his head back to look at him.

Swollen lips, pink from my kiss.

Green-blue eyes molten with desire.

A flush spreading over the freckles covering his cheeks.

"You aren't a bottom, are you?"

His smirk is slow and nearly sinister.

I shiver.

"I'm vers, baby." He nips at my chin. "I'll give twice as hard as I get."

Goosebumps rush over my skin, excited nerves taking over my gut.

"That's—holy shit, okay."

Mac's chuckle is deep and travels right over me, while his hands ease closer together.

Even over top of the denim, the feel of him teasing me shoots straight to my cock. The proximity of his fingers *exciting.*

This thing blossoming between us *exhilarating.*

"Yeah?"

I nod. "Doing it myself was awkward with the angle, but I liked it."

The admission has his eyes flaring comically wide before they roll back, and his head drops backwards.

"Fuuuuck." He drags me over his cock again. "Why'd you have to tell me that *now.*"

I smirk and smack a kiss to his jaw.

"Because you admitted that you'd like to do it for me."

He groans.

"You goddamn *tease*."

I lick my lips and pop up from his lap.

His fully tented lap. The erection barely held back by the material; the waistband lifted from his skin.

Mine is in no better condition, but it means nothing to me when my sight zeroes in on the darker spot near the peak of his pitched shorts.

"Keep staring at me like a starved man, baby, and I'll feed you your last meal."

My cock flexes behind my zipper and I gulp.

"I … I have to go feed my cat."

Mac blinks.

Then burst out laughing, a raucous and beautiful fucking sound.

God, I've missed it. Him.

This.

"Jesus, fuck, Tyro," he says around the rumble and pinches the base of his cock through his shorts. It pulls the material even tighter, showing full outlines of the blunt head and my chuckle dies off.

He's still shaking with mirth when he pushes to stand, his hand diving into his shorts and tucking his hard-on beneath the elastic.

It barely holds it back and my mouth waters.

"Let's go get your fucking cat."

Chapter Seventy-Eight

Jordan

SOFT PUFFS OF AIR flitter across my pec.

Tickles feather over my chin.

Weight and warmth blanket me, grounding me into the couch that's missing the lumpy cushion.

There's even the occasional tap against my toe.

The backs of my eyelids are washed out with orange, telling me there's enough light to fill the room, and yet, I can't find it in me to open them.

Raspy mumbles scrape over the otherwise silent room and my lips tip up at the corner.

It's just gibberish. Broken words and missed mutters.

My favorite way to wake up.

Skin to skin. Chest to bare chest.

His heart so close to mine that I swear they beat the same rhythm.

That part is new, but shit, it's now even more my favorite way to wake up.

Even better that he came to me like this in his sleep instead of wandering off to put pillows in the fridge.

"There were so many mornings that I woke up *ashamed*," I whisper, and tilt my chin to bury my nose in Mac's hair. I'm taken over by a toasty sweetness, the hint of rich smoke barely there but enough to make my chest swirl. "Wondering how the hell I was the one to wake up."

The arms hooked around my shoulders twitch.

"Then, one day, I woke up feeling guilty as shit for holding you back."

I thread my fingers into his hair and cup his head, holding him to me.

"I never meant to hold you back, Vida," I whisper softly, my voice too thick to do anything else. "I never meant to hurt you."

Pressing my lips to the side of his head, I inhale. Etching the scent of him to memory. Squeezing the imprint of him into my soul.

I'm not sure how long I stay like that, just breathing him in, but then he finally moves. Finally looks at me. Rolls his head along my pec until his chin is resting on my chest. His face is splotchy, and his lower lashes are damp.

My brow furrows and I gingerly cup his face. "Vida?"

He blinks and tears escape his brilliant eyes, but the corner of his lips lift in a soft smile.

"I thought I was dreaming," he murmurs, and my heart gives a mighty thump. "But you're here for real and I dunno." I think he tries to shrug, but the position we're in doesn't give much room. "It's got me feeling fuzzy as fuck."

My snicker burns up hot when a grin splits his face nearly in two. His smile so wide that his cheeks bunch up and his eyes squint.

It's the most beautiful thing I've ever seen.

I swallow hard against a sudden rush of nerves and speak the truth for him.

"You're goddamned *gorgeous*, Vida."

He's blinking when I brush some of the hair back from his forehead, his grin softening.

It's when I meet his eyes head on that I see the reddening and the moisture collecting again. His lips tip into something almost shy and he buries his face in my chest.

"I know it's kinda weird to call a man that b—"

"*No.* No." His head shakes against me, his sight clashing with mine. "Call me gorgeous or pretty or whatever the fuck *feels* right. Society can suck one."

Chuckling, I thumb over the wet trails down Mac's cheeks, ridding him of the dampness. "Okay."

"I like flowers, too. Just sayin'."

I nod, a lightness in my chest that I've never felt before. "Okay."

"And good morning kisses. I think. I don't know. I've never had one of those before."

Grinning, I cup his jaw and lean in, the tip of my nose feathering over his. "As you wish, mi Vida."

My lips brush his, light and gentle enough to have him huffing and slamming forward, knocking his teeth into mine. I chuckle against his mouth, the sound dying off when his tongue slips out and begs for entrance.

I let him in.

With tangled tongues and twisted limbs, my already-hard cock throbs against the thigh slotted between mine. He lifts enough to hover over me without breaking the kiss, and drags his leg along my length, pulling a groan from deep in my chest.

Hands wandering down his ribs and over his waist, I dip the tips of my fingers just beneath the elastic of the shorts he's wearing.

His tongue curls around mine as my fingers dig into the fleshy globes of his ass, his leg going over my hip until he's straddling me.

Only two thin layers of fabric separate us when he rolls his ass over my lap.

It takes all of my willpower to halt him with a hard grip to his waist.

"*Mac,*" I growl in warning.

"Jordan," he breathes right back, his pants flittering over my lips. "Trust me, baby."

My balls tingle.

He reaches between us, tugging down my waistband until my cock springs free. My balls are held up by the elastic when he plants another hot as shit kiss on me. One that leaves me dizzy and following after his lips when he pulls back, crawling down over my legs.

I'm dazed out of my mind by the smirk pulling up on one side of his face when I realize how far down he's gone, my brain finally catching up.

"Mac, you don't—*ahhh shit.*"

His lips wrap around the head of me, tongue dancing along the underside.

I suck back a breath.

"Goddamn," I pant out. "You're not supposed to—*ohhh fuck.*"

He takes me deeper. Deeper. Deep enough that I'm hitting the back of his throat, and my eyes roll into my head.

Goddamn, he can deepthroat.

But then he's swallowing, the muscles constricting around my cock like a squeezing fist.

"Oh my God."

Easing back, Mac teases the underside of the head again and a wave of chills breaks out over my skin.

It's like nothing I've ever felt before to have his mouth on me. It's so goddamn good that I'm close. So close that when his cheek hollows out and he sucks his way down my shaft, I bite my tongue. The inside of my cheek. Anything to distract me from blowing so fucking fast.

I'm *throbbing* when he pulls back, a trail of spit arching between my cock and his chin, my balls keyed up and tingling.

"Shit, look at you." I fist the base of my shaft and grip his chin. His eyes flare wide and heated when I arch my cock down, rubbing the head over his mouth. "Lips swollen." I thumb over the bottom one. "Face flush."

The tip of my forefinger brushes over his cheekbone. "Want me to feed you some breakfast?"

His eyes flare even wider and he's panting all over my cock as he nods.

I hum, my abs tightening.

"Open up, Vida."

He does and I slip the head back between his lips. His tongue glides along the entire underside, taking my length right back down his throat.

This time … his tongue sneaks out and teases along the very base of my shaft.

"Ah, *fuck*."

My chest pumps to keep up, my toes curling into the couch beneath us.

It's so tight and hot and *fuck*.

Then he's moving.

Short pumps that keep me buried.

Throat flexing over the head of me.

"Mac," I rasp out in warning and fist his hair.

That only seems to spur him on, increase the tempo, and he hollows out his fucking cheeks.

My abs bind up. My hips arch. My balls ache.

"Shit, Vida. Swa-sw—*swallow*."

He does.

And my release rocks me to my core.

Stream after stream pulses down his throat as fireworks burst behind my eyes and my hips lift from the cushion.

But it's not quite the intensity of the orgasm that's shifting everything inside me.

It's the way my chest lights up like an exploding star, demolishing everything I thought I knew and leaving behind nothing but him.

Every time with Mac has been mind-blowing.

But this?

It's goddamn life-altering.

Mac. Mac. Mac.

I'm starting to go soft by the time he finishes licking me clean and I come down, hauling him back up to slam my mouth to his.

There's nothing gentle about this one.

It's all teeth and stubble burn and the taste of my cum coating his tongue.

"How was your breakfast?" I ask when we finally break apart enough to catch our breath.

He grins something sly and devilish.

"Damn delicious, baby."

Chapter Seventy-Nine

Mac

H IS EYES ARE MOLTEN blue orbs, his cheeks a perfect shade of almost pink.

But it's not even the way that his lips are swollen from kissing me, the plush flesh reddened from my teeth, that has my chest swelling.

It's the goddamn *smile* on his face.

I did that. I put that there.

It's intoxicating to see, and I feel downright giddy knowing that it's because of me.

"You're staring."

"Am not." I snicker and adjust so that I'm propped on one arm beside his head.

Running my thumb over his bottom lip, I trace the smile with what feels like a chest full of caramel apples. I'm at the damn fair and I ain't ever leaving.

A creak has my brow furrowing and Jordan's eyes narrowing.

The snick of the door closing has my eyes flaring and my hands working to get Jordan's shorts back over his junk.

"Shit, shit, shit." Jordan whisper-hisses and pushes at me to get up.

"Macaroni?"

I freeze.

The sound of my mother's voice, too close for comfort, has me silently shushing him and falling back over him like dead weight.

"What're you *doing*?" he growls near silently next to my ear.

I ignore the chills and shift so that one leg is back between his. It feels like it would be less compromising to be found *not* straddling him while we sleep, at least.

Either way, it's too late to jump up now.

"Pretend to be asleep," I rush out on a breath and close my eyes.

The spread of his legs is wider than earlier and there's not enough depth to the couch for four massive thighs, and mine ends up hanging off the edge. Which only serves to dig my hard cock right into his hip.

"Well, isn't this sweet."

Something nudges my calf at the same time that Jordan's heart pounds hard beneath me.

When I don't react, my mother full on kicks my shin.

"Ow, devil woman!" I yelp and swing a scowl in her direction. "Is this how you wake up your injured son?"

Her hands are on her hips and her head cocks.

"Says the grown ass man that was pretending to be asleep."

I can't help the bark of laughter that escapes me.

"Ma!"

"And judging by—" she waves a hand in our direction, "—*this,* I'm assuming *sleeping* isn't the only thing that was going on."

I groan and bury my face in Jordan's neck. "Maaaa."

Heat radiates off of my sleeping buddy in *waves.*

"I'll give you fifteen to get decent. Then we're going for breakfast."

"*Ma,*" I groan out and pin her with a glare she shrugs off.

Somewhere in my apartment, a phone rings and my mother's sight trails to Jordan. "You might wanna answer that."

His swallow is so hard that I hear it click, and he nods.

I'm half a second from protesting, preparing to wrap around him like a spider monkey if only to get five more minutes of snuggle heaven, when he gathers me up like we aren't damn near the same size and lifts us off the couch.

If a man can squeal, that's exactly what I'm doing when shaky feet are planted beneath me and he leaves me standing in the middle of my living room.

"Shut up," I tell Ma, the heat of her stare burning holes in my back, my face aching from the stretch of my grin.

A slap lands on my shoulder, and I snicker.

"I'm just glad to see that smile, baby." I turn in time to catch her shrug. "But tell me to shut up one more time."

I snort.

"Love you, Ma."

"That's what I thought. Now go get dressed you heathen."

I mock salute the woman with a middle finger and head back to my room on light feet.

Throwing on the closest clean shirt and pants, I snag a bandana and tie it around my forehead as I step up to the sink in my bathroom. I'm halfway through brushing my teeth when I feel eyes on me. It's almost like a caress down my back and over my ass, but when I meet Jordan's gaze in the mirror, he looks almost shaky.

"Tyro?"

He jolts like I startled him, a flush rushing all the way down to his chest.

I spit foam in the sink and meet the reflection of his gaze. "You okay?"

"Uh." He clears his throat and shakes his head. "Yeah."

My brows furrow, but I rinse my mouth and the toothbrush to give him a second to collect himself. And it's for me, too.

I'm still leaning over the sink, focusing on my breathing, when arms band around my middle.

"I'm covering so you can go out with Marie." My heart skips as his chin rests on my shoulder. "But I gotta talk with Ian after that."

I nod, unable to do anything except place a hand on his tatted arm and trace over some of the abstract patterns.

Is this where we go back to the real world?

"You're wearing my shirt."

"What?" Looking down, I find the emblem of a gym on the front and shrug. "It smelled clean enough."

He snorts, his lips pressing against my thundering pulse.

"Do you know how hard it is to not touch you right now?" I bite my lip, and he nips at my neck. "To not taste every inch of your skin?" The swipe of his tongue leaves me shivering.

"Tyro," I groan out only to gasp when his hand feeds beneath the shirt and flattens against my abs. The tips of his fingers dip beneath the denim covering my rapidly filling cock, slowly lowering until I feel a digit on each side of my shaft.

"Pop the button."

I shiver and pant and do just that.

His hand lowers along with the zipper, cupping my balls and rolling them gently, pulling a moan from deep in my gut.

"This is the opposite of not touching me," I breathe out.

He hums and sinks his teeth into my neck. "You're the definition of temptation, Mac. Tell me to stop."

Shaking my head, I lean back until I feel him from shoulder to ass.

A strangled noise vibrates his chest, and he lifts my shirt with his free hand, pressing the palm over my heart. I'm not sure if he meant to, but the motion still has my eyes blurring.

Holding me to him, he wraps a fist around the base of my cock and jerks.

"Oh, *fuck*, baby."

Slowly, leisurely, he pumps along my length all the way to the tip, twisting around the crown then pulling back.

My heart pounds in my chest as I watch him work me over, his hands both holding me together while tearing me apart.

"I've got you, mi Vida," he rasps in my ear and a shiver rolls over my spine. "Come apart. I got you."

Head falling back to his shoulder, my balls draw up tight to the swirl of pleasure in my lower belly as I meet his glinting gaze in the mirror.

His tongue darts out, swiping a long line down my neck and I'm done for.

"J-Jordan!" I call out with rolled back eyes and ropes of cum shooting across the vanity.

"Fuck yes, Vida," he growls, the vibration rolling across my skin as his hips rut into my ass. "You're so fucking hot."

I jerk in his palm, the last bit of my release landing on his hand, and groan. "God, your *mouth.*"

His chuckle is deep. "You mean this one?"

I crack open an eye just in time to catch his tongue slotting through the mess in his palm.

He groans and my heart stops.

But then he's sucking my release from his fingers with fluttering lashes like I'm the best thing to ever touch his tastebuds and my entire body breaks out in goosebumps.

"Oh, God."

The hum of agreement shoots straight to my balls, and I turn in his arms, slamming my lips to his.

He kisses me breathless, fireworks going off inside my chest long enough to stop my heart and leave the ends of my hair tingling.

He pulls back and presses his forehead to mine.

"We should get moving."

My head rolls over his in what I think is a nod as I reach blindly behind me and snag the abandoned toothbrush from the countertop.

"I don't have an extra one."

He kisses me one more time and snags the offer, popping it between his smiling lips. "Thanks, Vida."

I nod and step out of his way, though I'm full-on melting inside.

He likes the taste of my cum and he's sharing my toothbrush!

Maybe dreams do come true.

Chapter Eighty

JORDAN

The bravado I was feeling from getting Mac off drained nearly as soon as we hit the street.

But it's at an all-time low as I sit across from the woman that raised him, at their favorite diner, with his hand on my knee hidden under the table, and her inquisitive glare aimed right at me.

As if this is some kind of meet the boyfriend thing and not just the two of them sharing a meal.

Oh, *and* I thought it was a great idea to agree to this for Sentry under the condition that Ian and I chat afterwards.

Which means my stomach is in knots and though my arm is on the back of Mac's chair, I'm anxious as hell that I'm going to miss something. Put him in danger. Risk his mother.

How the hell did I do this before?

"Jordan, dear, what have you been up to?" Marie asks, pulling me from my thoughts and I swallow.

You mean other than being hung up on your son? Having an existential crisis every time I look at him? Hoping he doesn't fall in love with anyone when I'm not around?

"Uh, the gym."

Mac snorts and squeezes my knee.

It almost comforts me. At least until I realize my thought pattern has shifted once again to what I feel for Mac and how this time feels like so much more.

More. More. More.

Blowing out a breath, I break away from the stare down with the internal excuse of scanning the room.

"I bought the gym I run," I amend. "It's been a handful and a half to figure out and fix up, but I enjoy it."

Marie nods and sips her mimosa. "So Ian requested you since Peach is on bedrest."

She's not asking, but I tip my chin in conformation anyway.

"And what about after that?"

I catch her glance sliding suggestively to her son who groans. "This isn't the Spanish Inquisition, Mother."

Their bickering begins to draw eyes from around us and I have to force myself to breathe. To focus.

Except all I see are Mac's curls, mussed by my hands. All I smell is that sweet scent of his enveloping me. All I feel is him.

His grip flexes on my knee again and I nearly jolt out of my seat.

"Shit," I mutter and avoid looking at his worried gaze. "Sorry."

The server choses that moment to interrupt and I'm thankful for the reprieve, however temporary.

Plates are doled out, the heavy scent of greasy meat and sweet syrup wafts through the air, making my stomach flip over itself.

I'm starving but not for food.

Aching from the amount of restraint it's taking to keep my hands to myself.

Mac. Mac. Mac.

As if hearing my inner monologue, his hand drifts higher along my thigh, his palm cupping my cock through the denim.

It takes everything in me to not react.

But that doesn't stop me from leaning forward, pressing harder into his hand.

God, what is wrong with me?

Swallowing hard, I shovel back the egg whites in front of me with a level of frustration that makes no sense to me. It's something I've never felt before, to be almost *angry* that it's food and not Mac on a platter for me to devour.

I want his taste back.

I *need* to feel him. To see him bare and begging to come.

Fucking fuck, I want to feel him inside me.

"When's your follow up?"

The question from his mother is like a douse of cold water to my supercharged libido.

"Two weeks," I answer.

"Actually," Mac starts with a wince when I throw him a look, "I moved it up. They said the earliest they were comfortable with was six days."

My brows shoot up.

"That's good news." Marie nods. "But why not wait, Macaroni? Give yourself the time."

"Have you met me, Ma? I can't sit around for fucking two weeks when there's nothing wrong. Remember when I was twelve and broke my arm?"

She snorts and shakes her head. "Beating on that damn drum two days later. *With the cast.*"

"You were so mad."

They're both laughing, and a smile is attempting to pull up the corners of my lips right along with them.

But ... *six days.*

In six days, I'll have Mac without restrictions.

No more going easy. Taking things slow. Making sure he's not hurting or worse.

He'll be free.

And for the first time in way too long, I think I might be able to breathe again.

Chapter Eighty-One

JORDAN

ARMED WITH A SINGLE warm can of soda that was difficult as shit to find and earned me the strangest look from Mac, along with a bag of peach rings, I walk into my old apartment with squared shoulders.

My lips are still tingling from the kiss Mac left on me as I left his place. He's just right across the hall, and yet, I'm still anxious to get back to him.

And nervous.

Nervous as fuck.

As suspected, Peach is nowhere near the place he's *supposed* to be and I snicker, dropping the bag of candy on his pillow.

Making my way back into the common areas of the place, I find Lugh and Ian sitting at the island waiting.

Drawing in a breath, I set the can down on the counter between them, keeping the structure as a barrier.

Ian's sight narrows and Lugh's nose twitches in his form of a chuckle.

"You know," Ian starts, palming the can and popping it open with a hiss. "You are somehow the *worst* and *okayish* bodyguard I've ever fucking had."

I snort. "Be careful, someone might think you're complimenting me."

Lugh's nose does that flaring thing again.

"Okay, smartass." Ian takes a swig of the warm pop, and I cringe internally.

"Said the psychopath."

He pins me with a glare and points around his can at me. "Why did I agree to this again?"

"Because you need boots," I answer seriously. "With Peach out of commission, you're down two guys."

"Three," Lugh chimes in and my brows furrow. "I'm sitting out with Peach."

I still don't understand that one but swing my gaze back on Ian. "There's two problems, though." He motions for me to spit it out. "The gym for one. I only have one employee and I'm not leaving it all up to him to take care of everything."

"Fine. So you'll spend some time there. You just have to convince Mac to go with you or get one of us to cover."

My heart pounds in my chest.

That felt too easy.

Which means this next part is going to be the worst part to hurtle with my former boss.

Dating a client is a huge no-no. Sleeping with one? Giant red flag.

Falling in love?

Even worse.

But when I don't have confirmation of any of that from Mac's side of things?

Yeah, my stomach is doing its best to not drop through my asshole.

What if?

"Second thing?" Ian presses and I swallow hard.

Here goes something.

"Mac and I are seeing each other. Or are going to be. I think."

My heart thunders as the pair stare at me like I just spoke another language.

Lugh picks it up first, signified by only a twitch of his brow and turns his sight on Ian who's still staring at me like he's waiting for the punch line.

"As in, sleeping together, Ian."

His brows furrow beneath his buzz cut. "Okay. And? You two were always doing weird shit together."

That makes me chuckle tightly.

"Look," I say stiffly as I lean onto the counter, arms crossed. "The *only* reason I'm telling you first and not him is because I don't want to fuck with his recovery." Ian's brows remain pinched. "But I'm in love with him and I plan on being his boyfriend if he'll have me."

There. On the table. Could not be any fucking clearer.

Ian snorts and I hold my breath.

I don't need the job. I definitely won't accept any money from the Thompson's because that just feels too weird.

But if I want to keep up with Mac? Be able to go places with him?

I don't want a third wheel.

Nerves or not … I know that I have him.

Through and through.

Breakfast this morning just cemented it.

Peach kept him safe, and I'd trust the bodyguard with my life in his hands all over again if I needed him to cover Mac when he comes back.

But if Ian's offering to give me my job back *and* be on Mac's detail, then I'm taking it back.

"That's it? Hell, I thought you were already doing that."

The breath rushes out of me and my eyes burn.

"You accepted that this whole time?"

Ian shrugs. "It's not ideal, but they aren't paying you. And if at any point you can't focus on keeping him and the others safe, then I need you to call it, but the bond between you jackholes was something I could never find for Mac. Every guard he had before you hated working with him. You're the only asshole that put up with his wild antics."

"He's not that damn bad," I argue with a pinch to my brow.

Another shrug. "Compared to the others, he seemed that way to them."

Shaking my head, I let it go.

"You're seriously okay with me dating him?"

"Who am I to say you can't?"

I catch Lugh nodding and something inside me warms over at the approval. It's not that I needed it, but knowing I have it … that they accept us … Mac and me together …

It's got my throat more than a little tight.

Me and Mac.

Holy shit.

"Thank you," I mutter and straighten, putting some space between us. "I will keep you updated on things. Just … don't tell him yet?"

With their agreements and a whole lot of blinking, I round the counter to shake their hands.

Except when my palm meets Lugh's first, he jerks me into one of those bro hugs with a slap on the back.

"Welcome back."

I nod when he releases me and turn to Ian.

Instead of a shake, he gathers me into his arms and squeezes.

"Thanks for coming back. And I'm sorry if I ever made you feel like I wouldn't accept you," he whispers, then releases me. "Now get to fucking work, kid."

More nodding. More blinking.

With my chest swelled to near bursting, I leave security's apartment.

And when I open the door to Mac's place across the hall, he's standing just on the other side like he was watching for me through the peephole this whole time. With my cat perched on his damn shoulder like a parrot turned guard dog.

It's the second-best thing I've seen all day.

Chapter Eighty-Two

JORDAN

"**T**ODAY'S THE DAY, BABY!" he calls out and tosses the sticks onto the bed he woke up holding this morning.

He was fidgeting, unable to chill out with the impending appointment, and instead of just waiting for him to fall on his face in his sleep again, I gave him the sticks.

He pattered all night long with his eyes closed.

But his ass stayed in the bed right next to me.

I nod and smile at Mac as he hobbles his way into his pants. He almost trips three times before plopping back on the bed and shoving his feet through.

For the last six days, Mac and I have been inseparable. Hanging out around his apartment, binge watching movies like our life depended on it, and making out when the temptation was too much. Just as we were before everything got all messed up, minus the sucking face, and I would be lying if there wasn't some part of me that was nervous to change it. To challenge it.

But the bigger part of me?

Well … it can't fucking wait to make this shit official.

The doc calls it progress on my part. I just think its impatience.

Now that I've had him, I don't think there's any universe in which I'd ever *not* be his.

"We're going to be late if you don't hurry up."

Hopping up, he scares the cat when he blows past to find his shoes that he left in the middle of the hallway.

Or, at least, that's where he thinks they are.

Meanwhile, he jets right past me even though I'm holding them in my hand.

Smirking, I follow his trail into the living room and hold up the Chucks. "Looking for these?"

"Dammit."

He snags them, bends to shove his feet in, then straightens and smacks a kiss on my lips. He's even running with them untied, nearly trips again, and bangs into the door with a laugh.

Watching him like this … it's like I'm meeting him again, some of the years gone by shaved away, his luminance following close behind him like a trail of star dust.

I snicker with a patter to my heart and follow the chaos, keys in hand. *God, I missed him.*

The drive is short and, thankfully, uneventful but the second the back of the hospital building comes into view, my nerves kick in.

All the what ifs roll through my mind, terrorizing me with the possibilities that this is too soon. That something's gone wrong. That maybe … with a second chance at life, Mac won't want to spend it with me.

It's irrational to think that, considering how he's chosen to spend every waking minute since he came back to me, but the fear is real. It stabs inside my chest, slicing me open with all the things from my past, reminding me of every time that things didn't work out.

Of all the times someone didn't come back.

"Tyro."

Blowing out a breath, I put the car in park and turn to him.

Despite everything, there's a soft smile on his face, something I don't think has left him since he woke up, when he reaches for me. Our hands clasp over the center console, his grip sure and warm. I'm still not used to it, him reaching for me like this leaving my organs tumbling over themselves, and I honestly don't ever want to.

Because if I never get used to this, then I'll never take it for granted.

"I'm good. It's gonna be fine."

My stomach flips, filling with little fluttering tingles.

"I know," I mutter and do a sweep of our surroundings before lifting his knuckles and pressing a kiss to the backs of each one.

"My little romantic baby."

I snort. "Little?"

His brow jumps and his grin morphs into a smirk. "Not little."

My chest swells.

I'll always choose you.

"C'mon, Tyro. Let's get cleared."

He's bursting from the car a moment later and I'm following after him with sparks lighting down my spine.

"Mac, hey."

Snagging his wrist, I pull him to a stop in the middle of the empty parking garage.

He cocks a brow at me, his eyes as clear as day as they assess me, his smile restored to its original brilliance so bright it takes my breath.

"You're staring."

I nod, agreeing as I step closer. Close enough that the toes of my boots meet his Chucks. Our fingers interlock. The backs of my free fingers brush over his cheek.

"I can't wait."

Green-blue eyes soften as they dance between mine.

"For what?" he whispers near soundlessly.

The corner of my lips tip up before pressing to his. I don't linger, though I want to. Instead, I pull back just enough that all I see is him.

All I've ever seen is him since the moment I laid eyes on him. I know that now. That there was no other way for this to end up. No universe exists without him and me. No story where the two of us don't make our own ending, together.

No way we don't exist just like this.

Mac and me.

"I love you."

His eyes flare wide, a gasp echoing off the concrete.

"What?" he squeaks with a tightening grip.

"I love you," I repeat, as I would a thousand times. As I have in every timeline to ever exist. "I'm in love with you, Mac."

A sound that I can only describe as a sob ekes through his parted lips and he dives forward, flinging his arms around my neck and squeezing.

"Is this a pity hug, or …?"

The laugh that he lets out is wet. Choked. But as equally good to hear.

"Psht," he scoffs out and tightens. "You'll never get my pity, Tyro."

Chuckling, I glance around before turning my face into his neck and press a kiss to his hummingbird of a pulse.

"But you have my love, Jordan," he whispers thickly. "You have for a while."

The sudden lift of weight has my knees nearly buckling.

"You and me?"

I feel his nod and my eyes water.

Tentative, soft, and so full of life, Mac turns to press his lips to mine and it's as if there never was a present without him. That all time has come together for just this moment.

That the universe has finally righted after so many years of being off course.

"You and me, baby."

Chapter Eighty-Three

JORDAN

AFTER A GAUNTLET OF testing and hours of waiting, Mac and I finally make our way into a private waiting room for the final analysis of his results.

It seems like overkill, but to the benefit of the staff here, they have argued at every turn that lifting Mac's restrictions so soon is unprecedented.

Because, of course, my drummer would not only challenge the norm, but also have enough sway to get the medical professionals in agreement.

As long as the tests all come back crystal clear.

He blames it on experience.

I blame it on his persistence.

Just like the rest of us say rodeo and Mac is just Mac, saying shit like *ro-day-o.*

His ass no sooner settles into a seat that the silence is broken up by people entering the room.

Except none of them are wearing scrubs or white coats and instead are several members of his family.

Rex and the twins. Marie. Then Aria and her sister.

They got my texts.

I smile to myself as he greets them.

What I don't expect is the house of a bodyguard, followed by the head of orange hair, to file in behind them.

"I want this kind of treatment," Peach remarks with smiling snark as he wraps Mac up and points at me. "You convince them to check him out early?"

I grin and stand to hug him. "That was all him. He'd still be in bed if it were up to me."

Peach's knowing smirk curls his lips as he slaps my shoulder.

"Then he's coming to my appointment after this."

Tipping my head, I couldn't stop the grin from widening on my face, even if I wanted to try.

Ian greets me next with a lift of his chin and a bump to my fist. "You good?"

I nod, the lightest I've felt in a long time.

"Yeah," I breathe out. "Thanks for coming to support him."

The man shrugs. "Not here for just him, kid."

That burning takes over the backs of my eyes. "Right. Yeah, uh, thank you."

Snickering, Ian steps aside and I'm smacked with the narrowed sight of Mac's twin accompanied by a second set of brown eyes in near slits.

"Broby!" Mac cackles and jumps on his back, momentarily stealing the second man's attention.

"Rex," I state and offer a hand that my drummer's brother glares at.

"Jordan," he greets with a deep timbre and grips my palm.

I give it back just as hard.

It's a contrast to the last time I saw the man, Peach laid out on a hospital bed between us, and I welcome it. *This* is the Rex Thompson I know. The overprotective brother. The loyal friend. Brave confidant to the man that I love.

I hope I never have to see another version again.

Mac comes back to my side when his brother relents to glaring at me from a distance and I smile.

The room continues to fill with each and every one of Mac's, and mine, extended family to the point that it's basically standing room only.

Anna and Leo. Lugh. Fin with Cedar and Jonathon.

There's an idle chatter that eases me, an aura of love circling around the space that's intoxicating enough to have me leaning into Mac close enough to whisper.

"Think they can tell I'm yours?"

He chuckles, the hint of a flush tinting his cheeks, and leans back enough to meet my gaze.

But then I lift my hand, palm up, fingers spread in offering.

His eyes go wide and glassy.

"You sure?" he mouths, and I nod.

"Of you? I'm *always* sure, Vida."

The smile that stretches his face wide is somehow still soft as he threads his fingers between mine and tucks our hands at his side.

"Hey, fuckbuckets!" There's just as many grumbles about his choice of language as there are chuckles as the room turns their attention on him. He's vibrating when he spares me a final glance, one last attempt to back out, before opening his mouth and telling our combined family; "Jordan and I are so gonna fuck after this, so don't invite us over."

"*Vida*," I snap with wide eyes and an immediate flush.

The smirk plastered on his face is devilish. "You knew what you were signing up for, baby. Now kiss me."

It doesn't matter that the room has exploded with laughter and claps, chatter and congratulations.

Possibly even a wolf whistle or two.

Because my drummer is fisting my shirt and hauling me close enough to slant his lips over mine and kiss me like his life depends on it.

It's the indecent kind. The passionate kind.

The everlasting kind.

And when my hand finds the back of his neck and holds him close, there is nothing else but us. No space left between our chests. No distance separating our hearts.

Just me and him.

Mac. Mac. Mac.

"Oh, my."

A clearing of a throat draws us back, but only as far as resting our forehead together.

"I'm looking for a Mac Thompson?"

"Present," Mac answers the doctor I can see in my peripheral and lifts a hand. "Tell me my brain's okay so I can keep kissing my man?"

The doctor covers a chuckle with a clearing of her throat as she comes up to our side, clipboard in her hands.

"I absolutely have to advise you to keep taking it easy—"

"And?" Mac interrupts and I nudge his head with mine.

"And all of the tests came back good. You're in the clear."

The relief that washes over his features cleanses me and this time, I'm the one hauling him back to me for another searing kiss.

He's glassy eyed and breathless when I pull back. "Let's go christen my apartment, yeah?"

The nod is immediate, the goodbyes are short, the drive even better when we pull out like a goddamn motorcade with Mac behind the wheel of my old Impala.

"I look damn sexy driving your car, Tyro."

He does.

"You better not put a scratch on her."

Chapter Eighty-Four

JORDAN

I'M ALREADY HARD WHEN I lock us inside my apartment, harder when Mac presses me back into the hardwood with his hands and lips all over me.

Blindly unclipping shit from my belt, I set my radio and holster on the table next to the door and cup his face once my hands are free.

His tongue slides along mine, taunting me with its talent as his fingers swiftly undo my pants.

"If I don't get your dick in me *somewhere*, I might burst."

Mac moans and nods, nipping at my lip. "Yes, that."

Except he's pulling my length free instead and dropping to his knees.

"Aw, fuck, Vida."

He palms my cock, pulling from base to tip before burying me deep in his throat.

"*Oh, fuuuuuck.*"

Washed out by toe-curling euphoria, I don't catch him encouraging movement until he's shoving my hips back only to pull me forward.

"You want—" I groan at the swallow around my crown, "—*shit*. You want me to fuck your face?"

The answering vibrations radiate up my shaft and settle into the swirl already tightening my abs.

Snagging his hair in both fists, I arch back, slipping my cock along his tongue until the tips meet.

"You sure?"

"Yeah. *Yes.* Yes. Fuck my face, baby."

A shiver prickles my hot skin when he licks his lips and I jolt forward, thrusting all the way to the back of his throat. Its slow and deep, each stroke cutting off his choked sounds. Blunt nails dig into my waist, pulling me closer, silently begging me to push farther.

My legs are already shaking when I palm the back of his head and tunnel into his throat until his nose is brushing my groin and his eyes water.

Not once does my man gag.

The moan that spills from his lips when I back off is downright filthy and has me popping his mouth off me to pull him to his feet.

"Bed. *Now*," he demands on a rasp before I can and a knowing tingle rushes over my skin.

Shucking off my clothes as I walk, I kneel on the bed naked and ready.

Mac's hands smooth over my shoulders, the heat of him blanketing my back as he pushes. I go willingly, bending at the waist.

It feels … weird. To be on display like this, especially when I feel him drop behind me, his sight even with my exposed hole.

And yet … There's not a single part of me that wants to shy away.

"Please tell me you have lube here."

Nerves and excited flutters mix in my belly, and I nod, flattening to reach for the nightstand.

My fingers just graze the drawer's knob when his hands grip my hips and yank me back up on all fours.

"Not yet."

It's all the warning he gives me before burying his face between my cheeks.

I yelp when hot wetness caresses my hole, jerking forward only to be pulled right back. Mac's tongue works its way over me, circling around the puckered ring at a hypnotic pace that makes me dizzy. Then he's adding enough pressure to drive me mad with want, my cock past the point of painfully hard as it hangs heavy between my thighs.

"Vida," I pant and press back. "*More.*"

Lips circling my hole, he hums and suckles, then spears his tongue right into the center. The tip plunges inside me and I cry out.

"Oh, *God*," I breathe and fist the sheets.

Mac works me open, thrusting his tongue in and out, stretching the tight muscle long enough that I'm panting, desperate, and leaking.

But then he's pulling back and tapping my ass and I immediately miss the warmth of him.

"On your back, Tyro. I'm gonna watch you fall apart on my fingers."

I scramble, flopping over so fast, I nearly roll right off the bed.

My chest is pumping when Mac settles between my spread knees, the smile on his face sinister and so damn sexy that I'm trembling.

He's already naked. His cock in his palm. His sight leaving trails of undeniable heat all down my body until it reaches my cock and flares.

The head's glistening with precum, practically pulsing with need, and purpling.

"Rimming? *Check.*"

I don't get a chance to respond because he's bending over me and wrapping his lips around my crown, suckling around the sensitive flesh.

"*Mac*," I groan out, hips arching, following his retreat when he leans back. "Stop teasing me."

His brow wings and his chuckle is dark.

It's sexy and controlled as he leans over, fishing the brand-new bottle of lube from the nightstand and straightening.

I could get used to seeing this side of him.

There's a glint in his eye as he slicks his fingers. A hint of mischief curling the corners of his lips when he runs them over my crease, finding my rim and swirling. I gasp and press down, chasing that feeling, wanting him to finally take that step so bad that I don't care how desperate I look. How needy I appear.

I fucking am.

"You ever been edged before, Tyro?"

I shake my head, body arching into his touch. "*No.* Please don't. God, fuck, just being around you is like being on the cusp without falling off."

The resounding chuckle tickles over my skin. "You accusing me of denying you?"

"Yes," I hiss and his tongue swipes over my slit, my hips jolting after more. "Just—*fuck*—please, Vida." The smirk splitting his face is smug. "*Please.*"

An airy chuckle puffs over my cock at his closeness, his blown greenish eyes locking on mine.

Without a word, Mac lowers his mouth over my cock at the same time that swirling finger dips inside me.

"*Ffffuuuckkkk.*"

It's like nothing I've ever felt before, having them both occur in tandem, and my brain short circuits with each inch Mac takes.

But when he curls that finger?

I see stars.

I'm so damn close to coming.

"*Mac,*" I plead and fist his hair. "Two. *Two.*"

Drawing back, he licks at the underside of my head as he eases the second finger past the first ring of tight muscle.

There's a slight burn. A stretch that's unfamiliar and I wince.

"Talk to me, baby," Mac murmurs, his voice shot. "How's it feel with two?"

I nod, panting, and lick my lips. "It's, um, good. Just kinda burns."

He nods and pulls back, adding more lube.

"Just breathe. Relax. Watch me."

Doing as he says, we lock eyes as those two thick fingers circle around the rim. He jerks me with the other, his tongue darting out to lick up the bead wetting the tip.

Slowly, his fingertips stretch me, the slickness of them just as hot as his mouth doing insane shit to my cock.

I'm so focused on the swirl of his tongue and the depth of his throat that I don't realize he's pushed past the final set of knuckles until his fist hits my ass.

The fullness has my cock pulsing, yet the burn keeps my orgasm at bay.

"So fuckin' tight, baby." Wiggling fingers make me shudder. "So good."

I bite my lip.

"Gonna move, okay?"

"Okay."

"Hey," Mac says on a groan, and I meet his darkened gaze that's swimming with something more than just lust. More than just desire. "You and me. Yeah?"

The breath I pull in is shaky, my heart stuttering as I nod.

Slowly, Mac pulls back, taking with him the uncomfortable burn and when he presses back inside, the sensation has changed.

And it's *good*.

I moan and press down, taking the digits deeper.

"Fuck, it's good," I rumble on a pant.

He does it again and my back arches.

"There it is," he rasps, his smile audible as he spreads my legs wider. "Fuck, that's so damn hot watching your hole take my fingers, baby."

My abs tighten.

He leans down to slurp up my cock, popping off with a husky laugh.

"Can't wait to get my cock in here."

He pumps harder. Faster. Curling those digits in all the right ways to have my lower belly swirling and my back bowing off the mattress.

"God, fuck. *Mac.*"

I'm gasping, my vision tunneling, my muscles tightening.

The pumps go short, the digits swiping over my prostate as Mac presses the pad of his thumb against my taint and I'm done for.

Gasping, I go rigid.

Toes curling.

Cock pulsing stream after stream onto my chest.

Hot wetness envelopes the head of me and I cry out as Mac captures the rest of my orgasm on his tongue.

It seems never ending with each pass of not just his devious mouth, but his fingers caressing that hot button inside me.

He's swallowing me.

Holy fuck, he's swallowing me.

Another wave has me rocking between his fingers and mouth, my vision nearly blacked out.

With abs even tighter and cries on my heaving breaths, my cock pulses against his tongue.

Mac. Mac. Mac.

"God … fucking fuck … coming *again. Mac.*"

He moans around me, taking every bit that I pump out as my ass clamps down on his digits.

I'm still leaking when he straightens, and I motion for him to come closer. "Bring it to me, Vida," I pant out.

He shakes his head, straddles my thigh with his fingers still buried inside me and spits the mouthful of white onto his free palm.

Slicking my release over his shaft, he fucks his fist fast and hard.

That's beyond fucking hot.

"Good ... fucking *God*." He pants and trembles, stroking my insides in time with his strokes over his cock.

He stiffens, swollen lips dropping open as thick ropes of cum shoot across my stomach and chest, mixing with mine.

"*Shit, baby.*"

Pumping the last bit of his release onto me, Mac finally slumps back on his haunches.

"Can I have my soul back?"

His brows pinch, still working to catch his breath. "What?"

"Y'know, since you sucked it outta my cock."

He sputters out a laugh that I grin at and grip his wrist. Easing him from my body, there's only a mild sense of discomfort, a slight pinch, as I sit up and claim his lips.

The taste of my release is strong on his tongue, turning me on all over again.

Or maybe it's the man himself.

My cock attempts to rally but ends up just leaking limply on my thigh.

"You can't have it back," he mutters breathlessly and slants his forehead to mine.

The smile that crests my lips is languid and *satisfied*.

"Okay."

Epilogue

Jordan

"**I** HAVE SOMETHING I need to show you."

Mac's soft smile smacks me right in the center of my chest as he looks up at me from the drum pad in his lap. Twirling the sticks between his fingers, digits that have worked me open multiple times over the last few weeks, he licks his lips and drops his gaze to the bulge in my sweats that just happen to be grey.

We've been taking things slow, his demands, not mine. Though I'll admit that I've enjoyed every second of him letting me find myself within us. Figuring out what I like and what feels incredible without any judgement.

Just … *slowly.*

"I'll take another peek, sure."

Chuckling, I shake my head. "Not that, Vida. We have to leave for this one."

It's something that I'd nearly forgotten about doing for him considering it was while Mac was on his European tour.

But when Peach called to tell me he'd finished working the piece I'd asked him to complete when they got back, my stomach rolled with nerves.

I think he'll like what I did.

Though I can't help but feel that I possibly overstepped.

Only one way to find out.

"Leave? Why would we *leave*?" He reaches for me, snagging my hips before I can deflect him, and pulls me into his lap.

Straddling his hips, hands on my waist, Mac leans in and slants his lips over mine.

I give in easily, opening up to him and letting each swipe of his tongue ease the nerves twisting my gut.

"I can still taste my cum on your lips," he nearly growls, my snicker getting cut off by him diving back in to lick and taste.

It's easy to get lost in the remnants of a sexy shower where I knelt for him, swallowed his dick, and *finally* got my fill of his salty-sweet flavor. Especially when my embarrassment of a gag reflex turned out to be hot as shit to him.

Gag on my cock, baby, he'd said.

And boy, did I.

"Vida," I rumble, fighting against the magnetic pull of him, only to lose and dive in for three more kisses to his swollen lips.

God, I'll never tire of kissing him.

"Tyro," he mumbles back and trails his lips down my jaw to my neck.

Pure strength of will is the only thing that peels me away from him, leaving puckered lips hanging in midair, as I climb off the bed.

"If you keep doing that, we'll never see sunlight again."

He snorts and presses a palm to his tented crotch. "I could live with that."

I feel the heat of his gaze follow me as I drop the sweats and replace them with jeans.

"Were those my underwear?"

Grinning, I thumb the elastic waistband up enough to peek out over the denim. Just enough of a flash of color to tease him.

"Goddamn you," he mumbles and darts up from the bed, grabbing me from behind and pressing kisses to the back of my neck.

Then he snags the waistband of both layers, yanks them down to slap my bare ass, and pats them right back into place.

My snicker is breathy and wanton.

Jesus, what has he done to me?

I feel like I'm ten years younger and falling in love all over again for the first time. Shit, most days I feel like I'm discovering sex with someone I care about all over again for the first time, and in some ways I am, but there's just something about this thing with Mac that is nothing like what I've known.

Hell, it's better than fiction.

"C'mon, Vida," I say with a smile that catches his eye once he's dressed, and hold out my hand.

He takes it, holding tight all the way through my empty gym, past Lemon at the front desk who catcalls us sexy daddies as we pass. Mac laughs and waves. I roll my eyes the rest of the way to the car.

After a quick check in via the walkie strapped to my ear, I toss a hand to the back of Mac's head rest and start backing up.

Mac's hiss from the passenger seat has me easing on the brake pedal.

"What?" His eyes are comically wide and staring right at the arm I have stretched between us. "I swear if you say some shit about my ink, I'm blaming you."

Mac blinks like he's coming back to the car and swallows. "What? *No.* Why would I say that about something I helped pick out?"

I chew on the inside of my cheek, an attempt at dampening the heat taking over the cabin of the car.

"Then why—" My voice cracks and I clear my throat. "Why are you *still* staring at it?"

Mac's plush lips purse, drawing my attention, and he sighs. "Be*cause,*" he almost whines. "It's fucking *hot.*"

"Me driving is hot?"

"No, no, no." He shakes his head and licks his lips as I maneuver us out onto the street. "*You.* Driving this beast of a classic. With *that* ink." His eyes roll back, and he grunts. "Looking like my fucking *wet dreams*, Tyro baby."

The flush creeping up my face has nothing to do with embarrassment and everything to do with the flames flinging between us.

"Go ahead. Pump up my head a little more, why don't you."

He slides across the bucket seat and dips a hand between my legs, cupping my cock. "Okay."

"Ah, shit," I groan and widen my knees only for him to retreat, tucking his hands in his lap.

"You ever gonna tell me what the soundwave in there is?"

Clearing my throat, I bite my lip.

"You ever going to tell me why you call me *tyro*?"

He snickers. "Hell no. You made me look up *Vida*. Google that shit."

I did.

Seven years ago.

It means beginner.

And while I wasn't fond of the reminder when I first joined Sentry, and Mac, now I'm pretty stuck on the endearment's accuracy.

Mac was the start of so many things for me. The entry to this life, his love, where I end up with him by my side. The introduction to my sexuality, my career, my business.

The life I always wanted but was too afraid to reach for.

It's almost as if he knew back then.

He might be my life, but I'm his beginning.

Pulling up to the back alley of Aria's boutique, I drive a little further down the lane until we're just behind the third storefront and park.

"*This* is what you wanted to show me?"

My nod is slight, my smile knowing.

"Exactly. C'mon."

Scanning the alleyway, I round the car and pull open his door, grabbing his hand again as it slams closed.

Palm to palm in the fading sunlight that paints the night in an orange glow, I tug his bandana down over his eyes and lead him into the back of the formerly empty building with my heart pounding and my skin prickling.

Fuck, I hope he likes it.

"Wait here. No peeking."

Leaving him in the center of it all, I run around the room to flip on the twinkle lights and neon signs I'd hung while I was ignoring that I was in love with him.

I don't make it to pulling all of the dust covers before I'm drawn back to his side by that ever-present draw only he has. He'll get the gist.

"Okay," I murmur and step to him. "If you hate it, I can undo it. So just … be nice."

He's vibrating when I cup his face and thumb up the material over his eyes. He blinks at me, pupils flexing with adjustment to the sudden light, and *gasps.*

"You didn't."

Biting my lip, I nod, stepping back for him to get the full view.

"You turned it into a real fucking arcade?!"

His voice cracks on that last bit as he swings around, taking in the addition of old school gaming machines all around the room mixed with a few of the newer ones. The color-splattered carpet. The posters and signs. A bar with only root beer on tap and every flavor of soda imaginable at the fountain once we refresh the syrups. There's even a candy display that's yet to be stocked.

When he spins back to me, his bottom lip is wobbling, and his eyes are misted over.

"Well? What do you think?"

Those tears spill over his lashes and he dives into me, wrapping his arms around my neck and kissing the air from my lungs.

"It's amazing."

Sniffling, I let loose a wet snicker and clear my throat.

"There's one more thing."

Mac pins me with a look that screams all the things his voice doesn't say. "When did you do all of this?"

I shrug and clasp his hand in mine, tugging him in the direction of the front. "When you were gone."

"You—" A choked sound cuts him off and more tears cascade down his face. "*Jordan.*"

The corner of my lips tip up and I pull him to me as we round the wall I added, making sure his back is to the still wet mural.

Good. Fucking. God.

I clear my throat and blink back the moisture in my own eyes at the sight.

Peach sent me a photo that absolutely did not do this justice.

It's perfect.

Grabbing Mac's shoulders, I pull in a composing breath filled with his rich, sweet scent and grin.

But, fuck, it's still watery.

"Okay, fuck, just turn around."

I push on his shoulders, and he spins.

Gasps.

Sobs.

"Oh my God," he whispers and grabs for me though he's not looking away from the painting taking up the entire expanse of the shop's front.

Wrapping my arms around his waist, I set my chin on his shoulder and hug him tightly.

He's shaking as he points, counting each drum painted into the wall, calling them by names.

It's so damn *real* it looks like a fucking picture hung on the wall, not a drawing of a touring drum set highlighted by rays of sunlight.

"Two toms, floor, snare … crash … bass—*This is my set.*" He trembles and I nod.

"Yeah, mi Vida. It is." My heart pounds with the final bit of this surprise I was certain I'd never be able to give him. "And, um, the windows behind us look in on this. You can see it from the street."

His shoulders shake and he tightens the grip on my forearm.

"Show me."

Keeping his hand in mine, I pull the covers from the windows, flip on the spotlight and guide him out the front.

His mouth drops wide at the sight, tears streaming down his cheeks.

"We could open it to the public, if you want, Vida." I watch as he stares in awe at the place. "All you gotta do it pick a name."

Mac turns to me, his breath hitching, and wraps his arms around my neck.

Then he's kissing me stupid and it's wet. Sweet. Full of so much passion and love and hope, that it makes me feel like we could withstand anything.

And after everything we've been through?

I know we could.

"Jordan, this is everything I didn't know I needed," he chokes out through a smile. "God, I love you so fucking much."

I nod and smile with my heart pattering a beat that syncs to his.

"Thanks for giving me the chance, Vida." I swipe the back of my knuckles over his damp cheek. "And thanks for loving me when I didn't even know I needed it."

The End

Is it ever really the end, though?

Check out The Chance; a special edition available direct from Rae Stone
including an illustrated cover and bonus content

Afterword

Holy Shit

It's here. It's finally fucking here, and I cannot believe it.

For two years, Mac and Jordan have sat on my mind, poking me with tidbits and storylines. Dropping hints and notes all over the place. Feeding me universe after galaxy filled with nothing but *them*. Mac and Jordan. Together.

Somehow.

It didn't seem to matter that their book was supposed to be the second one, but was rejected. It didn't matter that I scrapped the entire first version of their story and walked away from it. Didn't matter that I was told, on so many occasions, that I *shouldn't*. That *you can't*. That I managed to write two other books before coming back to them with a hesitant start and voices in my head that didn't belong.

I was nervous to jump into the MM world as an author after having written MF books. It was always the plan, the goal, but so many things had gone wrong up until now.

I'm fucking glad they did.

Because without all that, I wouldn't have learned to embrace the muse within the way that these guys showed me. I wouldn't have made the choices that I did. And I sure as shit wouldn't have found the amazing authors that have helped me along the way.

Jordan says it best when he finally admits he's in love.

There's not timeline where we don't exist.

They were so fucking right.

They just needed *me* to catch up. To be a better writer. To find the places where we were all welcomed with open arms and give them the HEA they deserved.

Finally.

This story is messy. It's infuriating. Sweet.

But so is their love and I'm so damn proud of them.

It's bittersweet to write this afterword, knowing that it means they're actually out in the world. Finding readers and making people fall in love with them like I did. Causing kindles to be thrown, and tears to be shed. To know that they finally, *finally*, belong to you now.

Where they were always meant to be.

I hope they gave you the ride they gave me. That their love sticks with you long after you close this book like they have for me.

Thank you for reading. For being a part of this journey.

From the bottom of my heart … Thanks for giving me and my boys a chance.

XO,

PS: If you enjoyed this book, please (pretty please?) consider leaving a review. They mean the world to indie authors like myself, AND they help other readers find me, just like you. Thank you! <3

Acknowledgements

Every book I have written wouldn't be possible without my number one, Mr. Stone. (I know you're gonna read this part first *insert eye roll*) Thank you for covering while I wrote. For encouraging me to keep going, even when I was told no. For being there to take care of shit when I was too occupied to do much but fall head first into this book and make it everything that it is.

To Beverly and your adamant support of Mac and his story. Jorge for breaking out the cymbals around the bonfire and helping me snap some sweet ass pics.

To my beta group, The Green Room, for all the love and support and feedback. I can't believe you guys let me steal those MM cherries. LOL.

To Heather, the editor of words and slasher of bad phrases. Thank you, thank you, thank you. This book wouldn't be what it is without you.

To Lyla for coming to the rescue on that arc formatting! You are a *queen*. Don't forget it.

To each and every author that I have come across along the way that has let me drop into their groups, share in their newsletters, and be the all around hype peeps that I didn't know I needed. And a special thank you to Brooklyn, Hazel, and Bree. This book would not exist without your support and love. I am forever grateful for all of you.

To Jordan for being the best PA I could have asked for. I had no clue that getting to work with you, getting to know you, would end up being the best decision I could have made. I'm so glad I found you!

To the readers. The arc readers. The street team members. And every person in between. None of this would be possible without you and I'm so fucking glad you're here.

Content Warnings

Things such as panic attacks, mentions of parental death via house fire, semi-flashbacks of a traumatic time, therapy, and a character having nightmares, all take place on page.

The following CW's may contain spoiler-like mentions. Proceed at your own risk.

Also on page is a car accident and subsequent injuries, including a hospital stay and required follow up appointment.

This is an MM romance, meant for readers eighteen and older.

About the Author

Rae Stone is native to the Midwest, from a town called Springfield, OH. While she no longer resides in the City of Roses, Rae is definitely a misfit of Suburbia that would rather paint her nails black and annoy the neighbors with her loud rock music.
When she's not elbows deep in writing, Rae can be found attending concerts with Mr. Stone, consuming romance novels like water, and letting her fur kids run wild.

Wanna connect? Find Rae on socials below!
Facebook | Instagram | Tiktok | GoodReads | Amazon | BookBub | Newsletter | Website

Need a place to discuss all things As Above?
Check out Rae's reader group here → Rae's Misfits of Romance